CW01277063

Plonk

An anthology of wine-inspired stories from the Red Wine Writers

First published in Great Britain by
The House of Murky Depths, 2014.

ISBN: 978-1-906584-60-3

www.murkydepths.com

Cover design and layout: Mark Badham-Moore.
Additional layouts Terry Martin

Printed in the UK by
Grosvenor Group (Print Services) Ltd
London

Contents

Introduction

Terry Martin

As a publisher of novels, magazines, anthologies, comics and graphic novels, a published author in my own right, and a member of the Red Wine Writers, it was a crime to me that the stories of this small group of talented and committed writers weren't available to any kind of audience. When I suggested at a meeting of the group that we should all contribute short stories to an anthology the reactions were mixed.

Writers, like most artists, can be notoriously unsure of their abilities and few of us like to accept the kind of criticisms that are so easily slung at authors; even Shakespeare and Dickens have had, and still do have, their critics. Thankfully, by the end of that evening a plan had been hatched and everyone was up for the challenge. Certain criteria were laid down – for instance, red wine had to feature somewhere; our introductions had to be no more than sixty words; there wouldn't be any poems – but, during the process of putting *Plonk* together, all of these seemed restrictions to making the anthology as entertaining as possible, and blind eyes were turned.

As a writing group the Red Wine Writers are no back-slapping pack of gossiping amateurs who meet to listen and glorify their work. Criticisms are often sharp and to the point but writers have to have broad shoulders and, while the learning curves can be steep and sudden, the lessons will undoubtedly make the writers stronger and produce better stories. The process that these stories have gone through has not only benefited the stories but given the group a realisation of the underlying talent of each of the writers, and given each individual a course in editing.

The stories in this anthology are as diverse as their creators and their styles, and vary in length from a thousand to nearly ten thousand words, not to mention the poems spattered throughout. Have no fear, there will be stories you enjoy. You will laugh, you will cry, you may even shudder at some, but even if a story isn't for you it will move you in some way.

For those interested in the group itself, it was originally formed from the nucleus of a writing course run by Emily Midorikawa. Several people have joined and some have gone by the way side but the die-hards have persevered and through the habit of sharing a bottle of red wine during the regular meetings the name has become synonymous with the group's ethos.

Terry Martin
2014

People often ask, "Are you still writing?" Any answer you give will involve guilt. Usually lack of progress is the main topic of conversation for fellow writers. Our monthly meetings at Red Wine Writers have been peppered with excuses of all sorts and our stories have only become this volume by breaking deadlines. The poem is for those of us who squander our time in procrastination.

Are You Still Writing?

Christine Dickinson

I might
tick off a list
tossed in my desk,
sign a cheque,
write off a debt,

scratch letters in sand,
use a word that's banned,
splash ink, waste paper,
create new litter.

I might
print out a tract,
mutter a fact,
spit in rage,
blot my page,

submit sagas of wit,
shred a volume to bits,
blow the whistle
in an epistle.

I might
trip up on rhyme,
waste all my time,
copy your verse,
pen something worse.

I might
have the last word
and not be heard,
pour a glass of red,
spend all day in bed.

I might rest my head,
read a book instead.

At the lights where West Elloe Avenue joins Pinchbeck Road in Spalding is one of those poster sites, filled with scarily big heads, advertising some commodity you probably don't need. I never took too much notice until the morning I discovered a blue eyed blonde Specsaver woman staring back at me and developed an infatuation with her. It took a while before I thought to combine Specsaver man, as he became, with the text message cock up that happened to, yes, me, one Christmas. In my case it proved innocuous but as a plot twist it had potential. As for why Becca, why a seventeen-year-old girl as the protagonist – why not? And ... well I've got three girls. One is, two have been, seventeen.

Me, Mercutio And A Bottle Of Merlot

Adrian Lazell

I'm in love with the man in the Specsavers advert. He's lush. He's here now. His picture propped up on Dad's cookbook stand – Mercutio. I named him after Romeo's mate. You know, the one who comes to a tragic end. Though they all do don't they? So it's me, Mercutio and this bottle of Merlot. I don't drink red wine normally but it's all I could find. What sort of a family runs out of alcohol on New Year's Eve?

The door bell is ringing. I'm not answering. I'm home alone. Well, not quite alone if you count Mercutio – which I do. Mum and Dad have gone to Aunt Spandex's party.

"It's tradition."

"It's boring." I'm seventeen and I've got better things to do – like sitting here with the man in the ad on the back of the Style magazine (Mercutio to me). He's slumping and I have to prop him up. Too much vino I expect – although his glass (I poured for both of us) seems untouched. Doorbell again – fuck off whoever you are. Oh and Happy New Year!

Zit has gone to the party. Zit is my fifteen year old sister (her birth certificate says she's Zoe but she'll always be Zit to me). Her boyfriend Zac has gone too. Everyone in the family loves Zac. Except me – he's a dork. Being astute you'll have noticed that, like Zit, his name begins with the letter z. I think that was the attraction. I can't think of any other reason. She's that shallow.

I haven't got a boyfriend; seventeen years old and no

boyfriend. Why? I'm pretty. I know that, though my nose is too big. And maybe my boobs, they get noticed too, usually. It just depends on what top I'm wearing. But unless I wear a burqa, or a balaclava, I'm stuck with my nose.

For the last few years I've gone with them but I'm really not in a party mood. Not after Christmas, or rather the sixth-form Christmas meal. And other than that meeting in town, the one I'm going to tell you about, and a sprint through a downpour to the corner shop to buy all the things Dad had forgotten for Christmas dinner (stuffing, bread sauce mix, crackers – everything basically), I've not been out. Mercutio arrived through the letterbox.

I need to explain the back story. We get boys in the sixth form – a High School perk. And the girls are all over them. Year eleven and below are silly, staring with fixed grins – giggling spotty cheerleaders. Some sixth formers play it cool, some of us chat to them, human to human. I did too, apart from Lex. To be honest I didn't notice him at first. He didn't sit near me. I'm doing French, German, History and English. He does dossy – Art, Music and Drama (oh and English). And he's a punk and I don't, or didn't, do punk.

Then, on a wet Tuesday night at the back end of November, my Mum gave him a lift. I didn't want her to but she's soft. He was stood alone at the gates. She stopped, lowered the window and asked if he needed one. It was torrential. His hair gel looked foul, running down his forehead. As he arrived on the seat I moved up against Zit, to give him dripping room. When Zit mentioned her detention with Clarkey he did an impression of the head that was spot on. And then there was the wink. It was the wink that did it, from the pavement outside his house – the gel wiped back into his fringe – and closing the car door. And it was clearly intended for me.

At Caz's party he sat with a very drunk little Joe (big Joe was away in Manchester on a uni open day) supplying him with refills of water and keeping him awake until little Joe's Dad came to collect him. And Caz said he cleaned up the puke, little Joe's puke, in her bathroom. That was above and beyond.

Next week in General Studies, when Miss Fisher dissed the seventies for being, Bowie apart, a creative desert, he gave a eulogy to Patti Smith which lasted for five minutes. And that got me to order 'Horses' from Amazon, even though I despise them for not paying their taxes.

He began to sit in our corner of the sixth form common room after that. He did most classes with Caz but not Geography. So while she was staring at Ordnance Survey maps and oxbow lakes we listened to Patti Smith, the Ramones and the Velvet Underground. And he asked me if I was going to the Christmas meal; which I was if he was, and he was because I was – I thought.

I wore black – black t-shirt, black bra, black skirt, black tights, black boots and black eye shadow too. Caz's mum was late picking me up and when we got to Shanghai's there were only two places, which were alongside the Joes, at the far end of the table from Lex. I was pretty annoyed about that. And as Caz was all over Big Joe, they may as well have shared a chair, I spent the evening fighting Little Joe for the Pinot Grigio and stuffing myself with prawn crackers. Lex stayed with his drama clique, who spent the evening doubling up and huddling to congratulate each other on jokes they didn't want to share with us mortals.

The meal passed as a blur until Caz reached out and squeezed Lex's bum as he made his way to the gents.

"Very seventies," was his response. He didn't seem too bothered.

"Oi," was my response, "hands off."

"You know what you should do, Becca?"

"What should I do?"

"You should flash your boobs at him." After Caz said this she narrowed her eyes at the drama queens. I think I looked doubtful. I tried to raise my eyebrows to my fringe and keep them there. "Okay me too. We'll do it together." She'd raised the stakes. It'd be one way of getting his attention I suppose. My eyebrows descended; it was hurting too much.

"I suppose ..." I held the hem of my t-shirt. "... If you will."

Lex returned.

"On the count of three. One." She looked at me. "Two." She grinned. "Three." I did it. Caz didn't.

Worse though, someone's phone flashed, while I flashed, and someone shouted, "Melons on the menu." Prick. Fuck. I covered up and, as I felt my face turning the full beetroot, retreated to the ladies.

"You okay?"

"Go away."

"I couldn't do it."

"I don't want to speak to you."

"I got scared."

"Fuck off, Caz." She did. And I came out fifteen minutes later, passing big Joe on his way to pee. "Nice breasts, Becca." That phrase not knowing whether to laugh or cry was about right. I parked myself on the bottom stair and dodged waitresses, until Lex arrived.

"You alright, Becca?" Not the brightest question really.

"Been better."

"I thought it was funny ..."

I said nothing.

"... in a good way." He sounded sincere. "Funny, daft, punk." I looked at him. He sat alongside and pulled me into a leathery hug.

"We're moving upstairs for the karaoke," he said. "Will you sing with me?"

"I've got a terrible voice."

"I don't care."

"Sing what?"

"Dunno – how about Perfect Day?" And we did. He sounded better than Lou Reed and I sounded like a pneumatic drill, as Caz put it. But she hugged me and I forgave her – Christmas and all that.

When Mum came for us Caz passed on the lift, saying big Joe would walk her home. It didn't dawn on me then that a taxi had come for the Joes half an hour earlier.

Someone is hammering on the door now. Don't they know I've got a doorbell? Okay – it's stopped. Think I'll retreat to the bedroom. I top up my glass; well not quite top it – there's not enough left in the bottle.

"I know it's a bit forward but fancy coming to bed, Mercutio?" He does. I pick him up, and his stand, and veer upstairs, then go back for his glass. It's 11.30 p.m. – thirty minutes of this crappy year left. I get changed, in the bathroom, out of sight of Mercutio – I'm not a total tart. I start on my teeth before I remember I'm still on the wine. Then I crawl under the covers, alongside Mr Specsavers. Well he's sitting on a pillow, so technically he's not under the covers. My phone is downstairs. Do I need it? It's switched off. I'll get it anyway. I stumble down, retrieve it and collapse on to the bed. My head will hurt tomorrow.

My head hurt the morning after Shanghai's but only until I found Lex's text: *Hope you got home safely. Call me soon. ;-) x*. Then my brain sped through its gears. Call me soon and a wink and a kiss – I loved him. I felt sick, but a good sick. This was going to be the best Christmas. What to say though? How to respond? It took a few goes.

I hate the Blackberry keypad and the tips of my fingers had grown fatter overnight. Eventually: *Home safely thanks – hope you got back okay too. I will call. Let's meet up...* One kiss or two? I went bold. He gave me one – I doubled it – *xx*.

There are voices downstairs; people shouting. I can make out a "piss off" and a "call the police". A gate slams. Quiet. Then the doorbell – should I go?

"I won't be a second, Mercs."

Mercutio doesn't seem intimate enough – not now we're sharing a bed. I take my dressing gown from the door but give up looking for slippers. The bell rings again.

"If I'm not back in five minutes," I say to the bespectacled figure on the pillow, "call the police."

My descent is slow. At the bottom I turn the outside light on; should have done that earlier. Through the door glass I see a silhouette, a man, and the line *Scaramouche, Scaramouche, will you do the fandango* plays in my head. Dad likes Queen – he's got no idea really.

"Becky."

Becky? No one calls me Becky.

"Becky, are you alright?" Mr Creepy, or Mr Creasy as Mum calls him, our neighbour can obviously see me too. He rings the bell again. I have to answer. I take off the chain, undo the latch and pull it back ten centimetres.

"Hello, Mr Creasy."

"Good Evening, Becky. Your Mum asked me to check on you. I think you've got phone problems."

No. My phone is deliberately turned off and the handsets on the landline got turned down when Aunt Spandex and the Spandex twins were here at half-term, so they could get a lie in, and nobody has thought to turn them back up. What Mum really wanted to know was, did I have a boy back? Well, fat chance. No offence, Mercutio.

"I'm fine. I'm doing revision."

"You're keen. It's New Year's Eve."

I know it's fucking New Year's Eve – that's why I'm in bed with my parents' last bottle of wine and the photograph of a man who, if I'm honest, Mercutio, is really much too old for me.

"That's me, keen student." I smile, then close my mouth, thinking my teeth must be stained with red wine. Does red wine stain teeth?

"I had to chase away a kid who was hanging around earlier."

"Kids eh?" I nod.

"We're having a party next door."

"Brilliant." Please go, then I can be Greta Garbo again (I do film club; I know about these people).

"Come and join us. It's New Year's Eve. A girl like you..."

A girl like what? "I'm fine."

"Don't you want to join us for Big Ben?"

Do I fuck? "I'm good thanks."

"Oh well." He looks at his feet and so do I. He's wearing slippers and it's starting to rain. "I'd best get back. So long as you're okay?"

"I'm dandy." I wrinkle up my nose in what would be a cutesy way; if I could do cutesy.

"Well, Happy New Year, Becky." He moves off.

"Happy New Year, Mr ..." I close the door, and think of saying creepy but I say, "... Creasy," because he means well, I think. And who else is going to wish me Happy New Year tonight?

Back in bed, the wine has gone and it's almost 2014. Good. We'll be rid of 2013.

Two days after the party I bumped into Lex and Caz in Claire's Accessories in town. Their backs were to me; his arm over her shoulder and her hand in his rear pocket. He returned a pack of body art crayons to the display and they turned.

"Becca?" She smiled and put her arms out in a downward 'v' and I got one of those as little as possible hugs where the hugger is frightened of catching something like aids or leprosy or humanity. Lex nodded.

"Christmas shopping?" she asked.

"Browsing."

"You recovered?" she reattached herself to Lex; completely brazen.

"Yes."

"You are a clown, Becca." Lex's hand squeezed hers and she looked up at him. I'd say he was trying to signal stop. She didn't stop. "Your texts to Lex."

What the fuck – how did she know? "Sorry?"

"Your texts to Lex." He moved away, to a bracelet carousel. "You do realise what you did?" She went wide eyed on me, "Don't you?"

"What did I do?"

"You answered your own text."

"I did what?"

"You answered your own text. You texted him on Friday night to see if he'd got back okay, then answered yourself on Saturday morning." She paused and smiled, Cruella De Vil style, then dropped it to deliver her punch line. "And then asked yourself out on a date."

Is it possible? I looked at my phone. Did it really fail to distinguish between texts in and texts out? Could I really be that dense? I knew the answer – technology wasn't my thing. Not with a hangover. He had never texted me. I had texted him. Twice. Oh God. I looked at the carousel but Lex had escaped elsewhere. I wanted the earth to swallow me but the Spalding earthquake didn't come. And Caz, my friend, turned witch, was smirking at me.

"You've got to laugh, Becca."

And that is why, as we approach midnight, my phone is turned off. It can't be trusted. The radio alarm clicks over to 00:00 – "Happy New Year, Mercutio." I give him a kiss. Now what? I watch the clock – 00:01, 00:02. 2014 is boring. I go to my desk, grab my laptop and bring it to bed. I go to Twitter and Instagram before Facebook. What's Mum's rule – only post when you're sober. And if I wish everyone "Happy New Year" they might guess I'm home alone. Unless I use my phone and that is out of bounds tonight. I get a notification – I've been tagged. I click to reveal. And I am, revealed that is, it's me, my plunge bra and boobs all over Facebook with a message *Happy New Year Becca, love Caz x* – the Cruella De Bitch-Witch. I untag the picture but cannot delete it. And she has 500 friends. No, make that 499. I hate her, hate, hate, hate, I fucking hate her. I close the machine and punch the lid. It hurts. I punch again. Then a spasm I cannot control takes hold and I shake, bawl, and burrow into Mercutio, my tears running all over his beautiful face and his perfect suit.

I have no idea what time it is, except daytime because light is sliding around my curtains. And Zit is sitting on the bed.

"Afternoon, Sis."

I grunt.

"Happy New Year." She's chirpy. "Mum made you a cup of tea."

"What time is it?" I'd look at the clock but my eyes are gluey.

"Five past four. What's that on your face?" I strip the magazine from my cheek and sit up.

"Mercutio I think."

"Mercuti-who?"

I take some tea from the mug Zit had been clutching. "How was the party?"

"Good, bad, well same old, same old really. Dad got drunk, Mum got cross. Aunt Spandex missed you."

"Aww."

"Think someone else did too." She is waving a piece of paper Neville Chamberlain style.

"What?" What is that?

"Something for you. We found it in the letterbox."

"A letter?" I take some more tea.

"From Lex."

I spill the tea and make a grab. "Give me that. Why are you opening my letters?"

She leans in to me. "It wasn't in an envelope idiot. It was written on an envelope, the cheapskate."

I grab it again and begin to read. Thankfully Zit stays shtum for a minute.

Becca – what can I say? I'm sorry about Caz – she should have shut up about the texts. I shouldn't have told her. I can't trust her and I guess you can't trust me. But you can. I've finished with Caz. Just a drunken mistake and nothing happened. I tried to call you tonight – is your phone working? And I called here tonight but guess you're out somewhere partying. Anyway, if you're interested, let me know. I'd like to take you out, for a meal, to make up for things. Lex x

Then, in a tiny scrawl of words at the bottom of the second side he'd added –

P.S. Those who have suffered understand suffering and therefore extend their hand. Patti Smith sang that.

"Oh, Lex loves you."

"Fuck off, Zit." I try to sound a grump but it doesn't work. I look from the letter to the remains of Mercutio. Life is about decisions and I am leaning towards forgiveness, which means, Mercutio, good as it's been, I'm going to give Lex a chance. If it doesn't work out I'll let you know. I kiss his torn face. Zit tells me I'm funny and I think – funny, daft, punk – I quite like that.

'Anguish' started life at a writing class in Harlow, Essex. At the end of each lesson we would be shown a picture and have to write a story within a thousand words by the following week. I often wrote more than a thousand but always edited it down to the required amount, an enjoyable exercise that every writing toolbox should include. You might smile to learn that this version of 'Anguish' is fifteen hundred words and a favourite of mine.

Anguish

Terry Martin

Spongers like her should be locked up. They were no good to society. No good to themselves. Ben Stains didn't think his views were extreme. In fact he thought most other people's tolerance verged on anarchy.

Through the café window he watched the vagrant woman as she wheeled her pram, full of her worldly possessions, along the high street, doing her late evening trash-can rounds before the daily town-centre collection robbed her of some unthinkable treasure. Her clothes hung with that same-colour-caked look reminding him of the mime artists he'd seen along London's Southbank, sitting or standing like statues, when he and his wife Lynn had visited the Eye. But they didn't smell. There could be no doubting she would. Just like the woman who had cleared a whole tube carriage on that same trip. That anyone could allow themselves to smell so disgusting had shocked both of them.

A piece of cereal bar caught in his throat at the thought. It took several minutes to recover from the resulting coughing fit. The few other customers in the café glanced at him disapprovingly. He refrained from giving them the finger, but the temptation was there. When his tickle finally subsided the old hag had disappeared, no doubt searching more lucrative bins. This thought merely caused him to dry retch and those at the nearby tables avoided looking in his direction.

Had someone suggested to him that maybe there was an element of jealousy in his almost fanatical hatred of an old woman he had never spoken to, he would have laughed and denied it without a thought. But she was free, and he wasn't. His marriage had not been the most successful although Lynn and he were still together, just. What responsibility for a tramp?

With a cup empty of both coffee and warmth, and a café that no longer seemed welcoming, Ben left to walk the last few miles home, dreading the usual moans and groans; unlike others, not looking forward to the weekend at all. He used to take home a bunch of flowers and a bottle of red wine on a Friday evening and he and Lynn would cuddle up in front of the fire to watch a DVD. That seemed years in the past.

Monday morning came way too soon, yet, in many ways, it was a huge relief. They had rowed nearly all weekend and his year-old daughter, Sarah, suffering from yet another cold, had kept them awake most of Saturday and Sunday night. Begrudging peace arrived when Lynn wheeled Sarah to the local park – the walk would do her good. No, she didn't want a lift. No, she didn't want him to come too, she wanted to be on her own. It had all stemmed from an argument about money – it was invariably about money, but not exclusively. Recent promotion should have made them better off, but where did the money go? He'd watched Lynn push the pram down the terraced street. The little plastic duck he'd bought his daughter, that she'd grown so attached to, hung from the canopy, bright yellow against the standard Mothercare dark blue. Lynn had stopped briefly at the corner of the street to speak with someone just out of view. Ben had been furious when his wife eventually moved off to reveal the filthy bitch of a vagrant. It was the first time Ben had noticed that Sarah's pram was identical to the woman's, but how could she bear to be near the filthy, stinking cow let alone talk to her?

Stressed out at work, with the extra responsibility, Ben had no respite Monday morning. A couple of silly mistakes resulted in his boss calling him into his office.

"What's the problem, Ben?"

"Still settling in, George. Won't happen again."

"But you were already doing the work before you were made up to IC." George was younger than Ben, had taken up the manager's position almost straight from university. He didn't have half Ben's experience, who did he think he was?

Ben hesitated. He didn't want to admit he was under stress; was finding it hard to cope, at work and at home. He tried to stop himself clicking the pen he'd brought with him. "I'm fine. Just a bit tired is all. Sarah's not been sleeping too well. Been keeping us both up."

"Do you think you could do with some time off?" George was looking worriedly at the pen, frowning at each click.

"Not at all. I'll be fine. You have my assurance."

George didn't look convinced. "If you need any help or want to talk about anything my door's always open."

"I appreciate that," he said as he stood, wanting to exit the room as soon as possible. "Thanks."

All eyes in the office looked his way, he could feel them, as he strode back to his desk. He threw his pen down and looked at his watch. Early lunch, he thought.

Having driven to work that morning, he decided to make use of the car and took a trip to the park to eat his sandwiches away from the office. If he didn't he'd still get hassled with phone calls and queries. His favourite bench gave him a panoramic view of the river. To his left, a variety of ducks and geese waddled along the bank or splashed in the shallows above the weir. Its continuing rumble always calmed him. Perhaps life wasn't so bad after all.

No sooner had this thought crossed his mind when, from around the back of an adjacent clump of shrubs, the old vagrant woman appeared, hood up on her pram, protecting her black plastic sacks from who knew what.

The cheese sandwich dried in his mouth, sucking out any last remnant of moisture. All his pent up anger and frustration seemed to channel itself towards the hag, as if all his problems could be blamed on her.

Even while a part of him knew this was illogical his emotions got the better of him. He flung his sandwiches, Tupperware box and all, into the raging water, slipping on the loose gravel of the path as he stormed back to his car.

A bent-back nail, as he opened the door clumsily, gave him pain enough to quell his anger somewhat, even to the point of realising his stupidity.

Leaning back in the driving seat he closed his eyes and willed himself to relax, surprising himself with a modicum of success. A gentle tap on the window brought him out of his reverie. He turned his head lazily.

"'Scuse me, dearie, but you're not supposed to park 'ere."

Ben was speechless. A fury he never knew he possessed left him gasping for words. Such audacity from the old woman! Who did she think she was?

He gave her a single finger, proud of his outward composure. Turning on the engine and simultaneously slamming it into gear, he reversed the car away from the reprimanding look, catching sight of her pram on the pathway beneath the weir. He looked from that to the old lady and smiled unpleasantly.

Her eyes betrayed her sudden realisation. Still smiling, and watching the woman's face, Ben methodically slipped the car into first. She was screaming "No! No!" as he floored the accelerator pedal, keeping it there as the car jumped the shallow kerb, shot across a carefully maintained flower bed, missing a statue of a long-forgotten local celebrity by mere millimetres, flattened the "Keep off the grass" sign before crashing into the pram. It lurched unceremoniously over the edge of the bank out of Ben's vision, but before it did a little yellow plastic duck swung out from the canopy. His insides knotted in an instant.

Ben hadn't needed to brake. The car had stalled to a halt on the brink. He was heedless of anything but what he had done. Why had his wife come to the park two days running? Why had she left Sarah on her own? These were just two of many minor thoughts that were consumed in his despair. He couldn't swim and he knew the currents hereabouts were lethal. He'd murdered his own daughter.

The old hag was running along the bank with the flow of the water screaming and waving her arms about.

Ben took the car out of gear and let the electronics open the windows as the front wheels edged over the bank. He closed his eyes, and took a final and unnecessary deep breath as the vehicle tipped forward into the foam.

His wife Lynn mourned briefly, but she soon found a new partner who was happy to accept Sarah as his own. The old woman had scoured the river for days afterwards and managed to find all her possessions except for the yellow plastic duck the nice young lady had given her.

Many hours spent commuting on London Underground can do things to the mind – and this story is an example of that; staring out of dirty windows and imagining something – anything – that could liven up the journey a bit! Why not a brief encounter with a long lost love?

Brief Encounter

Jane Crane

"Oh fuck it!" I shout, probably a bit too loudly as half a dozen heads turn in my direction.

I watch the back end of my train as it pulls away from the platform and curse my bad luck. I am going to be late for the party; a fact that won't go down too well since I am supposed to be the guest of honour. I consider using missing the train as the perfect excuse not to go, but decide against it. Instead I head for a graffiti covered bench at the far end of the platform and sit down to wait. As I sit I almost drop the bottle of red wine I am clutching to my chest. It had taken me ages to choose which bottle to buy and my indecision is the reason I missed my train and now find myself shivering on the platform. I don't really know why I bothered to buy wine at all. I'm going to a party being thrown in my honour – why am I bringing wine?

I watch as a couple walk down the steps and on to the platform. They are young and obviously very much in love. Although it appears that in this case love is being measured by how far he can get his hand up her shirt. The boy whispers something in the girl's ear and she looks over at me and giggles. I pray that they won't come and sit on my bench but to no avail. The boy plonks himself down on the opposite end of the bench and the girl climbs astride him. I check the platform display board, only one minute until the next train. There are a few people on the platform but I'm confident I will be able to find a seat on the train as far away from the lovebirds as possible. The girl is now making little moaning noises whenever she comes up for air and I realise that either her boyfriend is missing a hand or he has it stuck down the front of his girlfriend's jeans. I am mesmerised, not by the act itself but by the sheer brazenness of it. I don't know quite what to do. What is the correct etiquette in these situations? Shall I get up and move away or wait until he's finished and then offer him a tissue? I realise that the moaning has stopped and the couple are now staring at me staring at them.

"D'you want something love?" The girl is looking angrily at me. I see she is a lot younger than I first supposed. Her little face has the look of a petulant toddler wearing its mum's eyeliner and I feel the urge to take her to one side and have a conversation with her about self respect – but I don't. Instead I just shake my head, embarrassed, then get up and walk away.

For a second I feel terrible then I start to feel angry. How dare she tell me off? I'm not the one getting fingered on a train platform in full view of everyone! And she has the gall to look offended with me! I want to go back and say something but I don't. I don't like confrontation. Far better to bottle up your frustrations and keep them tucked away inside where they can eat away at you properly.

Thankfully at this point I see a train coming towards the platform. I decide to wait and see which carriage the young lovers get into before I board the train myself. Once they safely disappear into a carriage further back I get on and find a seat. I put the bottle of wine on the floor between my feet and place my bag on my lap with my arms folded protectively over it and over me. In all honesty I don't like travelling on trains much, I prefer being in my car, by myself, not having to share my space with strangers. But my friend Sarah had insisted I come to the party by train so I could, and this is a direct quote, "Get completely wankered for a change." I don't drink that much, in fact I don't think I've ever been 'completely wankered' in all of my thirty-eight years. Sarah had gone on and on about it for weeks so I eventually gave in and promised that I wouldn't drive to the party.

As the train pulls out of the station I see a woman, about my age, running to try and catch it. I see her sweaty, red face and I see her mouth the words "Oh shit!" I realise that was how I must have looked to the passengers on the train I missed. Not a pretty picture. I see my own face reflected back at me on the window. I look old and tired and my hair appears to have developed a life of its own. I unzip my handbag and grope around inside it for a brush or something to tidy up the mess and my vigorous rummaging causes me to kick over the bottle of wine.

"Oh bugger it!" I mutter and lean forward to retrieve it but it's already rolled under my seat. I kneel down and scrabble around to try and find it, my fingers moving across the sticky floor. I'm not surprised when the first thing my hand lands on is a discarded piece of hamburger. Eventually I find the bottle and get back in my seat. My hand is covered in fluff and ketchup and smells of a heady combination of grease and piss. I try to find a tissue in my bag to wipe off the mess.

"Can I help at all?" I see a hand reach through between the seats from behind me, clutching a slightly crumpled tissue.

"No thanks I'm fine" I say. I know I have tissues in here somewhere but I'm having trouble finding them amongst all the stuff I seem to have accumulated. I curse my choice of handbag. I'd bought one with plenty of compartments in the hope it would help me be more organised but in reality all it does is give me more places to lose my shit! I finally find the tissues and with a small sense of triumph I hold them aloft like a trophy.

The hand clutching the tissue retreats through the seats behind me whilst I busy myself removing the dirt from my fingers. The bottle of red is now ensconced between me and the carriage wall and I vow to make sure it stays there for the rest of my journey.

"Oh yeah, whatever, Granddad!"

"Stop bloody staring, you perv!"

The unmistakeable voices of my modern day Romeo and his Juliet float down the carriage towards me. I shrink a little further down in my seat and hope that they won't make it to my end of the train. No such luck of course. They find two seats across the aisle from me and resume their passionate face sucking. I marvel at how oblivious they are to their surroundings. The young woman sitting opposite them picks up her bag and moves away down the carriage to another seat. Her embarrassment seems to spur the couple on and their performance increases in both volume and intensity. I feel compelled to watch. I can't help it. It's like seeing a road accident. You drive past and you know you shouldn't look but you just can't seem to stop yourself. What is it about this spectacle that's holding my attention? Stupid question, I know what it is. I realise I am jealous. A thirty eight year old woman jealous of a couple of horny teenagers – how pathetic! It's not what they are doing that I am jealous of but more their complete lack of shame and embarrassment. They don't care who is watching or what anybody thinks.

"Interesting show, isn't it?" A man's voice comes from the seats behind me. I assume it belongs to the hand that reached out to help me earlier.

"I guess that's what being young and in love will do for you," I mumble, as I pretend to look for something in my bag. I don't want to get into a conversation with some random stranger about the antics we've just witnessed.

"In love, my arse – he wants into her knickers and then he'll move on," the voice replies.

I want to point out that I think the young man may have already jumped that particular hurdle but I think better of it. Arrogant git, I should tell him to keep his opinions to himself. The next stop is mine so I grab the wine, sling my bag over my shoulder and stand up, ready to fix the voice behind me with my best meaningful glare, but he is gone. I see a small group of people standing by the doors and assume he must be there waiting to leave the train. It seems to be taking forever to get to the next stop. I am in the middle of berating myself for getting out of my seat too early when suddenly the train comes to a juddering halt and all the lights go out.

"What the hell?"

"Bloody trains – what's going on?"

"Has someone pulled the emergency brake?"

The voices of confused and frustrated passengers all seem to blend in to one huge cacophony of complaining. Then, as suddenly as they had gone out, the lights come back on but they are dimmer.

"You always said I looked better in dim light, Jo." The voice in my right ear makes me jump and I instinctively take a step back, away from the voice. I catch my heel on something as I move and I can feel myself begin to fall backwards then a hand takes hold of mine and steadies me.

"I'm sorry. I didn't mean to make you jump like that. It's me, Jo, its Daniel. Don't you remember?"

"Daniel? "

I can't quite believe it, he looks familiar but there is something different about him. It takes me a few seconds to process it but then I realise.

"Where are those enormous glasses you used to wear? You couldn't see a bloody thing without those," I ask.

"Laser eye surgery. What can I say? It's a miracle. Are you sure you're okay?"

He is still holding my hand and I begin to feel a little uncomfortable so I remove it from his grip and begin picking at an imaginary piece of fluff on my skirt. When I eventually look up he is staring at me.

"Wha .... wha ... what are you doing here?" I can't seem to make my mouth form coherent sentences. This is too surreal. Daniel James does not belong on a train in my present.

"I can't really believe it's you to be honest," I say.

"I've been in London all day, business stuff, you know how it is."

I want to reply that actually no, I don't know how it is, but I still can't seem to make sense of it all. Then I realise something.

"That was you wasn't it? Sat behind me, offering tissues?" He nods and looks a bit sheepish.

"I was hoping you'd turn around – I saw you get on the train and then when you sat in front of me – I was trying to think of something witty and charming to say to you but ... well ... um ..."

"You ended up offering me tissues? Suave."

"Oh, piss off, JoJo," he says.

Before I have a chance to reply the train intercom crackles into life.

"We apologise for the delay, ladies and gentlemen, but there has been a power failure on the track ahead. Network Rail engineers are working to repair the problem and we hope to have you on your way very shortly. Thank you."

A chorus of groans and swear words fills the carriage but I actually find myself feeling pleased to be stuck on this train for now. I am in no rush to get to my party.

"Are you going somewhere special? Is this going to make you late for something?" Daniel asks. I shake my head.

"No, nothing special. I mean, just a party, for me, but I'm sure they will just go ahead and start without me." I can see Sarah now, effing and blinding about how she knew I wasn't going to turn up, how could I be so rude after she'd made all this effort? Blah, blah, blah. Well, I hadn't asked her to organise a party for me. I was quite happy just doing without but she hadn't wanted to hear of it. She'd cornered me in our little staff kitchen when she heard the news. Initially I think she wanted to make sure it was true, it had come slightly out of the blue for people, I suppose. Once she had all the details though then she went into full on party planner mode.

"You must let me organise something, Jo," she had said to me, "this event cannot go unmarked. I promise you I will keep it very tasteful and low key, just how you like things."

Tasteful and low key had turned into thirty women and the

function room at a hotel. I was grateful for Sarah's support, I really was, but sometimes she could be a bit of a handful. I don't think I even know thirty people so who the hell is going to be at the party anyway?

"We should probably sit down again. Don't think we're going anywhere for a while."

Daniel's voice interrupts my thoughts. I nod and we head for two empty seats near the doors.

"We'll keep away from the amateur porn show shall we?" said Daniel, as he sits down. "Unless you wanted to go back for another look – you did seem quite engrossed in it," he says. I shoot him a horrified glance.

"I was not!" I say, as I feel my face begin to warm up. "I was just amazed at their lack of shame, that's all."

Daniel chuckles. "Yeah, sure, that's what it is – straightforward righteous indignation." I give him a wry smile in response and take my seat. I'm not sure what to say next. The silence between us seems to go on forever and the harder I try to come up with something to say the less I can think of. I look around the train carriage for some inspiration, what on earth for I don't know; perhaps I am hoping that the poster talking about the importance of checking for STDs will spark off a lively conversation? After what seems like ages, but is probably only a few seconds, he finally breaks the silence.

"So, how have you been?" And there it is, probably the most annoying question in the history of civilised society. How had I been? What is the correct response to that question after such a long time has passed? We haven't seen each other for nearly twenty years; how do you sum up that much time in a handy conversation sized package? It's probably more polite to just say a benign "I've been fine thanks, and you?" but, unluckily for Daniel, I find myself in a slightly more expansive mood.

"Well, let's see. My best friend, that's you by the way, ups and moves away when I'm eighteen and I never see him again. I meet the love of my life at twenty and then become a widow at thirty.

I never achieve my ambition to become an Oscar winning actress and I've been stuck in the worst job in the world for the last ten years. How about you? How have you been?"

Daniel is staring at me with a look of total shock on his face. He opens his mouth to speak and then closes it again. He does that so many times he is beginning to look like a goldfish and I find myself talking again to fill the silence.

"Sorry .. um .. that was unkind of me. Not your fault. Don't know why I told you all that really. It's probably the shock of seeing you again after all this time. Ignore me. I'm fine, honestly. My life is good. Thank you for asking."

I punctuate the last word with a bright, more than slightly fake, smile, which I hope has made up for my bad behaviour. Daniel still looks more than a little uncomfortable but he manages to speak.

"Jesus Christ, Jo! You still know how to surprise me, even after all this time!" He shakes his head and looks at me. "I'm so sorry about your husband. That must have been awful for you."

"Car accident, nothing special," I say, by way of an explanation. That must sound harsh but that's how it had been; nothing extraordinary just a driver not paying attention. That had been all it took to bring my whole world down around my ears. Daniel takes my hand and holds it between the two of his. His hands are warm and soft and I enjoy the feeling of him. I think maybe I'm enjoying it a bit too much though so I pull out of his grip and try to change the subject.

"What about you? Where have you been for the last twenty years?" I ask, "It was like you dropped off the face of the Earth, no one knew where you'd gone."

"Well, after Dad died Mum wanted to move back to Glasgow to be nearer to her family and I went with her." He shrugs. "I couldn't leave her on her own so I applied to Glasgow Uni and we lived there for three years."

I remember how much of a mess Daniel's mum had been after his dad died. She started to drink a lot, and sleep a lot too, stopped going out, stopped doing shopping. Daniel would spend so much time at our house that my dad joked that he ought to charge him rent. It had made me so angry back then, to see his mum neglecting him so badly. But I hadn't really understood the depth of that kind of grief at the time. I did now.

"How is your mum?" I ask.

"She's good. She got married again. His name's Patrick. He's a good guy. He's Canadian so that's where I've been for the last fifteen years or so. He married mom and we all moved to Vancouver." I realise why I hadn't recognised his voice straight away. There is a definite trace of an accent; not all the time but just occasionally the trans-Atlantic twang creeps in and takes over.

It is hard to reconcile this new Daniel with the gangly, awkward nerd I remember. We had been friends since we were five. Daniel's family had lived two doors away from mine and we had gone to all the same schools growing up. He had been like a brother to me until puberty hit and hormones became involved. Almost overnight he went from being my best friend to my unrequited love. I loved Daniel James with a passion that may have bordered on obsession but he always insisted we should just stay friends. I tried to make him change his mind many times. I still cringe at one particular incident, right after his sixteenth birthday party, when I decided to get naked in his bed and offer myself to him. *How could he refuse?* I thought. But refuse he did.

"You're not still thinking about my sixteenth birthday are you?" he asks, interrupting my thoughts in the middle of that horrendous flashback. What the hell? How could he possibly know that?

"You always used to twist your hair around your finger whenever you were embarrassed or nervous. The only thing I could think of that you could be embarrassed about with me was that night after my birthday party." I lean forward and put my face in my hands.

"Oh god!" I mumble into my palms. "I can't believe I still feel so bad about that, even after all this time. You were very nice about it though. You even helped me zip my dress back up. I was mortified!"

"I was an idiot," he replies matter of factly. That makes me smile. "I think I was worried I'd get it wrong and be a total disappointment and then you'd never speak to me again."

"So in order to mask those feelings you went and spent the next year getting it on with Janice Hooper at every available opportunity," I reply. Janice Hooper – the school slapper. Big boobs, no brain and even less shame. I am pleased to see that it is now Daniel's turn to look shamefaced.

"Bloody hell, Janice Hooper. I haven't thought about her in years. What was I thinking?"

"Don't ask me, I never understood it. All I knew was that you rejected me in favour of that big breasted trollop and I was back to being just your mate."

Daniel's relationship with Janice had lasted for a year, right up until his dad died suddenly from a heart attack. After that Daniel became too much like hard work for Janice and I was the only one who stuck it out with him while he grieved. We had become close again but within six months he was gone. His mum gave the keys for their house back to the council and they disappeared without a word. I was so hurt; he hadn't even told me he was going, let alone where. My mum said she was pretty sure that they had headed back to Glasgow but she hadn't known any more than that.

"I thought about coming after you," I say. "I even bought a train ticket to Glasgow. I don't know what I thought I was going to do once I arrived. Wander the streets until I found you I guess."

I remember thinking that I would know where he was once I got to Glasgow, like I would somehow be able to track him down through my sheer force of will. In the end I decided that he obviously didn't want me to find him, if he had then he would have told me he was leaving.

"I didn't have a chance, Jo. I knew Mum was up to something, there had been lots of calls to my grandmother in Glasgow, lots of whispering down the phone. The next thing I knew I came home early from college and she was getting in a cab! She was going to leave without me, Jo!" I watch him talk and while he does he keeps his eyes firmly fixed on the carriage floor.

"She had packed my stuff and was going to leave it at your house, said I would be better off without her but I couldn't lose her as well as dad, so I jumped in the cab and that was it. I knew you would be upset that I had just gone and I figured you probably wouldn't want to speak to me after that so I kept away."

I want to say something to him, to tell him that is a load of shit; that I would have wanted to hear from him no matter what but I find I can't. It all suddenly seems like so much old water under too many bridges. I don't have the energy to care. I have other things on my mind. I don't want to be looking backwards when I have a future to think about for the first time in what seems like forever.

"I'm getting married tomorrow!" I blurt out. Daniel looks surprised. I'm not sure why I felt the urge to say that to him. He didn't need to know that, did he? I could have gotten off the train – when we finally make it into a station – said goodbye and he would never have known.

"Wow. Another surprise, never a dull moment with you is there? So this party you're on your way to?" Daniel says.

"My hen party, apparently," I reply.

"And the wedding is tomorrow?"

"Yes. It's in the afternoon at the registry office. It's not a big deal. Simon didn't want to make a fuss as it's a second marriage for both of us. He said it would be a bit vulgar to do a big church thing at our age." I'm rambling.

I see Daniel raise an eyebrow at that last comment. He looks like he is about to say something but decides against it. I am grateful for that – I really don't want to discuss it – I have made my decision and I'm content with it. Besides, I have my reasons for not wanting too much fuss either. You don't ever really want to advertise the fact that you're getting married just to avoid being alone. People would think I was crazy, or totally desperate, to get married again for companionship rather than love but I have made up my mind. I had followed my heart before and look what had happened. Simon understood this. He felt the same way I did.

"So how did you meet him?"

"We met at a bereavement group I went to after John was killed."

"Aren't there rules about members getting together or something?"

"Yeah, why? Are you thinking of going along to see if you can pick up some grieving widow action?" I ask. I expect him to laugh at my joke but he doesn't. His mood seems to have changed.

"Very funny. I'm just curious that's all."

"We didn't get together until about eighteen months later. We had both left the group by then so nobody cared."

I remember my first date with Simon. He had spent most of the night talking about his dead wife – it was very romantic. I think I realised then that I would never be the love of his life, nor he mine, but we understood each other and liked each other's company. It was better than being single in a world where coupledom is king.

Daniel and I sit in silence again for a few minutes but unlike earlier, this silence feels familiar and comfortable. There were lots of times we would just sit like this, especially after his dad died. When we were teenagers we would go and sit on a bench at the top of a dry ski slope that some idiot built by the side of the A13. There was a concrete path that snaked all the way around the back side of it and it took you right to the top. At night the view was pretty cool; the street lights and car headlamps all below us, they looked so pretty you almost forgot you were on top of what had been an old rubbish tip in the middle of East London, right next to a busy motorway.

"They demolished the ski slope, did you know that?"

For the second time in our short conversation Daniel has correctly predicted where my mind has meandered off to. I'm not sure I'm comfortable with how well he knows me and I'm starting to feel a bit like a bug under a microscope. I keep my gaze locked on to the floor in front of me and that's when I notice that one of his shoelaces is untied. It makes me smile. It reminds me of the Daniel I remember, the little boy. He was always tripping on his feet, usually because one, or both, of his shoes were untied. He always had grazed elbows or scuffed knees. My mum would sit him on our kitchen worktop and dab at whatever new injury with spit and kitchen roll and then put plenty of Germolene on as a safety precaution; you could soothe everything with Germolene she used to say and we had believed her.

"Your shoe is untied you idiot. Mind you don't trip up, Daniel James." I nudge him gently with my shoulder.

"Daniel James. That sounds so weird now," he says. I give him a puzzled look.

"Mum changed her name when she got remarried and it was just easier for me to do the same. Patrick's been really good to me so it seemed the right thing to do." He sounds sad, and I put my hand on his arm to reassure him. He covers my hand with his and looks at me.

"Are you in love then, Jo?" he asks. I'm not sure what to say. I could lie and say yes and then that would be it or I could tell him the truth: that I don't want, or need, to be 'in love' anymore.

"Simon is a good person, Daniel. He takes care of me and I take care of him. We get along quite nicely together, it works for us."

"So you don't love him?"

"I don't see how that's any of your business really," I say, pulling my hand away from his arm. He shakes his head.

"It's not I guess. But I would like to think you were happy. You were my best friend too, Jo. I cared – care – about what happens to you." I want to stop him saying anymore, I don't need to hear his opinions on my life and what I'm doing; he had given up that right a long time ago. I change the subject.

"So what's your name now then?" I ask. For a few seconds he just looks at me and I assume he's trying to decide whether or not to go along with my attempts to divert the conversation away from me. Finally he says,

"It's Daniel Campbell. I use James as my middle name now, just so I don't feel like I've abandoned dad totally."

"That's nice. It's a good, honest name." He opens his mouth to speak but the nasal voice of the train driver interrupts him.

"Ladies and Gentlemen, this is the driver speaking. The engineers have fixed the fault and we will be moving again in a few minutes. Once again we apologise for any delays."

I take a deep breath and stand up.

"Well, Daniel James Campbell, it's been really nice to see you again. Take care of yourself and tell your mum I said hello." He stands up with me and we are face to face for a few seconds. I don't know what to do now; should we shake hands? No, too formal. Is it wrong to kiss him goodbye? I can see he feels as awkward as I do so I lean up and kiss him on the cheek and then I turn and walk over to the train doors. I don't look back. I just stare at the dirty walls of the tunnel as they move slowly past. I look at my reflection in the dark train window and over my shoulder I can see Daniel just staring at me.

I hold my breath, willing the train into the next station. I want to get off and get away before he can ask me any more questions. I haven't had to explain my decision to anyone up until now. Agreeing to marry Simon has given me a feeling of calm and security that I haven't felt for a long time, like I'm finally back in control of my life and the course it's taking. That was until today. Now I feel unsettled and unsure of myself. If I can just get off this bloody train and get to my party then everything will be fine, I reason. There are people there waiting to celebrate my great news and I need them around me now to drown out my doubts with their congratulations and air kisses.

The train finally stops and the doors begin to open. I don't wait for them to open completely; I force myself out between them as soon as the gap is big enough and take in a great lungful of air, like a deep sea diver deprived of oxygen. I walk quickly over to the stairs that will take me up and out onto the busy street. I'm halfway up when I hear a voice calling my name, asking me to wait. It's Daniel. I turn and see him at the bottom of the stairs, trapped behind a group of men in suits. I give him a small wave and then turn and carry on up the steps.

I reach the top and fumble in my coat pocket for my ticket. My heart is pounding so hard in my chest that I think the whole world must be able to hear it as I stick my ticket in the barrier and walk through.

Out of the station and turn left, out of the station and turn left, that's what Sarah had said and I repeat it over and over like a mantra as I walk towards the station exit. If I can just make it out of the station then I can lose Daniel amongst the crowds and traffic noise and then everything will be fine. Everything will go back to normal and I will forget my doubts and forget how good it felt to just have him hold my hand again after all these years.

I can see the hotel on the other side of the road just up ahead and I can see Sarah standing on the steps looking in my direction. She sees me and waves and then gestures at her watch and mouths the words "Where the fuck have you been?!"

I pick up my pace a little and step into the road and straight into the path of a cyclist. Everything seems to move in slow motion from that point; I see the panicked face of the cyclist as he sharply swerves to avoid me and I feel two hands grab my shoulders and pull me back onto the kerb as the bicycle whizzes past. The cyclist is shouting and gesturing to me as he speeds off down the road but I can't make out what he is saying. I'm sure it isn't particularly complimentary though. I know it is Daniel's hands on my shoulders even before I turn around.

"Christ, Jo! What the fuck? Why didn't you look where you

were going?" he shouts, as he turns me around to face him. He looks pale and angry and shocked all at the same time.

"I wasn't thinking I guess – too busy rushing to my party." I give him a weak smile. He is still gripping my shoulders and he has his face so close to mine. Before I can move out of his grip he pulls me into a hug and squeezes me so hard I think he might crack a rib. Over his shoulder I can see Sarah standing on the hotel steps with her mouth wide open. The realisation of how this must look to her hits me and suddenly I feel so angry ... with Daniel, with Sarah, with Simon, with my whole stupid life. I keep my arms firmly by my sides and when he realises I'm not hugging him back he lets me go.

"I'm not some dumb bloody heroine in a crappy romance novel that you need to rescue, Daniel!" I shout. "I'm fine, I don't need anyone's help, not least of all a man I haven't seen in twenty years!" His jaw clenches and his hands fist by his sides.

"I'm not trying to rescue you from anything other than your own stupidity!" he shouts back.

I'm not sure if he means my near miss with the cyclist or something else but I don't care. I know what I want to do right then, in that moment. It is so clear it takes my breath away.

"I have to go now. Goodbye, Daniel," I say, as I turn and walk away. Sarah gives me a wave and a relieved smile as I cross the road and make my way towards the hotel. I see the black cab idling by the kerb with its orange light glowing like a beacon and I climb straight into the back of it. Sarah's smile changes from relief to confusion in a split second.

"Where to, love?" the driver asks me.

"I don't know yet. Can we just drive and I'll let you know when I've decided?"

"Fair enough sweetheart, it's your life."

As the taxi pulls out into the flow of traffic I look out of the back window. Daniel is just standing there, watching me go.

"Yes" I say, to no one in particular, "It most definitely is my life."

This was the second story I wrote in Emily's class, redrafted many times since as I've gradually learned how to say more in fewer words (I'm still learning!). It's the one closest to my heart because it's a tribute to my mum.

Ducks And Swans

Julie Williams

An old friend stood at Mum's front door, arm in arm with her husband. Lavinia had phoned the day before to ask if she and Roger might call on their way to a great-niece's wedding. Sister of an ancient earl who'd cashed in the family Rembrandt and chanced away the proceeds at Monte Carlo, Lavinia exchanged cards with my mother Jean every Christmas. It was fifteen years since they'd last met.

"Darlings, how lovely!" Mum carolled from her chair when I showed them into the sitting room. It might have been a stranger talking. Her voice hadn't sounded so full of life, or so posh, since I could remember. With a jolt, I realised how subdued she'd become. When you're with someone practically every day, changes in them don't register. She wasn't aware of what was happening to her and I wasn't either, not really, but I sensed she needed my support. This reunion was a big deal. I'd left my baby with a friend, tidied the house, washed the best teacups and set them on a low table in front of the fire.

Lavinia bent for a kiss. "Jean, it's been an age. How are you, darling?" Straightening up was a slow job for her. She was still holding Mum's hand when I excused myself to make the tea. A stage whisper followed me to the kitchen, "... very proud of her, a wonderful wife and mother and a brilliant career as a writer, too ..."

The sputter of the kettle drowned out the rest but as ever my cheeks grew hot at the shameless puff. I'd repeated that I was only a reporter on the local paper more times than I could count. On my way back with the teapot and a homemade cake on a tray, Mum's bright new voice stopped me mid-stride: "They named the baby after me, but I'm afraid the poor child's going to grow up with a figure like her other granny. That woman has the biggest bottom you've ever seen."

Their laughs sounded genuine. I adjusted my expression to indulgently amused and hoped this version of my mother was the Jean that they remembered.

Lavinia and Roger were settled side by side on the sofa opposite Mum. He ran a finger round his collar as the twenty-five-degree fug impacted on him. Lavinia, sober but celebratory in dark blue, kept her back straight and her knees neatly together. Narrow black patent pumps with grosgrain bows across the toe completed her wedding outfit.

"Jean's been telling us you have a daughter now," she said. "Grandchildren are such a delight, aren't they?"

Mum would never pick up this cue. Someone had to.

"Tell us about yours. We love little ones, don't we, Mum?" I said. I'd cut the cake and handed it round. Mum took a massive bite out of her slice and certainly wouldn't be able to talk for a while. I'd wanted her to be mother with the teapot, but now I saw it would be too much for her and that I'd have to be in charge. Lavinia focused on each of us in turn as she gave the lowdown on the youngest Hons in her family. Dry and witty without a wasted word, it was a masterpiece of social narration sadly wasted on its audience. Mum was too busy enjoying her cake to concentrate and I'd become preoccupied with the side table where Lavinia had set her plate.

It was early nineteenth century, walnut with barley-twist legs, and Roger had presented it to Mum on her fortieth birthday. One Saturday night, misbehaving with a boyfriend, I'd put a bottle of red wine on its gleaming top and nothing could shift the purple ring it had left. Lavinia's cup rattled on its saucer as I put it down to cover the horrid stain. Had she noticed it? Probably.

Mum finished her cake and seized her chance to talk while Lavinia drank her tea. "Julie helped herself to your precious snuffboxes when we came to tea one day, Roger, remember? You used to call them your bibelots." She leaned forward with a roguish twinkle and patted Roger's bony knee. "She'd hidden them in the little basket she carried everywhere and when we got home she tipped them out on the floor as presents for her teddy. What a little character, and she hasn't changed a bit – you wouldn't think she was fifty-six to look at her now, would you?" I was thirty-six, but I let it pass.

Exhausted by this effort of memory and exposition, Mum fell into one of her armchair snoozes and, after a minute or two, Lavinia stood, took my arm and steered me outside to the garden. We left Roger on the sofa across from my sleeping mother, blinking through his glasses at the Times crossword puzzle which he'd discreetly withdrawn from his jacket pocket.

Lavinia pointed her long, straight nose at the winceyette nightie I wished I'd remembered to take off the washing-line – Mum would never have been caught in such a pickle, even a year before. She shook her head slowly.

"Dear Jean, her ducks were always swans." She spoke inwardly, as though this particular duck wasn't standing next to her on the lawn. Her words hit a tender spot in me that still smarts to this day. I knew what picture we presented: a declining old lady; a busy daughter struggling to keep up with her mother's growing needs; a situation that shouldn't have been allowed to continue. Finding her friend so diminished must have been a shock and Lavinia, eyes still sharp and wise though watery with age, was finding her own way of dealing with it.

Mum had often told me how they met, years before I was born. I imagine it was curiosity that prompted Lavinia to ask Mum in for tea when she called with a collection envelope for a blind babies' charity. Being Mum, she'd have exclaimed at the beauty of a flower arrangement in the hall and I know she crouched on the doorstep to play peekaboo with shy little

Beatrix, Lavinia's eldest, who was hiding behind her mother's skirts. Once inside, Mum no doubt expressed heartfelt admiration for the Georgian silver teapot, crooked her little finger when she held her cup and chinked its rim with her spoon when she stirred it. Not a shred of self-consciousness intervened between the impulse and the word or deed, and I bet Lavinia itched to know where all that sunny self-confidence came from.

Over the years Mum must have enraged her but she never showed it. Lavinia had investments in South Africa yet she only gently demurred when Mum, fired up by a bishop's talk to the Young Wives, spoke out with passion against apartheid. Mum joshed the unworldly Roger for never having tried to find himself a proper job while Lavinia exemplified her own oddly motherly attitude to his lack of ambition by repeating: "Roger wasn't brought up to earn a living, poor lamb." Worst of all, Mum palled up with their Nanny, Yvonne, and used to meet her for tea in Fullers on her day off from the nursery. That simply wasn't done. Despite these irritations, the friendship endured.

After Roger inherited and the family moved away, Mum wrote long letters to Lavinia as she later did to me. Each letter in her clear, forward sloping, upward-tending hand, peppered with exclamation marks, maintained the illusion that she was still there in the room, talking, talking, but listening, too. And the never-ending conversation left the reader in no doubt that she and hers were clever, beautiful and special. That her ducks were all swans.

The story of The Ugly Duckling always made me cry. No-one supported him when he was picked on for being different. He spent a long winter alone on a desolate marsh trying to work out what he'd done wrong. Dad, who used to read to me at bedtime, would pass me a tissue at the end and say: "Look, it's ended happily. He's found out he belongs with the swans and now he's going to be fine," but I wouldn't be comforted, mostly because the 'duckling's' fate hung on a random stroke of luck. Out there on his own, the odds were stacked against recognising himself as the handsome swan reflected in the water. Without help, it was a miracle he made the connection. He could so easily have endured a lonely lifetime without a family and without becoming the best he could be. Poor duckling. He didn't have a mum like mine.

In 1968 as student protests swept across the US and Europe, we were in Exeter's most opulent department store, shopping for something for me to wear at the Freshers' Disco. In the changing cubicle Mum's formidable double-D chest and big personality had me squashed up close to the mirror. Our reflections jostled before us – me in front; small, slight, shifting my weight from one bare foot to the other. I thrust one hip forward at a time, hypnotising us both as the geometric pattern of the dress I'd tried on fused and separated. Mum beamed over my shoulder, taller in the four-inch heels she always wore, her face vivid with delight. Dresses of all colours were piled in the corner and a rattling bunch of coat-hangers crowded out the only peg on the wall.

"Darling, this is the one. Black and white is very chic, and you're so slim. You'll wow the boys in this. Believe me, I know what wows the boys!"

Mum pulled the curtain aside and gently pushed me out. My father was perched on a delicate gilt chair next to a mannequin in a mink coat.

"You look lovely, darling." He beamed his approval. "It's a bit short, maybe, but you have the legs for it. Not quite as good as your mother's, of course, but a fine pair of pins all the same."

So the op-art minidress it was. Dad wrote a cheque and soon afterwards his Rover 2000 dropped me back on campus with my carrier bag. I knew what Mum's expectations were for me that night.

She wanted me to take her place in the pictures from her youth she'd painted in my imagination. I'd be at the centre of a group of immaculate young intellectuals, dazzling them with my repartee, keeping each in thrall with a word, a glance, a dip of my pretty head on its swan-like neck. I would dance with all who asked. I'd be kind to my plainer girlfriends and try to get them partners. Above all, I would be the unattainable quarry. Men would chase me, not I them.

Of course it didn't work out like that. The disco volume drowned out all intelligible speech and it was no longer cool for boys to look smart. The world had changed a staggering amount since the 1930s when Mum was young and there was much to learn. It was a long time before my inner swan got close to spreading its wings. When it did emerge it can't have been the kind of bird Mum had hoped for, but she never let on.

I tried to keep the hurt from my voice. "What do you mean, her ducks were always swans?" Lavinia shook her head again then looked at me with piercing directness.

"I love Jean. She's one of my dearest friends. She and I were girls at the same time in the Thirties but our girlhoods were sooo different. I was the one born with a silver spoon in her mouth. Life was suuuch fun for me – coming out, the Season, without a care in the world. Jean didn't have my freedom, my opportunities. But she made sure anything was possible for you when you were a girl. You know she can't go on like this, don't you?"

I spluttered. "I know, I know, but what can I do? She's used to living here, in this house. She loves the baby. I can't just ..."

"You've got to be practical. She wouldn't even remember that she had a pan boiling on the stove, would she? Has she started wandering into the road? You must address this before something frightful happens."

Lavinia took my arm and led me back to the house, her elbow

against my side as fragile as a bird's wing. My mind was racing. She hadn't told me anything I didn't know in my heart. In this small house overstuffed with a lifetime's furniture I'd gradually taken over responsibility for Mum's shopping list, her cooked dinners, her outings, a series of unreliable gardeners and one saintly home help. I'd sat at the table with her as her Biro snailed across Christmas cards to friends, urging her on when she glanced up for reassurance mid-word, occasionally asking me who she was writing to. But in both our minds she was still the boss, mistress of her own house, my mum, Jeanie's grandma. This would have to change. Lavinia had made it official.

In the late 1980s, there was no reliable diagnosis for Alzheimer's and the first two nursing homes where they told us they could cope with a 'confused' old lady proved quite unable to handle Mum. Luckily staff at the third understood that patients with senile dementia remain individuals, each with their own personality, each affected in a different way by the medical problems which cause it. She was happy there until she died, three years after Lavinia's visit.

Perhaps a month before her death she started to withdraw into herself and lose her interest in people. Up to then she remained as communicative as ever, her clear voice informing all corners of the residents' lounge of the unparalleled brilliance of every member of her family and explicitly comparing us with the poor specimens other people had visiting them.

On the day I remember best, I'd passed round a bag of jelly babies in a feeble attempt to deflect the other residents' hostile stares. Jeanie squealed much too loudly. I thought we'd be thrown out. It was all Mum's fault. The two of them were playing peekaboo and I caught Mum beaming across at Jeanie just the way she'd beamed at me in the mirror the day of the Freshers' Disco twenty years before, her face aglow with love and hope.

I wanted to explore how love and loss interact with hope and friendship. I love France: its food, wine and culture. I was lucky to tour the vineyards around Beaune in a chauffeur driven Rolls Royce, lent to us for the day (another story perhaps).

Last of The Vintage

Siân Thomas

Mason stared at the twin bottles grinning at him in the dim light of the cellar. There should have been a solitary bottle of this last vintage remaining. How could he have got it wrong? There were definitely two in the rack in front of him.

He had completed his inventory several weeks ago, taking pleasure in the thought that only the more mediocre wines would remain, except of course for this last bottle, his favourite Côte de Beaune vintage.

To most people, discovering a double pleasure would be a bonus; another bottle would surely keep the other company. What was the hardship in that? But Mason knew that precisely one bottle would suffice for him. Two would ruin the delicate balance he sought. He shuddered. It had to be just right this weekend. The last thing he wanted was to botch the job or, even worse, to leave someone the impression that he had needed to bolster his courage.

He scanned his memory. Yes, Hugh was definitely to blame. Mason had been in the cellar making up the inventory when his Philistine nephew had called. The persistent clamour of Vivaldi from the mobile had filled the small space, demanding Mason's immediate attention. He must have miscounted the bottles then. It would all be Hugh's soon anyway, the house and its contents, but not this vintage. Mason was adamant that he would not leave his nephew even one of these bottles.

Mason brushed one hand over their necks, his fingers feeling the grains of dust and grit that had built up over the years in the cellar. He lifted out one bottle and wiped it carefully with his sleeve. Crimson hues shot through moss and petal greens as he caressed it in his hand. He remembered the same shades of light as the sun had set languidly over the vineyard on the outskirts of Beaune that early autumn evening four years ago. He and Amy had watched the labourers toiling over the vines, as they used the remaining light to finish gathering for the local domaine. Later the proprietor had insisted that he give Mason and Amy a few bottles as a parting gift to mark their honeymoon.

Amy had loved travelling in France, sharing the driving of the battered Deux Chevaux through the vineyards around Dijon. Neither of them had known it would be her last visit. Only two years later she had been diagnosed; she had fought hard to stay with Mason, but gradually her body had transformed into a fragile husk, unable to bear her fluttering spirit.

Mason sighed. What should he do with these two bottles? He replaced the bottle to lie next to its partner. For now, let them rest there together. He wanted to consider this carefully, but he knew he had left himself little time.

He had planned it all meticulously for this weekend. Early that morning he had watched his neighbours, Mr and Mrs Price, preparing to depart for the weekend, arguing over the satnav route as they filled the car with cases and presents for the grandchildren. Finally, doors slammed, gears crunched and the car bounced angrily out of the cul de sac. Silence had closed in quickly on the London street. Even the park opposite had remained empty of dog walkers and joggers at that hour. A cat slunk along the top of the low brick wall in front of the other adjoining terrace house whose shutters were closed like pendulous eyelids. Claire, the freelance photographer who owned the house, often left it empty whilst on foreign assignments.

Mason sat at the kitchen table, fingering his wedding band. He could no longer remain here without Amy; it was time to move on. Mason tried to twist the ring off his finger, but it was too tight. He pushed the chair away and walked to the sink, letting the cold water run fast. Just a matter of a few minutes, he calculated. To his satisfaction it took just three minutes for the ring to clatter against the side of the metal sink. He snatched up the ring before it could escape, placing it on the draining board, and switched off the tap. He needed to get on and sort out his paperwork in the office.

At his desk he glanced at the photograph in front of him. Amy leant on the side of the rickety Deux Chevaux, one arm tucked around a bottle - that same vintage. Her teasing eyes still mocked him now, as they had in that captured moment. She had threatened to open the bottle for their picnic, and he had insisted that the wine was too immature, that they must keep it. Now he wished he had let her have her way. He smiled and touched the pale indentation on his ringless finger. Amy would disapprove, but she would understand nevertheless. Readjusting the laptop to screen off the morning light, he pushed Amy's picture to the side of the desk. There was still plenty to sort out, including deciding what to do with the second bottle. Amy's voice rebuked him, "Just drink the bloody thing!" Shaking his head he placed Amy's photograph face down on the desk.

Mason was surprised when he heard the hall clock strike twelve; he had been so immersed in clearing away files which would be unnecessary from now on. He felt thirsty, and ready for a bite to eat before tackling the next task. He closed the laptop firmly and drew back the chair. As he moved away from the desk the two distended bags of shredded documents that lay at his feet rustled.

"They'll have to go before lunch," he mumbled to himself, aware that his quest for order had almost become an obsession. He would have to take them outside now.

The cold air cut through Mason's thin shirt as he carried the bags into the garden. Already tight green shards had penetrated the damp soil as spring struggled to assert itself. A blackbird with a beakful of worms danced across the path, pausing in front of Mason before skittering towards the shed.

A wail rose from the other side of the low garden wall. A cap of tight curls appeared for a few seconds above the bricks, then disappeared. The wail reached an even higher pitch. Mason stared, fascinated as chubby fingers grabbed the top of the bricks, followed by the same dark mat of hair, and this time, a round face. An open mouth confirmed the source of the frustrated outburst.

The boy raised one leg to straddle the wall, puffing furiously at his efforts. A triumphant smile flickered towards Mason as the boy managed to right himself. He wobbled. Mason dropped the bags and dashed forward, arms outstretched to steady the tenacious explorer. Warm fingers pressed into his own pale flesh as the boy used Mason's arm to pull himself up to stand on the wall. "Voila! Merci monsieur," the boy attempted to make a bow. Mason laughed, but held on firmly to the boy, impressed by his determination.

"Fabian? Fabian!" The boy's mother saw the gaunt grey haired man reach out to pick up her son. She flew across the lawn, and snatched Fabian away from the stranger's grasp. "Let him go! Get away, what are you doing?" Her heavy French accent fired the words at Mason. The boy's legs swung in the air and he vanished, small feet landed on the path and clattered away towards the other house.

Half-buried memories thundered into Mason's consciousness. He fought them back whilst he removed the bags from the path and placed them in the bin. Then panic rose in his throat, he tried to quell it, but the cool air inflamed his lungs; he swung round and fled inside.

Slowly over lunch Mason remembered how much Amy had wanted a child, and his own persistent ambivalence until it had proved too late. Why had he held back? Now he wished he had someone with him of their own flesh. Was that being more selfish, to rely on an innocent life to bear your pain and carry forward your hopes?

The door bell broke through his thoughts. Mason was relieved to be spared the nagging self-recrimination to which there would never be the right answer. The frosted glass in the hall revealed the slim outline of a woman, hand poised to ring the bell once more.

He swung open the door; it was Fabian's mother. He half expected another angry volley from her, but instead she swept into the hallway as Mason retreated in astonishment. Then she smiled. Glorious warmth shone in her tawny eyes, fixing Mason to the spot. The narrow space filled with her thick perfume, redolent of pungent spices from a bazaar.

"I am very sorry. Please forgive my rudeness earlier. Fabian explained you'd stopped him from falling." Mason relaxed as the scent of warm cinnamon wove itself around his temples. He stared at the tense young woman who seemed unable to gauge how he might respond.

"I have been so worried about him. He is so headstrong, just like his father, and Fabian misses him so much whilst he is away. Sometimes it is very difficult for me. It will be better when James is here with us."

He smiled, remembering Fabian's persistence. The woman's shoulders relaxed, she held out a hand to Mason.

"Please, you must come and join me and Fabian for dinner tonight. We are celebrating our first evening here, and I would like us to be good neighbours. We're staying here at my sister-in-law's for the next few months until we get sorted. You know Claire, of course."

Mason took her hand and nodded as he recalled the few occasions he had bumped into Claire.

"Good, then we will see you around seven? Just a simple supper. My name is Véronique by the way."

She had taken his nod as acceptance of her invitation. It was too late to correct her. Yet Mason knew he had not wanted to refuse her. He was drawn to the woman and her child like a solitary boat to a safe harbour. Véronique's warmth reminded him of Amy's own spontaneity. He smiled, knowing that Amy would have beaten Véronique hands down in any attempt to make a stranger welcome. Anyway, what difference would a few hours make out of his schedule?

At quarter to seven Mason returned to the cellar and took one of the vintage bottles from its resting place. Somehow he felt that his new neighbour would appreciate the fine wine and it would make a fitting welcoming gift. He was sorry that he did not have anything suitable for the child; perhaps another time. He shrugged. If he stuck to his plan, there would be no other time.

The shutters had been put back from the windows and a warm glow emanated from the downstairs rooms as Mason walked up the path to the front door.

"Maman! Notre voisin!" Fabian greeted Mason as he arrived.

"Fabian, what did I tell you? Remember, now we are here in London, you must speak English like Daddy."

"Yes, Mummy." The boy grabbed Mason's hand and pulled him into the living room. The floor was strewn with Meccano parts. "You must help me. I am building a crane to fix things. It must be ready for when Daddy gets here."

Mason handed over the bottle to Véronique. He knelt down, picked up one of the parts and handed it to Fabian.

"I hope you don't mind," Véronique said. "He insisted on starting this as soon as we arrived. He's worried it won't be finished in time, but goodness knows when James will join us. James has been volunteering with Médecins sans Frontières. He's due to finish his stint out in Syria, but we haven't heard from him. No text, nothing, and I ... One of the other field hospitals was bombed only a week ago."

She sighed, rubbing the boy's curls. Fabian shook his head and tried to swat her hand away, intent on his task.

"Careful, Fabian." Véronique balanced the bottle in her hand, twisting it to read the label. She looked up at Mason. "This is really special, you know that? Did you mean to bring this tonight? Shouldn't you be saving this for the right occasion?"

"I did; well no, I had a hunch that you might appreciate it. Besides, I have another one at home."

"Really? You obviously know your wines then, not bad for an Englishman." Véronique laughed.

"And you are a native of Languedoc?" Mason was sure he had correctly identified her accent to the southern region of France.

"Yes, I come from near Carcassonne originally, but James and I have travelled around a lot. We met as students at Montpellier. You know it?"

"I used to visit France regularly, particularly the wine regions, but I don't travel now. In fact I took my wife to Dijon and we visited the vineyard where this wine came from on our honeymoon. I was keeping the wine for us, but I don't have any need now." Mason stopped. He didn't usually talk to anyone about Amy.

"Claire told me about what happened to your wife. She said it was very sudden. I am sorry for your loss. I can't imagine how it has been for you. I worry about James when I don't hear from him for just a few days."

Mason nodded, staring down at Fabian who was concentrating on the delicate operation of fitting a bucket to the dangling suspension chain. Each time he tried to fix it the chain would swing away from him. Mason bent down and held the chain firmly for the boy.

"I tell you what. Let's save this bottle for when James comes. We can have a proper celebration then. I've got another bottle in the kitchen; let me just fetch it."

Fabian smiled at Mason as the bucket swung gently on the chain. "Mummy, look! We've nearly finished!"

The simple supper turned out to be sumptuous, each dish

surpassing the last, from tiny lamb pies, delicate jasmine rice bejewelled with cranberries to a rich cassoulet. Mason enjoyed sampling the dishes, many of which were familiar to him from the time he'd spent in the south of France. Finally his revived appetite was satisfied. He pushed back his chair. "Really Véronique, that was marvellous. I couldn't eat another thing."

"But you must Mason, we still have cheese and dessert." Véronique looked disappointed.

"I'm sorry. I've got out of the habit. Perhaps I should be going anyway. I'm keeping Fabian from his bed."

"Nonsense! He's used to staying up with grown-ups, and you must try my special dessert. I will train you up, and then you will be ready for one of my feasts, won't he Fabian?"

Fabian looked sleepily at Mason. "Mummy is right. You are too thin, Mr Englishman."

Mason laughed, surprising himself. Both Véronique and Fabian joined in, and soon the trio were tucking into Véronique's créme Catalane, a fabulously light custard flavoured with orange.

Finally, Fabian pressed his face into his mother's side and mumbled. "Fabian you can go to bed now ... and yes, I am sure your new friend will come and visit you again." Véronique winked at Mason, and hoisting the boy onto her hip, carried him out of the room. "I won't be long," she murmured. "He's almost asleep."

Mason retrieved the bottle of wine and poured the remains into the two glasses. He couldn't remember the last time he had felt so at ease. Perhaps he would come over tomorrow and help Fabian complete his construction.

A mobile phone rang. Mason glanced up; there was no sign of Véronique. Should he answer it? Where was it? He located the mobile behind a pile of books on the floor.

"Yes, quickly! Answer it, Mason!" Véronique called from along the hallway. He picked up the phone and pressed it to his ear. He bit his lip in concentration to make out the faint voice and its message. Véronique swung around the doorframe, and grabbed the phone from him.

"James is safe. They say he's left Syria and is en route to Paris. His connecting flight will land at Heathrow early tomorrow morning."

Véronique shrieked and grabbed Mason's arms.

"There, I told you! Tonight was just a warm-up, and when James gets here we will really celebrate!"

"But won't you want to be on your own, the three of you?"

Véronique put a hand on her hip and smiled at Mason. "There'll be plenty of time for that tomorrow. How about you come over the following evening? I will have lots of time to prepare a feast, and James will want to meet you. And then we can open that lovely bottle you brought."

"No really I can't. Tomorrow I – ," Mason stumbled. It was too difficult. How could he explain to her? He sank into the sofa, shaking his head.

"Mason what is it? You are busy? You cannot make it?"

Mason groaned. "I shouldn't have come here tonight. I hadn't planned to. Now everything is getting too complicated. I don't know..."

"What's complicated about making new friends?" Véronique sat down and took his hands in hers. "Now tell me about Amy."

Mason's fingers fumbled with the keys, struggling to unlock his front door in the chill of the night. He had forgotten to leave on a light. The wall was cold as he felt for the switch in the hall. Winter was making a final attempt to hold on, but Mason smiled, remembering the bird gathering food for its young.

He paused in the kitchen to retrieve his wedding ring and placed it on his finger. It fitted snugly, the cold band warming quickly. He went into the office and picked up the photo frame on his desk. He brushed a finger around her face, and then pressed his finger to his lips.

"Thank you Amy." He set the frame upright on the desk. He knew for sure that she would like the idea of the old vintage celebrating a new friendship.

Tomorrow he would look in the loft for his old Meccano set. He was sure it was still there.

Many difficulties after a death are to do with practicalities as well as coping with grief. Daisy has resources Rodney and Fay are unaware of otherwise this would have been a longer story. Two characters from 'Crossword', Lucy and Tina, appear in 'Planting a Tree'. They live down the same close as Daisy and Jane. I haven't met any of the other neighbours yet but I hope to.

Planting A Tree

Christine Dickinson

Daisy leans on the window sill and gazes at grey roofs and the yellow brick walls of terraced houses. She hears the regular swish-swish of cars spraying through the puddles and heading for home. It is not dark enough for lamps to be lit even though she has set a candle flickering on the window ledge. The lavender perfume soothes her headache, though her nose is sore and swollen. She has no more tears and the chill she feels might just be the start of a common or garden cold. Nothing she can make a fuss about while Jane lies under the white duvet flecked with its sweep of bright pansies. She notices that a wind has got up and has blown a plastic bag into the small tree they'd planted three, no four, years before to screen their front room. It was Jane who had spotted the grey backed leaves unfurling just a week or so ago while she waited for Daisy to make her bed up with clean sheets.

"Would you believe it, do come and look," she'd said, hugging a faded pink robe round her like a shawl. "They were only buds yesterday and now our tree is covered in its tiny ferns. Soon it'll be flowering. We'll have white stars in our garden again."

And they'd stood side by side, not quite touching, revelling in what had been their private marker for the onset of spring. They'd chosen the juneberry together for its small size and the coppery leaves it shed in the late autumn. Usually Jane organised the garden and Daisy was content to help out but Jane said a tree changed the landscape and it had to be a joint project. They'd spent hours discussing varieties before Jane spotted a selection labelled amelanchier at the Baytree Garden Centre just before the winter. They'd picked out and planted their tree the same day, wearing their wellingtons to firm the compost round its roots one dark, drizzly evening.

A click and the bang of the front door draws Daisy's attention from the window back to the bed. She anticipates the nurse, probably Fay as it's a Tuesday, clip clopping up the stairs and announcing what a fine day it has been, despite the rain. As she stoops to smooth the wisps of dry hair away from Jane's mouth and eyes, her heart beats faster. The lack of a greeting means that their visitor is Rodney and he'll be heading for the kitchen and the kettle. Daisy feels him stalking the house, bristling like their cat, Tiger, when he senses an intruder in the garden. Jane's son is the only other key holder and he comes and goes as he pleases. His visits make Daisy feel like a guest who has overstayed her welcome especially now Jane is in the last stages of her illness. Daisy shrugs the thought away. He moved out to a house of his own years before she moved in, and there is no time for a confrontation.

Every floorboard creaks as Rodney mounts the stairs. Daisy sits by the bed resting Jane's palm on hers as if they are sharing a prayer. She strokes hand cream through each finger, massaging the bones under the tissue, reaches the wrist and circles it between digit and thumb. The concentration and the scent of geranium with lavender has calmed her so that, when he pushes the door open with his foot and fills the doorway with his bulk, she's able to look up and arc her mouth into a smile. Rodney flashes a gold capped tooth at her and holds out her tea. Daisy, her hands full, gestures to the window sill where he lets the mug slap down after tiptoeing across the room in his steel capped boots. Tiger, who has yet to live up to his name, uncoils from the foot of the bed and springs towards the doorway. She hears the crash and rattling of the cat flap, sighs and hopes it won't be wrenched off its hinges again.

"Sorry 'bout that," Rodney stage whispers and pulls an oil stained rag from his pocket to mop up the tea spill. "Being here, it's like me fingers and thumbs stop working."

He has to pull his shoulders and thighs together as he folds himself into his mother's reclining chair. It's the one Daisy now thinks of as hers after the hours she has spent waking in it, dozing and watching the bed. She opens her mouth to tell him that there is no point in lowering his voice for Jane but Rodney is still talking through glugs of tea. She clenches her teeth, lays Jane's hand under the sheet and screws the cap back on the tube. Her half mug of tea has dark patches floating on top, rather like the age spots she'd been studying a minute ago on her own hands. When had the first one arrived? She didn't know. And had it come fully formed or just gradually grown its own tan and marked out boundaries over the weeks, months or days? She blinks and looks across at the face of an old lady on the pillow. Jane has been her closest friend and companion for almost eight years. How has it all come to this?

Rodney mumbles through a staccato of phrases with the odd gruff note breaking through the thick air. Spikes of his black hair are flattened by rain and blades of grass have stuck to the soles of his tan leather boots. After each gulp of tea he wipes his mouth with the back of his hand, displaying a hairy forearm with a tattooed bracelet of barbed wire.

"So, how much longer do you think? I got this job coming up over Birmingham way. Might need a week or so to sort things out. Pays well though."

Rodney waves a hand in the general direction of the mound on the bed topped by his mother's tiny head with its tufts of white hair.

"She's okay is she? Need anything, do you?" He sits back with his hands on his knees but his shoulders are hunched forward so that a flop of belly is clearly visible under a blue and white football shirt.

Daisy thinks Jane's breathing is easier but maybe it's Rodney's presence muffling the sound. He doesn't have to speak to fill a room and she often wonders how such a petite woman managed to produce an offspring as four square as her son. She knows nothing about Rodney's father except that he walked out of their lives leaving Jane with their baby boy.

The chair squeaks as Rodney levers himself up as if to remind Daisy of his unanswered queries but he's already upended the last dregs of his tea and is looking towards the door.

"Don't worry about us," she says. Her voice is croaky. She pulls a tissue from her sleeve, clears her throat, and remembers that she's not spoken to anyone else since the delivery man knocked that morning. He'd brought, at last, the book of short stories she'd resorted to ordering online since they no longer browsed the bookshops. Daisy started to read fiction aloud, especially after Jane lost interest in Radio Four. They'd imagine themselves in nineteenth century drawing rooms critically reading the latest work in progress. Daisy could pick up the threads of their current read between her friend's frequent naps. It reminded her of the early days when they'd found common ground discussing books. Jane accepted her eccentricities, her shyness, and they'd soon become allies. Retirement was a new adventure. They'd even braved group sessions together, practised French and Italian and, in a mad moment, joined a crochet class.

"Nuffin' I can do, then?" Rodney is scratching the side of his head as if to rid himself of further questions. Closing her eyes, Daisy drops her chin to her chest and shakes her head.

"Well then, better be off. You'll know where to find me." She feels the wafting of air and realises he is waving his phone under her nose. "Always on call, that's me. I'm yer man."

Daisy swallows hard. She's not needed a man for a long time. The plumber they'd employed to convert the bathroom was a woman, newly qualified, cheap, cheerful and competent. Her flare of anger is dampened, as always, by her understanding of a mother who couldn't do enough for her son and her love for Jane. She looks up to nod and stares into the striped bulge of his stomach.

"Don't worry, Rodney. Your mum doesn't need anything. She's on so much morphine. It must be a couple of days since, well, since she even opened her eyes."

"Ah well, bad business altogether. So I won't be around for a few days. Can't be helped," says Rodney, backing out of the room. Then he stops, takes a pace forward and pats the duvet.

Daisy thinks she hears him say, "Chin up old girl," and wonders whether he means her or his mother. Then he's gone, leaping down the stairs with a vigour he'd not shown coming up barely five minutes before.

Daisy swirls the tea round her mug trying to dissolve the skin and then gives up. It's too strong anyway. She sniffs, wipes the back of her hand round her eyes and thinks of the meditation they both practised during yoga. Kicking off her shoes she plucks Jane's worn dressing gown off the door hook. There is ample room to pull her feet up in the still warm armchair and tuck the worn candlewick round chin and toes. She lets the memories churn over her, a wash of pleasure and pain.

"Sorry I'm late, Daisy. You okay?" Fay stands surveying the room from the doorway rubbing her hands together. She chuckles. "I had an argument with a catheter. Well, not one as such but you can picture the scene."

Daisy could and smiles despite being startled from sleep. Fay can always lift her mood, and Jane's too when she'd been more alert. These nurses' visits have been essential both for Jane's personal care and for the valuable minutes spared to visit the corner shop or chop vegetables. It surprises her how long everything takes when there are only two hands but still two mouths to feed, three if you include the cat as Jane most certainly would. Tiger might be back waiting for supper now that Rodney has gone or would he be climbing up next door's bird table? Daisy wonders about her status now Jane can't fuss over him. He'd been a one woman cat.

"Shall we have a cuppa?" Fay says as she takes her patient's pulse. "I'd love one if you can spare the time, this being my last call of the day."

Daisy knows how Fay likes her tea, well brewed but with plenty of milk and, if it was the end of a difficult day, two sugars.

"I'd love that too," she says, uncurling from the chair and replacing the dressing gown on its hook. "I must have fallen asleep. See you downstairs in a bit."

Jane only drank herbal teas and has her own blue and white striped pot which is in its customary place by the kettle. Daisy likes Earl Grey but Jane can't stand the smell and said it turns her stomach to see it drowned in milk so, if she has it at all, she drinks it without. In the kitchen Daisy clasps the family-sized teapot warming against her chest and studies the variety of packets lined up on the shelf. The camomile and peppermint might be useful for visitors but who else did she know who drank rooibos? Then the heartlessness of making an inventory stops her in her tracks, the pot slips and she just catches it before it hits the work top.

"Damn, damn and blast," she hisses and digs her nails into her scalp as if to punish the brain for not controlling the mouth.

Daisy turns her attention to brewing their tea, adds an extra bag for luck and squirts a generous dollop of Jif into the sink. Scrubbing at the brown stains and grease will keep her occupied until Fay clatters into the kitchen to claim her drink. Since Jane has been in her own time zone the household rituals of meal times have been suspended. Daisy has reverted to the hand to mouth way of living that started in student days and stopped when she was married. She left her husband because of his violent temper and it was years before she could enjoy cooking again. Daisy shudders and rubs harder. She has never seen Fay miserable despite the bleakness of her job caring for people in the last stages of life. Jane had talked about her own funeral, told Daisy she had appointed her as executor along with Rodney and exchanged all the last words she needed with friends.

"You'll have enough to do," Jane said in that dry, clipped tone of voice she always used when doing business. "Rodney's not much good at that sort of thing so it will all fall to you. There'll be no reason to argue if it's come from me."

She handed Daisy the keys to her bureau and told her to take care of the contents.

"Childe and Stokes know my wishes. I've always used them if I've needed a solicitor in the past. There'll be no nonsense with them."

Jane has already drafted a letter to inform friends of her death and Daisy knows that the only reason now for wanting to hold on to the present is the close bond they've formed with the carers.

Daisy is wiping under the pots of basil and coriander which have leaked after she watered the dried out soil when Fay drops her bulging workbag on the floor behind her. Fay seizes hold of the teapot first and pours two mugs.

"I need this," she says, collapsing onto the cushioned chair with a grunt. "I'm sure you do too."

Daisy notices that the cream surface of the small table where she and Jane used to scan the newspapers at breakfast is speckled with tea and crumbs. She's careful with the dishcloth and tries not to disturb Fay's elbows.

Fay leans back and puts her mug on the damp surface. "Come and sit down. Take a break. You should recharge your batteries."

"I've not done anything for days. Look at the place. There's dust and grease everywhere. Jane wouldn't like it."

Daisy balls the wet cotton in her fist and flings it towards the sink. Its brief flight ends as the cloth catches the edge of window sill and the remaining energy spills out across the cold tap. She perches on the stool with her back to the radiator but, despite the damp in the air, there's no heat in it and she shivers.

Fay pushes the fringe of red tinted hair away from her eyes.

"Have you started to think about yourself, your next step? It's hard, I know, because you've only been thinking about Jane but soon, and it will be very soon, it's going to be about you and what you want."

Daisy's lips feel sticky; her mouth is dry. She scrapes her teeth together as if she's chewing and then swallows. She remembers Jane remarking on the habit she has of grinding her teeth.

"Well, don't laugh. I do know I want Tiger and Rodney doesn't. He told me he can't stand the smell of cats and he'd be for having the whole house professionally cleaned as soon as possible. He's not a bad chap. He's just a bit blunt that's all." She unwraps a hand from her drink and waves in the general direction of the stairs. "And he wants all this to be over."

"That's what worries me," says Fay. She empties her mug and stoops to fumble a folder further into her work bag.

Daisy wiggles her toes into the moccasins she now lives in, and slaps across the tiled floor. She retrieves the long stemmed wineglasses from the top shelf, pins a bottle of Chianti under her arm and stands tapping her nose with a cork screw.

"Goodness, Daisy, take care or you'll have your eye out!" Fay straightens up and nods in the direction of the two crystal glasses. "They're a sight for sore eyes. Got someone coming this evening?"

"No, not now. Not today. Jane and I went bargain hunting on our city break to Venice in the spring last year. We loved the feel of them and the delicate carving. Those two were the only ones like that." She pauses. "Red or there's a Chardonnay in the fridge?"

"Mmm, Italian red. Well then, just a small one. There's no one at home, just a ready meal and the iPlayer but I've got to drive. How can I say no to drinking from such a precious and pretty glass."

Daisy's eyes are wet when she sits opposite Fay but she's smiling.

"Jane and I first met at the vets you know. I was having Felix, my old cat, put down and Jane had just got Tiger from the Cat Rescue Centre. We got chatting and then she waited with me."

Daisy pauses to swirl her wine and admire the glint of rosy stars as the cut edges catch the light.

"Rodney had his own life and she was lonely. I was in a house, rented rooms so it didn't seem like my home. We met again at the bookshop for coffee and just got on. Jane had just lost her lodger and offered me the chance to move in. It suited both of us."

"Have you anywhere to go back to? I was wondering where you'd live."

"No. This is our home and there's still Tiger..."

Daisy's voice trails off as she looks through to the tiny utility room, the back door and the draughty cat flap. Tiger's favourite tins of fish mingle with the bleach, garden twine, secateurs and the dried beans Jane had saved from their last crop of runners in the autumn. Staying would be as hard as going but she wouldn't be breaking any of her promises.

"Life will be difficult enough for you without having extra changes. Coming to terms with living on your own is a challenge." Fay pauses. "I've had to do that more than once. I know how tough it is."

Daisy tucks a loop of hair behind her ear and looks from Fay's mottled red cheeks to her eyes and notices they are a warm brown. Daisy's eyes are barely blue but it suits her narrow bones and thin hair the colour of ash. She pushes her index finger into the back of her scalp and corkscrews a tail into a sausage. It's another bad habit which has amused Jane. Her hair is greasy. How long is it since she's given any thought to how she looks?

"Jane and I," she says, "we're not a couple. Not like that. I was married just the once. No kids. We had a lot in common, and the same sense of humour, I guess." She grins. "Rodney thinks I'm odd."

Fay shows both sets of teeth and her upper gums when she laughs and her chest shakes through the pale blue polyester of her overall.

"Nothing to worry about there then," she says. Half rising, she touches Daisy's upper arm. "Let's look in on Jane and then I should go. But I will ring you before I'm back on duty. See how you're doing, both of you."

"That's good of you. There's something Rodney doesn't know."

Fay wraps a warm hand round Daisy's knuckles, white against the fragile glass.

"There's always secrets in families. It's healthy."

Two weeks later Daisy is slopping water into the cafetiere and refilling the kettle for another pot of tea. She's left Fay with a cheerful group of older women in the front room, their cheeks pink from drinking wine in the afternoon and the effort of smiling. They've all agreed with Tina, a forthright and kindly neighbour, that the service was just right. It went exactly as Jane had planned it – not glum but a celebration with a reading from Rossetti and anecdotes from two book club friends told with the wry humour she would have appreciated. The sandwiches and iced cakes from M&S have eased the sharing of reminiscences of previous happy hours and high teas discussing their reading and the light it sheds on their lives.

The kettle comes to the boil. Daisy hears the note change but lets it switch itself off. If Jane were there she would take over the tea making leaving her to daydream. But her work is done. Her talent for anticipating and smoothing over problems cannot be relied upon in any future event playing out in the house. The heavy footsteps overhead can only be Rodney prowling his mother's bedroom. All afternoon she's been aware of him frowning as if there is a conversation he can't quite hear. Daisy nudges Tiger from her lap, opens the window, fills her lungs with the damp air and exhales. She pictures Jane in her striped bobble hat and scarf with her worn rucksack turning to wave before she shuts the gate. The window frame has swollen with all the rain and won't shut without a slam. Tiger shoots out of the cat flap. Daisy sighs, washes her hands and assembles the mugs.

Daisy is glad to see the back of her chatty neighbours, Tina and Lucy. They are the last to leave apart from Fay who arranged to have the day off so that she could offer to help clear up. Lucy's excitement about the imminent birth of twins in her family was uplifting at first but now her voice sounds discordant without the rise and fall of other conversations to muffle the shrillness. Daisy follows the two sturdy forms towards the gate but, before she is able to say her final goodbye and comfort her eyes with a glimpse of Jane's colourful flower bed and their favourite tree in bud, Tina shrieks and points,

"Flippin' heck! That's quick work. You never said!"

Lucy pulls at her friend's arm but it's too late. Daisy turns and faces the zigzag red and orange script of a 'For Sale' sign for Wicken and Pollock Estate Agent planted close enough to brush against the slender branches of the juneberry. She lowers her eyes to assess the damage where careless feet have crushed yellow tulip heads into mud. Sweeping her arm over her forehead as if making a backward wave she brushes past Fay in the doorway and takes the stairs two at a time.

The front room is tidy and the kitchen less so when Daisy thinks about Fay and comes downstairs. There's an open bottle of Jane's favourite, an Italian Pinot Noir, on the table with some newly washed glasses.

"I didn't know where to put them," says Fay, adding a plate to the stack already draining.

"That bottle won't keep. I shouldn't have left you to do all this."

"That's what I'm here for and there wasn't much. Your neighbours cleared most of the pots."

"Let's have a drink," says Daisy, reaching to the top shelf for the crystal flutes.

Fay shakes her hands free of suds and dries each finger thoroughly before pulling out the nearest pine chair. She strokes the carvings in the stem of her wine glass and catches Daisy's eye across the table.

"It must be an hour since Rodney went for a quick pint. He said he'd be back shortly."

"Cheers," says Daisy, "and thanks. You're a good friend."

"I mean to be. I've been thinking."

"Dangerous. It rots the brain. Get this down you. Do you have to rush off?"

Fay shakes her head. "I've been thinking about your situation and I think I can help."

"You don't know what my situation is."

"I don't? Well, I'm guessing then that you will be looking for a home just as I'm looking for a lodger."

Daisy's cheeks turn pink and the flush spreads down to her neck. Before she has time to reply the front door bangs open. Resting her fingers lightly on Fay's wrist she whispers, "You're so kind," and they look up to see Rodney blocking the doorway. Tiger smacks his head so sharply through the cat flap that it swings wildly and snaps off its hinges.

"Not disturbing nuffin', am I?" says Rodney, reaching for the kettle. "Brew up anyone or are you gals sorted?"

He's still wearing his grey suit but the tie is dangling out of his jacket pocket and the buttons are opened far enough down his chest to show a patch of curly hair nestling round a heavy gold chain. Fay retrieves her hand and holds her open palm towards him.

"Hi, I'm just here to help Daisy clear up, make myself useful.

I'll be off soon. It all went off rather well, I thought, just as your mother would have wanted."

"You think so? I never knew what ma wanted. Still, that's that. Gotta get this place out of me hair. I'm on the move. Gonna get meself a place in Spain. "

Fay clips the table sharply with her glass.

"Don't go." Daisy touches Fay's shoulder as if to press her into the chair. Fay sits on her hands and focuses on the outline Rodney's toes make in his patent leather brogues.

"You put my home on the market."

"Sorry old gal. You knew it was coming. I meant to tell you meself, but I know them estate agent guys and they said they'd do me a quick sale. Favour to a mate. Get things moving, like."

"This is my home, my home and Tiger's." Daisy paces each word and enunciates each syllable. "We are not moving. If you'd been here we could have spoken about this before your mother's funeral."

Rodney's mug looks small grasped in his meaty fist and his colour is high. He gulps his tea.

"You thinking of making trouble? I let you do all this how you wanted, kept outa yer way. But I wanna move on, see, and so must you."

"Listen, Rodney. My life has moved on and so can yours. You've not looked at the will, have you? To prevent complications your mother specified that I should stay here for my lifetime."

Daisy is not sure who looks the most shocked. Fay and Rodney both stare at her and Rodney's jaw is working as though he is chewing a lump of gristle.

"In any case, I can buy you out," Daisy says, taking a slug of wine.

"You'd never get a mortgage." Rodney doesn't say 'at your age' but the words hang in the air.

"I don't need one. When I sold my old house to move here I

paid off both our mortgages. I've also funded the major improvements – kitchen, bathroom and the conservatory. Childe and Stokes have all the documents. Jane insisted that we kept everything to do with any investment I'd made in the house."

"You mean it's gone, all me bloody inheritance? I'll not believe it. Ma, she would've said."

"Your inheritance is safe but it will be in cash, as soon as we can get to the solicitor. It's only that you don't own this property."

Tiger chooses this moment to stick his head through the cat door. He steps over the detached plastic flap and sniffs the air. Fay clicks her tongue against the roof of her mouth and pats her knee. He licks her hand and jumps on her lap.

"I'm allergic to that 'effing cat," says Rodney.

"When his time comes your mother wants, wanted, his ashes sprinkled with hers under the juneberry in the front garden. You know, that tree just by the 'For Sale' sign."

"I think she cared more for that bloody animal than she did for me."

"It's just easier to show love to a cat. A pet always needs looking after. You know how much she loved you."

"Can't get me head round it at all." Rodney is shaking his head from side to side as if desperate to unclog his brain. "Why didn't she tell me?"

"She did try. More than once. In the end she wrote you a letter but I've not had a chance to give you it. I'm sorry. It shouldn't be me telling you."

"You think I've put me great big foot in it again."

"It really doesn't matter," says Daisy quickly. "The main thing is your mother wanted what was best for you so, of course, that's what I want too."

She tries to look him in the eye and smile but Rodney is examining the floor, his upper body slumped against the worktop as if it is holding him upright. To fill the silence Daisy is tempted to fiddle with her wine but she holds herself still and waits for him to speak.

"So, I've gone and jumped the gun a bit. With the sale."

"A bit but it's okay, no harm done."

"I can take that board with me. Tell Wickens the sale's off. Call in tomorrow, shall I?"

"That'll be good. Your letter's just inside the bureau. On top, you can't miss it."

"I'll fix that bloomin' cat trap too."

Rodney levers himself up and sets off for the hallway. As he swings round his heels squeal and leave a black streak on the quarry tiles. On his way out he slaps Daisy's shoulder and grunts. It could be a thank you, she isn't sure. He raises his hand in Fay's direction and, moments later, the front door shudders behind him.

Tiger, purring while his chin is scratched, doesn't turn a hair. Fay looks up at Daisy and grins.

"So the answer to taking the spare room in my basement flat is a no, then!"

"I've got more space here," says Daisy. "I might take on a lodger myself. Tiger's really taken to you, hasn't he?"

She reaches for the bottle of Pinot and empties it into their glasses.

Names have been changed to protect the innocent and names have been omitted completely for the not-even-close-to-being-innocent. I nearly died that evening ... I'm glad I didn't.

Impact

Mark Badham-Moore

It's been a bad few days for Bill. Extend that to years, what with finding out about *her* affair and the after effects.

Right now he feels his life is similar to one of those complicated domino displays he watched on Record Breakers – some pieces had fallen as predicted in multi-coloured glory, but others were scattered as if a dog had run riot. It seems like he's at a constant divergence, one path threatening to send him off a cliff edge but, tantalisingly, another reaching new heights of creativity, with Roy Castle there blowing his trumpet.

This evening, he's not sure what plastic rainbow beckons. However, it's Thursday evening – badminton, in the Community Hall.

He'd arrived home at six, after another depressing day at work. Two days before he'd asked for a necessary pay rise. He'd been refused.

Showers are forecast, but he has to play. He needs to repeat last week's performance; his side had won every game. That had never happened before. Physically, he's ready, but he has to shake off the job; the cycle ride will help. He's six miles from the Hall. He can cover that in less than twenty-five minutes.

Including a phone call to his son, he has just over an hour to get ready.

The kitchen's in a state. When he gets back he knows he'll be up till the early hours cleaning and washing dishes, so that when he brings his son back tomorrow, it won't be a complete pigsty.

Bill ignores the garlicky, peppery aromas of the last three evening meals: overlaid, enticing, yet slightly sickly.

Upstairs he switches on the stereo; world news takes his mind off his own. Still no divorce. More debt because of his bloody dead car. A litany he does his best to blot out.

Downstairs, the cat-flap goes 'clik-clak'. Padded thumps follow as his cat lands on the bottom stairs. He shouts affectionately, "Hello, Willow."

He comes out of the bedroom, undoing his shirt and watches as she comes up three steps at a time. He smiles. She is one of the few happy threads left, although six months ago he had two cats, until Willow's brother disappeared.

Now he has one black-furred, friendly face to feed. The cat mewls in her own particular way, pushing at his hand. He keeps her away until the cat food, assaulting his nostrils, is messily arranged for her eager appetite.

"Damn," he says to himself. It's nearly seven. Willow ignores him. The clock ignores him, its orange colons flashing without pause.

Back in his room, Bill disposes of the empty sachet and finishes unbuttoning.

He wonders if it's raining outside, but doesn't check. He slips on his t-shirt and socks. He's proud of his weight loss since *she*'d left. Fitter too, back to how he'd been, his child's lifetime ago. It's for Charlie's sake and his own sanity that he picks up the phone. Most nights, he tries to call his son. Charlie stays over most weekends, Bill's own selfish pick-me-up, but not last weekend. He selects the number and presses to dial, holds the handset to his ear, the tone hard and repetitive. It rings and rings and, well-practised, he counts ... up to ten. Hanging up he puts it in its cradle.

I'd better see if it's raining, he thinks, and goes downstairs to the front door, checking the time again. It isn't raining.

Fifteen minutes to get out of the door, to play those winning games. He can hope can't he?

He shuts the door and grabs what he needs – rucksack, bottle, racquet, lights, reflectors, jacket, waterproof (just in case) and money.

Ten minutes later he's ready, turns lights off, puts on his cycle helmet and steps out, closing the front door behind.

"Oh, for goodness sake." It's properly raining, something between a downpour and drizzle. Not enough to stop him.

Attaching his lights he wheels his bike to the road, front lights illuminating willow trees to his left and rosemary bushes on his right.

It's quiet outside. Dark too. No street lights. He mounts his bike to once more embark on a journey that he's completed many times before. It's almost automatic, but he knows that the straighter stretches attract the worst drivers. It's why he doesn't listen to any music.

Still, he makes his own kind – the whistle of the wind overhead, the rhythmic tyre rubber and his own voice. Sometimes he sings to himself, snatches of songs he's heard during the day, an improvised pedalling song, or talking out loud about story ideas.

In his head the ride is divided into five minute stages.

Stage One. From home to the first village. By the time he reaches the end of Stage One he's pedalling steadily, the spitting rain falling monotonously.

At least, he tells himself, it's not getting heavier. His glasses are still clear, which is a blessing and the village street-lights allow him to relax a little. He feels confident about winning, but not arrogant enough to think he can repeat his winning streak.

He heads past the Post Office. Stage Two. The monument, the derelict pub and then returns to open fields. His lights tentatively illuminate the grass verges, even as he swings left, right, left again, following the curve of the road.

Concentrating, he cycles between opposing houses and then past the entrance to a large packing plant where articulated lorries come and go all day and most of the night.

Now he's into Stage Three. This is the darkest part, where large sycamores arch overhead, their size only curtailed by the constant passage of lorries. He's often had to avoid fallen branches snapped by a lorry's roof. Not tonight though. The road bears left, trees only on his left now, the night dull and damp.

A relatively straight stretch follows, heading toward the A63. This is the road where, a few years before, *she*'d had her accident and had almost gone to prison. He wonders how different things might have been. ... He shakes it off, pedalling that little bit faster, putting road and memories behind him.

He can hear the A63, the steady thrum of lorries and the orange glow of lights at the staggered junction. Before the T-junction he looks behind and crosses the clear road, jumping his bike onto the pavement. It only extends a short way along the tiny slip-way, but it's in-line with the traffic island he needs to use.

Stage Four. Here he has to join the traffic on the A63 for two hundred metres before turning onto the road that will take him to the hall.

Still astride the bike, Bill inches forwards, looking intently to his right.

"Come on, come on," he says as cars whistle by. There's his gap. Nothing coming, not for about a quarter of a mile. He wheels over, looking both ways, and, as he reaches the raised island with its two stumpy plastic obelisks, he can see it's clear left. Staring hard to make sure, for the first time annoyed with the rain as a few drops hit his glasses, he jumps up with both feet on the pedals, pushing down with his right while turning the handlebar right to get to the far edge of the road. He glances down and behind his saddle to check that his red light is still on. Feeling relieved, he straightens up.

Bill hears the steady approach of a car and then he sees it, beside and passing. Seconds later, he hears the roar of another car approaching. This one, a Mini, gives him plenty of room. He's nearly at the next traffic island. Everything is bathed in the lithium glow of the street-lights and he hopes that the rain is easing off. Passing the island he can hear something else approaching. He's not sure what, but it's very fast.

The gap is being closed by a white van. It's too close to the white borderline, too close for both van and cyclist. As its bumper comes in line with the rear wheel of the bike, a hand's width separating them, there's no change in its trajectory.

First, the bumper hits Bill's right foot. Second, immediately after, the left wing mirror smashes into his saddle and lower back. Plastic shatters. Bones and vertebrae crack. Metal snaps. The sound isn't particularly loud, the results are instantaneous – Bill and saddle are separated from his long-serving bike. Back arching, his helmeted head slams back and bounces off the side of the van, then forward momentum sends him tumbling through the air.

Handlebar shuddering mechanically, the bike plunges into the water-filled ditch set back from the road.

Bill's route is almost as direct, but the force of the impact sends his unconscious body flying at a more acute angle to his previous direction of travel. At the apogee, the saddle disengages and lands between road and ditch. Bill carries on, a human shot-putt, turning, twisting over, head following feet, landing face down in the bottom of the water-filled ditch.

When Bill's head struck, plastic on metal, the driver finally realised that something was amiss, and the van swerved ever so slightly, but didn't stop.

There isn't silence afterwards. There's the gentle fall of rain, the mundane sound of cars, drivers oblivious to what has just happened.

The road isn't busy enough, not at this time of night.

Minutes pass.

Further along from the motionless bike lies Bill's body. His landing has left his legs fully submerged in ditch water and he's face down, covered in mud.

More minutes pass.

More rain falls, more cars drive by.

Slowly, consciousness returns. He spits muddy ditch water. He's soaking wet, cold and very confused. He can't remember the last ten minutes of his life.

"Who did this to me?" he thinks.

Instinct makes him push, to lift himself up. Self-preservation drives him to get out of the mud and ice-cold water. Pain, however, makes Bill cry out as his left collar bone grates in response to his attempted use. He realises that his left hand remains gloved, but his right is bare, freezing, but he can work with it, without agony. That's how he manages to stand up, by pushing with only his right arm on muddy grass until, swaying, he stands knee-deep in the cold, cold water, feet numb. Head numb, his first words are: "Who did this to me?" A whisper, then shouted, "WHO DID THIS TO ME?" There's no answer, not an echo.

He's confused. Astonished. He can remember cycling, eager to play, the cream-coloured Mini passing, then nothing. An utter void refusing to yield.

Right now, he knows he isn't going to get any answers. He needs to get out of the ditch, attract somebody's attention, or worst case, walk to a house.

His left arm limp and useless, Bill leans toward the road side of the ditch, reaching out, trying to find some purchase. With greater difficulty he raises his left leg to push himself up. His right leg almost gives out, but he perseveres. His hand slips on the mud. He can feel the cold so much and in glancing right he sees the outline of his bike, its red light still flashing.

He loses count of the number of times he scrabbles around in the mud, grass and road debris. Although he can't see it, his saddle is only a short distance away, plastic and metal embedded in the earth.

He stands up as straight as he can.

Blinking, unable to feel his feet, he stifles a sob, "Somebody help me." He raises his right arm, waving it. Legs rigid he says it louder, "Somebody help me," repeating, repeating, until he's shouting, but he's unheard.

He only stops when a flashing blue light appears and halts nearby. He's so sure, sure it must be for him.

His arm falls, mud drips, it's all he can taste.

At least, he thinks, it's not my blood ...

... *Oh no, Charlie, I'm not winning ...*

‘Scar’ was originally written a few years before Plonk was conceived, the result of a free write exercise while completing a Creative Writing module for my Open University BA (Hons) Literature degree. The rest of the Red Wine Writers thought it was a worthy contender for Plonk – though they initially preferred the free write itself. After several edits it passed muster.

Scar

Terry Martin

Ben had run from the pub still clutching the broken bottle of Merlot that moments before had cut a jagged motif into the unshaved flesh of his brother, Steve. A cheek wound millimetres away from blindness. Flecks of redness – scarlet and maroon – splattered his white shirt, though from the car park spotlights it could have been tar. It looked good in his eyes. Felt good too. At least, it had in the adrenalin-filled minutes following his berserk attack. The shirt had been an inspiration for many of his paintings afterwards and still surfaced in his work.

Ben liked pubs, not that there were many around anymore. Even the cigarette ban hadn't kept him away. Nowhere else held that social interaction that a little alcohol induced. Not being a particularly sociable animal, yet yearning conversation, the 'local' was his crutch. Pub smells always brought back vivid memories, less haunting than satisfying. Ben lived that fight every day. Regrets? About the pink and smooth pattern in Steve's cheek that must have reminded his brother every morning of Ben's deed? Not at all. Steve's scar was physical. Ben's had been forming an unhealthy crust long before the fight.

They had been in their early twenties. Steve a council official climbing the local government ladder with his honours degree and bold assurance; Ben, while no less intelligent, an artist whose medium was oils and whose confidence seesawed with every success and failure.

Ben was aware of the chip that had grown steadily on his

shoulder. His clothes had been mostly hand-me-downs until secondary school when Steve's uniform was grammar school, and Ben's comprehensive. Steve was encouraged to go to university, Ben had wanted to attend art college but found himself with an apprenticeship in a practical job. He regretted listening to the advice of the school's careers officer who insisted, without any knowledge of his talent, that art wasn't a route to a real job.

"You won't make a living out of being an artist. What else would you like to do?" At the time he was too immature to have the strength to challenge such negativity and lacked belief in himself. When he grew his hair long he felt he'd lost his father's respect entirely, though his mother was more understanding. He was her baby. Steve was their successful son. Sure, they still gave Ben their support but it always seemed like an apology.

'That's a great piece, Benjamin, but who's going to want that in their living room?"

They were at the opening of his first mini exhibition in a room set aside for local artists in the town hall building. Though his brother worked there, he'd been too busy to attend. Ben's father was commenting on one of a series Ben had painted at his favourite spot on the rolling hills to the East of the town, which stretched its rambling way to the other side of the valley. From the vantage point overlooking the town he could turn one-hundred and eighty degrees and the countryside was unblemished save for the occasional farm and small barn. Coppices clumped themselves randomly amidst the meadows to mimic the thick and ancient woodland to the south. Ben's style was still developing and he had been experimenting with light and colour in a new way, giving his pictures an abstract quality.

His father, in almost the same breath, added, "Steven's been put in charge of a new team from the planning department looking into the feasibility of a bypass." The pride in his father's voice cut into Ben's psyche, a kernel falling on the fertile land of frustration and disappointment. That same evening this weighted comment, remembered in the heat of debate, led to the fight.

None of Ben's friends or family had spoken to him since, at least not in a civil way. The town hall never hung his work again. Fifteen years give a month or so. What had it all been over? The bypass. An argument over a road and the countryside that would be eaten up and ravaged by the diggers. Ben believed that was just the beginning. A retail park would follow, a consequence of the bypass. Inevitable. Fresh wounds through fields and woods outside the town becoming a cancer, spreading concrete and garbage, attracting even more traffic, even more pollution, congestion, road rage. Rage. That inner demon that he had once, and satisfyingly, allowed to surface and that would not let him rest. A simple name-calling that he never forgot. Childish, harmless. Thoughtless, painful.

"That's progress, Ben. Live in the real world instead of your arty, farty world. Go join your hippies in the trees. ... Like monkeys."

Steve's friends, the audience he had been playing to all night, roared with laughter at the remark. Their apparent support for his brother's intentions to carve up the countryside only fuelled Ben's anger. Even the landlord, across the worn oak bar, joined in. It seemed like the whole pub was filled with the derisive sound of monkeys, ridiculing his beliefs. And that was when Ben's frustration, amplified by drink, stripped him of his self-control. Steve's celebration at his advancement became a bloody riot. Ben could not even pretend the bottle had mysteriously appeared in his hand. He had lifted it from the table and sought the edge of the pub's brick fireplace to ensure a first-time break before turning on his brother.

While Ben held his own principles in high regard he was still drawn to the inevitable designer park. He could purchase his art materials at discounted prices. Years later on one of those visits he saw Steve shopping there, his jagged trophy clean-shaved in macho arrogance. Ben's anger boiled up again. This time he turned away, despite a resurgence of passion. As one of the demonstrators back then, Ben hadn't been naive enough to think their tree-house lives would actually stop the steamroller of progress, but he'd had hope. Their frugal and precarious protest was a futile attempt to stop the road from being built. Ben's involvement was far more personal. It was the scenes that now remained alive and vibrant only on his canvases that he'd wanted to save. Given another broken bottle he would have decorated the other side of his brother's face.

There are people whose glass is usually half full and rarely half empty. Jenny Edmonds, an artist and potter from West Pinchbeck, was one such person. She collaborated with me on a pamphlet of poems and drawings in 1992, the year before she died. It would have pleased her, as it pleases me, to see her name in a volume of short stories about her favourite tipple.

The Artist

Christine Dickinson

Her smile was a beam of summer,
a burn framed in a frizz of hair,
a gash splashed across a canvas.
She'd wear flared skirts, a clash of scarves,
dash in, sloshing a glass half full.
She'd chuckle a gripe off its course,
bellow a laugh when all seemed lost.
She'd flow over the boundaries,
hug you tight like an envelope,
wave you off like a slash of breeze.

My heart went out to the man at the next table. He was struggling to make friends with a boy whose mum was his girlfriend. I guessed it was the first time the mum had brought them together and this meeting really mattered to all three of them. The interplay of emotions in this quite common situation fascinated me.

Bernie and Allegra

Julie Williams

I hesitate before I step into the warmth of Bernie's kitchen. The room glows a welcome and the oven sends out little puffs of roasting beef and potatoes, the perfect match for my rioja. I set the bottle down on the table. It's laid for three, with red napkins flaring in the wineglasses.

"I thought we'd relax more in the kitchen, love." Bernie has sneaked up on me. She doesn't mean to surprise me. She's deft and quiet in her movements, like a sleek mother cat. I reach for her, but she dodges, picks up my bottle and puts it on the dresser.

"Er, why?" I'm stretching out an empty hand, like a child that's had its lolly stolen.

"I've got champagne. Your wine'll go lovely after."

"Hang on, Allegra doesn't approve of booze. Those sixth form binges. You've always said."

"She'll be fine with it. It's an occasion, you know?" She comes close and I regret my snippy tone. Her dress under the apron is black, its neckline a modest scoop. I tuck in a satin strap that's strayed on her shoulder, and breathe in her perfume.

"Not every day you meet your future stepdad for the first time," she says now, and tries for a laugh.

"You didn't put it like that, did you? For God's sake, Bernie."

"Course not. She asked me who'd been staying weekends. I said come and meet him."

"Simple as that?"

"Not quite. I had some persuading to do."

"Bribery?"

"Wasn't easy. But. Asking like that, I think it means she's ready. Good, in't it?"

I take her upturned face in my hands and kiss the small crease of uncertainty on her brow. I put my arms around her and give her a squeeze.

"It certainly is," I say."So what have you told her about me – about us?"

"Not much really. That you teach English at the college. I'd have said more but she stopped me. Said she wanted to make up her own mind."

"Sensible girl," I say.

"She'll be here any minute." Bernie is glancing at the clock."Promise me you won't mention her dad."

"At all? Or what you told me last weekend?" An anguished look is all the answer I get and there's no time to argue, even if I wanted to. "Not a word. Don't worry." There's something missing from the table. "Any horseradish in the house?" I ask.

"Oh, no, it was on my list. Too late now, sorry, lover." Bernie's over by the sink, washing carrots. "She was supposed to be here same time as you."

"Teenagers," I say.

I find a corkscrew in the dresser drawer and retrieve my bottle of wine. Cork drawn and bottle replaced on the dresser, I sink into my favourite kitchen chair. I watch her slit open a net of sprouts and peel the blemished outer leaves from each floret. I ease down an inch or two, relaxing at last. She slices a stack of carrots and brushes the bright discs into a pan. Job done, she turns to the clock again and notices where I'm sitting.

"Davey, that's Allegra's chair. Sorry, lover, but would you move? I know it's yours at weekends, but ... she might mind, see?" Bernie's from Bristol and becomes singsong West Country when she's excited. I don't sigh or look askance, I get up, walk round the table and perch on the high stool opposite that'll be hard on my knees when I pull it in to eat. One of its legs barks a warning as I shift on the seat. Her mobile buzzes on the table and she snatches it up on the first bar of Dancing Queen.

"Hello sweetheart, everything all right? Where are you?" Her shoulders drop a fraction of an inch. "No, that's fine. No problem. It'll keep. We'll see you then. Love you."

"What?" I've climbed off the stool. My hand's in the small of my back as I stretch.

"She didn't say why, but she'll be an hour at least. Too long for the joint. It's ready to come out and sit, now. The spuds'll go leathery. She's such a punctual girl usually."

Bernie pulls on her oven gloves. A blast of heat and rich roasting aromas follows the click of the glass door. She heaves the tin out and bangs it down on the hob. The potatoes are golden. She cuts a nick out of the beef's slick dark crust. Perfect pink.

"You'll work your magic and it'll be fine." I hope I don't sound so bright that it grates. I reach for the rioja. "This is what we need, our Friday tipple," I say, the bottle in my hand.

"No, Davey, not for me anyways." She shovels the roasties into another tin and slams them back in the oven. She's staring at the beef as though it can tell her how to keep it rare and tender. I put the bottle back and now I need something to do with my hands. I go to the sink and turn the tap. There's a mixing bowl and kitchen cutlery in there to be washed. But not by me. Bernie leans over, turns off the tap and reclaims the Fairy Liquid from my grasp.

"Why don't you leave me to it," she says. "You could get the horseradish. The cream one's nicer." She switches on the top oven and pulls out a shelf to make way for the beef, frowning slightly.

"All right," I say,"she'd better have a good excuse, though, don't you think?"

"No, Allegra doesn't do excuses, and she wouldn't like me to ask. She's always had such definite ideas, even when she was a tiny scrap. You go, Love. Bye."

I give my scarf an angry tug where it's snagged on the hook. I call goodbye round the door as I leave and turn up my coat collar though it really isn't that cold outside.

I get back within the hour but Allegra has beaten me to it. She's sitting in our chair and it dwarfs her like a throne. I flourish the jar of horseradish before I realise Bernie's not looking, then set it carefully at the centre of the table. '

"Allegra! Fantastic, it's so very good to meet you." It's too early in our acquaintance for kisses so I'm ready for a handshake. She offers me her slim white fingers and I have to stoop to take them briefly before they are withdrawn. My hand detours to my right trouser pocket, where it seaches in vain for some keys to jangle.

"Hey, Davey," calls Bernie, "that's good timing, that is! Allegra's only just arrived." She is draining sprouts in a cloud of steam at the sink.

"Actually, I've been here at least ten minutes, Mother." Allegra hasn't inherited the husky contralto I love. The voice is higher in register, cool and dry.

Bernie's neck flushes pink in a heartbeat. I want to go over and kiss its tender nape but I have Allegra to deal with. Regular features, angular cheekbones, creamy skin with no makeup, remarkable pink-gold hair tucked neatly behind the ears. The eyes refuse to meet mine. My stomach tightens as I walk round the table to claim my place on the stool. Bernie catches my arm as I pass her, and gently leads me back.

"Now Allegra, say hello to David, nicely." She's still holding my arm and she's shaking. "Get up," she says.

The girl stands and puts out her hand for a formal handshake. She and I look at Bernie, whose head is tilted in my direction. Allegra's gaze follows obediently. Her eyes are grey-blue under brows so fair they are almost non-existent. My students this age are altogether more robust-looking creatures, but I'm not sure they are stronger. Her delicate nostrils twitch and I'm aware that I smell of the pub.

"Hello, Mr -"

"It's David."

"Sorry, David, it's just we don't call our teachers by their first names at school. It feels strange."

"I'm not your teacher though, I mean, we're practically ..."

"Family. You were going to say family, weren't you?" Almost a whisper, for my ears only.

"Davey, will you break the bubbly out the fridge and pop the cork for us? I'll get the glasses." Bernie is about to open the wall cabinet. I scuttle off on my errand and I'm holding the cork down with both thumbs, foam escaping over the lip, when I rejoin them at the table. She's lined up three flutes in a row. I release the cork and let the bubbles flow into them softly, one after the other. We both pick up ours, Allegra's stays where it is, on the table. She's the only one sitting down.

"A toast, to the future. All three of us," says Bernie. She and I raise our glasses. She gives me a wink so fleeting I almost miss it. Smiling like idiots, we glance down at Allegra's bright hair, then at each other, and take a long draught apiece. Allegra makes a tiny tutting noise.

"Come on, Allie, you've had champers before, and liked it. Why don't you two get to know each other and enjoy your bubbly while I finish the meal?" Touching Allegra lightly on the shoulder, Bernie drains her flute and leaves us. I clamber on to my stool.

"So, what set books are you doing for A/S – you are taking English, aren't you?" Allegra pulls a face combining boredom and disbelief. I stumble on. "Look, I don't care, but it matters to your mother. Just take a sip. It's our toast." She pushes her champagne flute towards me.

"I don't want it, it's all yours." Plates clash across the kitchen. I get to my feet to help Bernie, who has laid them out on the worktop and started to carve. The beef crumbles as she tries to slice it, and the potatoes resemble old brown shoes in need of a polish.

"Delicious. Best time of year for sprouts," I say, spooning out generous helpings on to the plates. I grab the carrots' pan and am touched to see Bernie has glazed them, maybe with honey and butter. "Gorgeous carrots." I share them out too. Bernie is concentrating hard on stirring a small pot on the hob, her hair in tendrils and her face damp and shiny. I carry the laden plates to the table. She follows me and pours gravy in concealing pools over the beef for each of us. She and I sit and start to eat.

"Mmmm, your gravy," I say, reminding myself of the kids in the Bisto advert, but meaning it. Her alchemy with meat juices has brought the meal back from the brink, and I'm relishing just about every mouthful.

Allegra has scraped all the gravy off a grey sliver of meat on her fork. She holds it up, then loosens it from the tines with her knife and lets it fall. She sets her knife and fork down together on the plate.

"I'll try and find you a nicer bit of beef in a minute, Allie, but there's nothing wrong with the veg, see." A tremor on the last word.

"Don't call me that." Allegra lifts her fork and taps a potato. There's a small knock on wood sound, and she reunites her knife and fork without exploring further. According to Bernie, she's never had a nickname at school – she prefers Allegra, no exceptions. Her dad calls her Princess, but it seems that everything he does is okay with her. The irony of it.

"Look," I say. "If this meal isn't entirely to your taste, it's nobody's fault but yours. You were an hour late with no warning." Bernie and I have both stopped eating and she's getting up from the table.

"At least I didn't roll in from the pub, reeking of cigarettes and booze."

"I can't believe how you're talking to Davey. Where's your

manners?" Bernie has turned from the worktop where she's been trying to hack in to some sweeter meat at the heart of the joint. Allegra jerks her head in my direction.

"He started it. He's got no right to tell me off. How could you do it, Mother? Reject Daddy and split up our family, and what for? The likes of this pathetic old man?" The knife and the skewered sirloin slam down on the cutting board. Bernie's eyes are awash. When she told me how her marriage ended, she said Allegra must never know, it would destroy her. The 'happy family' myth that rushed in to the vacuum is costing Bernie dear.

"Now just a minute, young lady." I hardly recognise the reedy tenor as my own voice. Bernie deserves better from her champion.

Allegra pushes her small furious face towards me across the table, a pink spot on each cheek.

"Just a minute? How dare you, with your teacher pose and your 'young lady'? You'll never take my father's place, he's twice the man you are."

Bernie brushes her face with a forearm and is tugging at her apron strings, pulling the knots tighter in her haste. Feline sureness has deserted her.

"Did you really think Daddy and I didn't know he was sneaking round here, Mother? Ever since it started – two years, is it? We didn't take him seriously. Compared with Daddy, who would?"

"Sweetheart, you knew, all that time? We thought – I thought – better to wait until you was ready. It was to protect you ..." Bernie tails off miserably.

Allegra misses a beat for effect. "Yeah, right."

Middle-aged and roughed-up by the years, I'm certain that Bernie and I have found true love and that's what I'm risking. It's like risking my life. But heart thumping hard against my ribs, blood rushing in my ears, I know what I've got to do.

"Yes, that is right, Allegra," I say. "Your mother will go to any length to protect you from hurt. Take Daddy for example."

"No, Davey. Stop. You promised me. Come away, Allegra." Bernie's got her by the wrist and she's trying to drag her out of the room. Her thistledown daughter proves the stronger. She's sticking to hear me out.

"I want us both to hear this, Mother. He's going to really show himself up now."

"Daddy's story was in the newspapers," I say, shaking my head at Bernie who's cupping her hands over her daughter's ears. "But you were too young to read them. You lived in Bristol then, and Daddy used to drive your babysitter home. They had sex in his car. Her parents found out and reported it because she was only fourteen. He was jailed for it. Your mum would've had him back for your sake, but he couldn't face her. For all I know, he still can't." Allegra has her head down and her eyes scrunched shut as I finish but I judge she's heard enough. Bernie is standing behind her like a guardian angel. She hunkers down to draw her close but is shrugged away. She looks up at me, they both do, dazed and bleary from weeping.

"I want you to go, Dave," Bernie says.

I'm still perched on the wonky stool and clutching my knife and fork, both streaked with gravy. It's possible I've been waving them around. I replace them carefully. I lever myself to my feet by pressing the heel of each palm on the table top. The scarlet napkin drifts to the floor and I let it lie. Can't risk making an undignified exit now. I've done the right thing. It's been painful for me as well as for them, but they'll thank me for clearing the air between them, once they've had a good cry. They'll be able to talk to each other honestly at last. I consider saying as much to Bernie, who follows me out of the room, but while I'm putting on my coat I see her face.

She thrusts the bottle of rioja at me. It feels wrong to leave after dinner without a word to the hostess but it seems I don't have an option. Out on the pavement I turn to say goodnight, but she's shut the door.

It's been a week. I can't reach her on the phone and my texts and emails are getting no response. I've written her a letter, here in my coat pocket. I've left the car as usual round the corner by the pub. It's already dark and a spit of rain slurs across my glasses. For a second my heart lifts, the way it always does on Friday night when I'm counting the doors along the terrace to Bernie's. There's a light behind the kitchen window blind. Just lift the flap on the letterbox and push the envelope through, then go. It's heavy one end with my key. My hand's shaking and I fumble it. The flap clatters as it falls. I turn away and head back for the car.

"Is that you, Dave?"

The door's open, the light's streaming through and she's standing there, the envelope in her hand.

Closer up, she appears puzzled, stern.

"I'm so, so sorry," I say. "I've been a fool. I lost it with Allegra. I should never have told her what I did. Not my business. Unforgiveable."

"Oh Davey," she says. She moves inside to make way for me. Her voice is sad.

I stay out on the pavement. "Your key's in there. I didn't want you to think ..."

"I didn't. Come in." Her arms are open and everything becomes clear. We hug and kiss and cry, all at the same time. I've come home.

Alongside the cliffs just south of Bude, north Cornwall is a collection of cottages and a farmhouse. The location is real. None of what follows actually happened but, for me, Jack, Ruby and their friends exist too. And they are a circle of friends who have, perhaps, stayed in touch beyond the group's best-before date.

The Going

Adrian Lazell

The walk along the wet sand, the Atlantic washing over the bride's feet as she hitches her dress, the wind catching the groom's jacket, spray hitting faces, gulls crying over the photographer's calls then, drained flutes retrieved and cameras collected, guests are herded back up the sandstone path to eat.

I hang back at the sea, turquoise-grey against the beach, blue as it merges with the sky, watching it breathe in and out, in and out, before following orders and the others. The curl of the hill embraces the cottages and farm-house which are, as Beth cried out on arrival, divine. Every bed is over pillowed, every bathroom over towelled and every fireplace over logged. Though, as this is a Cornish summer, we may be burning them before booking out. Every corridor brings a dozen encounters. This is the world's most over populated hamlet. Humanity, as in people, is crammed into every cranny and quite a few nooks. They're all here.

And I love each of them, or at least feel a fondness for them, foibles and all. This wedding is also a college reunion, and drawing out old passions. Look at us, a group of actors coming back for a delayed sequel – overplaying our roles.

Luke has his guitar. Out on the cobbled courtyard Paul's campervan is full of body boards, not quite enough for the whole assembly but one between two would do it. And Andy, the host with the most, money at least, is ignoring Heather, his new bride, to do the refilling rounds, making the waitresses redundant. It's good to see him back on form. Chrissie, blonde, fringy, flirty when drunk, waves at me from the cleared square of dining room that's become a dance floor. The crow's feet are pressing a little deeper than when I last saw her and the sacks under her eyes will be full in the morning but she is still delicious, as a friend. She's also scatty and I imagine unreliable as a partner. Or she would be for anyone but David, our one absentee – a conference in Dubai has kept him away. Their marriage seems to work because they're rarely together and when they are they just ignore each other. But you don't know do you – or at least I don't. I can't see inside other people's marriages, even those I've lived alongside.

Nic leans across me to be topped up by Andy. She's so dependable, a security blanket for all of us, organising the photographs, the march to the beach and back, speeches – the de facto best man. She asks me how I'm doing and with this being a wedding, which heightens emotions, and us being mates, she means the question. I reply with I'm fine and head into some blandness about how good Andy and Heather are together, before she gets called to join YMCA.

And Beth, my Beth, mother of my boys, wife of nearly twenty years, long dark hair artificially straight, artificially dark these days, is mingling. Her love of life, zest for it, that's real enough. She leans into the lapel of the goatee bearded brother, I think, of the bride – Simon maybe. Laughter ripples through her body. God she looks happy.

My glass filled, I thank Andy. The music ends and Nic announces that Luke is going to lead a sing-song. Sing and song are two words that should never be used together. I drain the glass and examine the dregs. As Andy's attention has passed to the performer I am able to slide along the goblet laden table, grab a half empty bottle of claret, and make for the door and cobbled courtyard. Nic will be organising games next and they will include forfeits, the kind that lead to kissing strangers. The fun part of the evening is upon us. I loathe it. Aren't we a little old for all this? Or is it just me? Better to be scarce, to disappear into the night for an hour or three.

The day has closed and a broken slate sky sits over the cottages. The appeal of this place is its rejection of modernity; a mythic rejection as we all used sat-navs to locate it, checked our smart phones for signals on arrival and plugged our iPads and Kindles in on reaching our rooms. But the trail to the cliff-top, unaccompanied and lit only by the waning moon, offers something authentic. Waves break on the rocks below me. An owl calls out – you don't get many owls back in Orpington. Man is less obtrusive here and that suits me fine.

The bottle and glass are propped against a clump of Cornishness, something turfy, a miniature grassy knoll. I spread my hired jacket to avoid grass stains on my hired trousers, the flawed logic of the act occurs to me too late. After five minutes I adjust to a prone position, my shirt lying against the jacket lining, my trousers on the bare grass. Something crawls on to my back – there is life here. Then a hand touches my shoulder.

"Mind if I join you?"

I recognise the voice and turn my head to see Ruby kneeling alongside, causing a rapid increase in my heart rate. Unexpected is an understatement.

"Of course," I struggle with the sense of the words, "not."

A fresh bottle of red and a glass are arranged in front of her. She smiles – her hair just a shade short of black swept from her forehead and strung out on the breeze. The moonlight gives her olive skin a bluish tint, but still more Mediterranean than north Atlantic. Her eyes crinkle in the corners; her cheekbones catch the best of the light. Something about her is rodent, but a very attractive rodent; Disney rather than James Herbert.

"Andy looks happy." As I say this I want to erase the words.

"At least he won't be accused of going for a trophy wife." She smiles. I love her spikiness. I always have.

"Is that bitchy? I think that's bitchy." Heather isn't a looker, I think that's fair to say. But she's lively and loud and good company, so long as you agree with her opinions – which on education, immigration and hunting I don't, but on food, wine and holidays in France I do.

"I think Chrissie is going to be suffering in the morning," I say.

"She's asleep."

"That's early – she was dancing a few minutes ago."

"She's under a table. Someone must have pulled her trip switch."

We share the smile of friends who know the script; from a quiet beginning a few drinks take Chrissie into shouty, sing-along territory, and then her battery gives up and she finds refuge on a chair or pile of coats or, tonight, under a table and she sleeps until dawn, when her hangover arrives. I push myself up to sit alongside Ruby – my infatuation now, as she has been for over half my life. We each went off to get married elsewhere, became parents and yet stayed in the same circle. And everything went unspoken.

"It's beautiful here."

"Best part of the weekend," I say, my look holding her eyes for a moment. She glances away at the strip of moonlight splitting the ocean and I think she's embarrassed. Then she looks back and grins. So attractive. So unavailable.

"You know what would make it better though?" As I say this my stomach rolls. I'm sixteen again, an age when it hurts to speak to your crush.

And she seems to be wary. "Jack." It's my name but she is saying it as a warning. So I pocket the suggestion of a kiss and save it for later, or never.

"What would happen now if we were all meeting for the first time?"

"In what context?" As she says this she turns her face and sweeps stray hair behind her ear.

"Oh I don't know." I haven't thought this through. "Speed dating?"

"Do you mean would I go for Andy and would you end up with Beth again?"

"I guess."

"Or, to be blunt, would I go for you?"

"Because you already know I'd go for you."

"I don't like games like this, Jack."

"Why not?"

"Because I'm not a keys on the table kind of a girl. I never understood the appeal of swingers." She's holding my right hand in both of hers, our eyes meeting. "And there is Heather to complicate things." She takes a hand away to put more stray hairs in their place. "Besides, I'd never do speed dating." And she's being honest, she wouldn't, she wouldn't need to. She'd never be short of offers and it wouldn't be her style. She'd want romance not one-liners.

The sea crashes below us.

"I'm surprised no one's gone night-swimming," I say.

"There's still time." That smile again. Oh I could commit crimes for that smile. Or take risks I wouldn't consider for anyone else.

"Well, Ruby, we," I glance down at my suit trousers and back to her, "we could go skinny dipping."

She leans in to me to nudge me off balance. "Dream on."

"My whole life seems to be made up of dreams."

"I suppose," the moon catches her eyes, "it could be fun."

"It could be brilliant."

"And cold. How much wine have you had?"

"Enough."

"Too much I think."

Looking at my brogues I feel overdressed. I guess she is right. We could paddle.

"I should have married you, Ruby."

"Where did that come from?" She feigns shock but then smiles.

I say nothing.

"You're very sure of yourself with me aren't you?"

"Didn't used to be."

"Repressed is the word I'd use."

In stages I get to my feet, grab the remaining wine and offer it to Ruby. She shakes her head. I fill my glass and take a step nearer to the cliff edge. I feel a bug on my calf and try to shake it away, spilling wine on my shoes. What is wrong with me? I say all this now but not then, nothing then.

In the library at college her bare feet caught my attention first. Who goes barefoot in the library? I visited the library more and more frequently. She supplied me with Maltesers. I bought her coffees. Two months of that. In December, waiting by a notice board for a break in the rain we dared each other to audition for a college production of Pygmalion. Colonel Pickering – not bad for my only venture into acting. Ruby, of course, got to be Eliza Doolittle. And first day at rehearsals we met Andy Munroe who happened to be playing Henry Higgins and from that day I became number two; the best man but one. Andy fox-trotted in, landed the lead role, spent the spring opening the batting for the college eleven, organised the Summer Ball, and went on to get a first in Economics and be head hunted into the city. I think I'd have preferred it if he was a shit. Then I could have just despised him. But he had a joie de vivre that swept up Ruby and she was gone. I just lived on shed loads of envy.

"Jack, what are you doing out here?" I turn to find Beth along with the bride's brother. "Have you met Simon?"

Handshakes are exchanged.

"Alone?"

"Apparently." It seems I am, or had been.

"So what are you doing?"

"Waiting for the sunrise."

She looks at me as if this is odd, and then looks at Simon for back up. I notice that they are holding hands. What the hell – I'm her husband. I stare at their locked hands and then at Beth but she must be too drunk to realise what she's doing.

"Okay, well, just wanted to check on you." She looks to Simon. "We'd better be getting back. People are going to bed."

"How's Chrissie?"

"She's out for the night. Andy just about carried her up to her room."

"Just about?"

"He's a little drunk. Funny day for him really ..." As she speaks, Beth lets go of Simon's hand to brush something from her face. "... being the anniversary."

"Funny day to get married," I say.

"Anniversary?" says Simon. I look at him. Beth looks at him too and they re-join hands.

"Ruby, his first wife –"

"She died," says Simon.

"She died two years ago this weekend."

Simon shrugs then scratches at his beard. He clearly didn't know.

Beth rattles out an explanation, "Brain haemorrhage, sudden, coming back from the school run, something went pop and her car veered over the carriageway into a lorry and ended up in a hedge."

"That's tragic," says Simon, and I want to tell him to fuck off with his hand on my wife's and his feigned sorrow for my friend.

"Surely Heather has explained all this," I say.

He shrugs. "I knew Ruby had died. That's all."

"And you didn't think to ask more."

The silence becomes awkward as it continues. I break it, "Have you heard from the boys?"

"A text that said they're fine. Right, Simon, let's get back inside." Beth puts on a plastic smile and gives a puppet's wave. Simon takes his hand from his beard and pushes it into his rusty mane, then, unsmiling, turns with her. A few steps later he puts the brakes on, pivots and calls back.

"By the way, Jack my boy, you're facing the wrong way."

"Wrong way?"

"Yes – you're facing west. ' His eyes are smiling. "The sun rises in the east." He nods, draws his free hand up and gives a flicked salute.

"Thank you."

"Don't mention it old sport." And the pair climb away towards the distant buildings.

"Old sport." I hear a laugh behind me. "He thinks he's Gatsby." Ruby has returned.

"We were just talking about you."

She ignores this. "He's right though. You need to be on the other side of the cottages." I bite my lower lip. "Up on the hill. Then you'll see the sun come up."

On the wall of my guest room is a quote from a Thomas Hardy poem The Going. He wrote it after the death of his wife Emma:

'You were she who abode

By those red-veined rocks far West,

You were the swan-necked one who rode

Along the beetling Beeny Crest,

And, reining nigh me,

Would muse and eye me,

While life unrolled us its very best.'

These cliffs are Hardy's cliffs; the red-veined rocks far West. I look at Ruby. She is my Emma. Only she isn't. She is Andy's Emma, or Andy's Ruby, or she was. My head is a mess. It might be the wine. Andy's response to death is to get back out there, to dive head first into the sea and bob back up with a new catch. Second anniversary of losing her – I'll get married again. No thought, no reflection.

There is a scene in Annie Hall where Woody Allen asks an elderly couple how come they're so happy and the old lady replies, 'Because I'm very shallow and empty and I have no ideas and nothing interesting to say.' And the old man is the same. They are a perfect fit. But with Andy and Ruby it couldn't have worked like that – Andy might be a little one dimensional, but there was always more to Ruby, much more.

I think of how she'd once eye me, even after she became forbidden fruit. And these memories, mixed with a little vino, have conjured up a ghost, a spirit, a kindred spirit.

Two dewy sets of footprints lead back to the farmhouse. I feel guilt.

"She feels neglected."

"She's got company hasn't she?"

"Neglected by you."

"I feel neglected."

Ruby is right though, Beth does feel abandoned. Maybe she's always been my runner's up prize, second place to a ghost. A sliver of ice touches me; a black dog trying to take hold. I need to shake it off. I listen to my lungs take in and expel chilled air.

How long since I invested in my marriage? I'm thinking really invested, committed, as opposed to the lip service; the standing order of forced exchanges I give now. I take a step towards the house. My head is full of cotton wool. Thinking has become hard work. How old are the boys? Fifteen and seventeen – so it's had a decade and a half to decompose. Each evening I go to my laptop and she to hers. We don't do conversation.

I catch the chorus of a tune playing in the house – *Everyday I love you less and less.* Not quite true – we stopped loving each other long ago. Now we live on a plateau of civility and indifference.

"Do you realise what a catch she still is?" says Ruby.

"Simon does." But I realise it too.

"Go after her, Jack." I turn back to my ghostly companion. "Woo her."

"Woo – that's a good word." This conversation is going somewhere I hadn't planned. If I've dreamed up Ruby why can't I control what she says? She smiles. The curl at the corner of her eyes warm and inviting. She moves close, leans in and kisses me on the cheek, then gives me the best, most solid hug imaginable.

"You, Ruby, you're a catch."

"I'm not available. Beth is. Go after her, Jack." She moves past me, throws an arm up to give a loose wave, and then drops it alongside her black dress. I watch the curve of her shoulders in the moonlight, the curl of her back – a little more concave than in her Eliza days and the movement of her buttocks – not a pear, an apricot perhaps. She sashays up the slope in her high heels, doing a night time coastal path as if on a red carpet and I wonder how? I've seen her on red carpets too, arm in arm with Andy, making small talk to guests at the Roxy, and then large talk to art house film producers about Bergman, Fellini and Tarantino. She took over a decaying art nouveau cinema when it was close to death and made it the hub of weekends in town. Her vision and Andy's money, in that context it worked. And me – what could I offer? I went into criminal law. I thought it would make me noble, an Atticus Finch of the Home Counties. Instead I'm cynical, impatient and in debt. I assume the worst in every client and hate myself for it.

"Where are you going?" My words seem to strain to reach Ruby, but she's still there, not quite merged into the night.

"To speak with Andy."

"You can't."

"Why not?" She has stopped and is facing me from, maybe, thirty metres away.

"Because you're dead." I say the last word in a softer register, letting it drop into the breeze, but she's heard.

"I'm speaking to you aren't I?" She's not fazed by being reminded that she's not real, "you coming in?"

"No – I might relocate to the east, take the hill and see the sunrise." In the distance a door crashes.

"Jack." She has taken a few steps down the path but is still raising her voice to reach me. "Andy is up there getting married, getting drunk but getting through it. You, you Jack ... you're lovely, sweet." Don't call me sweet Ruby please. "But you wallow." Even my own ghostly creation lectures me. She is getting closer. "You take pleasure in your own misery." I feel her hand on my cheek. "Maybe Beth isn't your problem. Maybe your problem is in here." She wraps her knuckles against my forehead and widens her eyes – two brown discs staring at me. The wind whistles through me. She slips her hand from my face. "I love you, Jack ... ," she smiles, "... as a friend." And she turns to retrace her steps. "Go after her, Jack, and win her back."

I follow each move until she merges into the shadows. Then realign my feet to face the Atlantic, listen to the water break and think of her. Surely there was more than just friendship. But I fool myself sometimes. I do that in court too. I lose what is real and what is fabricated. Not good because my job is to reduce everything down to the known. Ruby's a memory now and destined never to be more than that. I think of Beth, and then of her and Simon.

A gull sweeps past. The sky is brighter, the sun, behind the hill, must be rising. The house is without lights, asleep. I consider this, then pivot to search out the beach path. I walk and slide, grabbing tufts of marram grass to stop myself tipping.

Repressed, she called me repressed. My shirt is always buttoned to the top; my tie straight, Jack Rowland, forever Mr Reserved – except once, long ago, with Ruby and in the early days with Beth. The dog is upon me. I hate these thoughts. I need to shake them, wash them away.

My jacket spread over the sand I sit and draw my legs in to untie the laces of my left brogue, slide it free and then my sock and deposit it inside before doing the right. I stand, unbuckle my belt, drop and fold my trousers and place them over the shoes, hesitate then pull my pants down and fold them on top. Then my watch, cufflinks, tie and shirt are left in a pyramid on my pants. I look each way along the beach but there is no company. I rearrange the pile to hide the cufflinks and timepiece, though only a Seiko, in my shoe. I take a breath, then another and when, after ten or eleven, I find myself no closer to the ocean I decide to count myself in. The numbers from thirty are internalised but, by the time I reach ten, I'm screaming and at five I begin a run towards and into the waves, take the cold plunge and a mouthful of salt water and start swimming away.

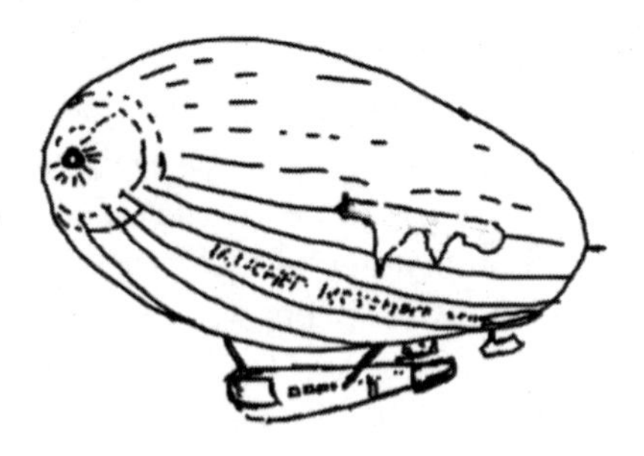

A version of 'Maid In Heaven', an alternative present (technology is over one hundred years behind our own timeline), initially appeared in the anthology *Wordland 3: What They Saw In The Sky,* published by Exaggerated Press. This version has some minor edits due to suggestions from the rest of the Red Wine Writers.

Maid In Heaven

Terry Martin

It wasn't so much the splutter of engines that made Private Veilleux look up but the rattle of musket balls against metal. No more than sixty feet above him a young mechanic, about his own age, in a makeshift harness, hung precariously from the side of a dirigible frantically fiddling within one of the engine housings, ducking instinctively every so often as bullets ricocheted off the iron surface. It was Veilleux's first glimpse of the enemy. At least the kid hadn't suffered an eight-hour tramp through the mud-sucking trenches that zig-zagged to the front line.

Until then the trench had been eerily quiet save for the occasional zing-thwack of a sniper's bullet hitting a sandbag and the muffled crack of a musket that followed. Veilleux and, it seemed, his fellow *nouvelles recrues* were keeping their thoughts to themselves and their heads low, heeding the warning that had been drilled into them by Sergeant Proulx during their four weeks' training. The sergeant had somehow managed to switch from no-holds-barred taskmaster to caring father within seconds. Veilleux's feelings towards him were a mixture of hatred and love in equal proportions. Veilleux was pretty sure that the rest of his platoon felt the same way and marvelled at how someone could garner so much respect in just a month.

Veilleux and his lifelong friend Bernard were half squatting, half leaning against the joists that kept the sides of the trench from tumbling in and burying its occupants alive. Anyone travelling along this section also had to duck under crossbeams to compensate for unusual subsidence.

Veilleux wondered if Bernard was regretting their decision to join the army. They'd had aspirations of emulating the great Dr D'arc whose inventions had inspired the revolution to finally free France from centuries of English rule. Their enthusiasm had been further whipped up by the taking of Paris, but dreams of joining *La Résistance de l'Air* had been dashed despite Veilleux's degree in aeronautical engineering. Footsoldiers were in greater demand. During their training they'd heard that Dr D'arc had either been killed or captured and the front had stuck on the borders of Normandie. It seemed likely the English would retake their European capital.

Further along the trench an officer shouted to stop firing at the airship, to save ammunition, but his commands went unheeded as they continued to maniacally ram the Minié balls into their muskets, hurriedly aimed and fired. Veilleux's instinct was to stop them, although he doubted they had any chance of hitting the young lad. A cloud of strong smelling cordite, incongruously reminding Veilleux of Christmas crackers, began to deploy itself along the bottom of the trench. Beside him, Bernard grimaced.

Debris, of what must once have been wings, fluttering lifelessly like forgotten washing along the sides of the dirigible, suggested it was some kind of airship-biplane hybrid. Having studied aeronautics and enjoyed the hands-on engineering experience in the university's hangars in England, Veilleux was more fascinated with the craft itself than the young mechanic. It was about forty foot long and fish shaped rather than symmetrical with a gondola that looked too big to be supported. Two engines, one either side at the rear of the craft, were without propellers, though there was still momentum, perhaps from a secondary power unit within the gondola.

Stencilled between the keel's rigid joists on its rubberised outer skin, where normally you would see a name, 'Launched November 2014' suggested it had seen a lot of action in the last two months. Veilleux was disappointed that he'd heard nothing about a prototype aircraft. But then, he wasn't in *La Résistance de l'Air*, he was just a foot soldier.

A whoop of success, followed almost instantly by silence, made Veilleux look back at the boy. A lucky shot had smashed through his skull dripping blood and brains onto the fields below as his body swung upside down like a damaged pendulum; a grotesque trophy of marksmanship. A high-pitched wail, cutting to the heart of everyone who heard, echoed across the front from within the gondola. Veilleux could just make out hands pressed against one of the airship's observation windows in the base of the car, and the face of a distraught young woman, before the damaged craft continued its dying descent deeper behind his own lines.

Death was new to Veilleux, and the kid had looked so young. Bernard still stared up as the dirigible disappeared, the grimace set in stone. Two soldiers vomited nearby, their spew soon lost, both physically and odorously, into the calf-deep mud of the forward trench where boards had been ripped up for firewood. Veilleux couldn't remove the image of the girl's stricken face or the gruesome memory of her compatriot's death. What was a girl doing in the middle of a battlefield anyway?

"Settle down," were the quiet words Sergeant Proulx used as he moved along the trench between the huddles of soldiers. He had been medalled in the Empire's army, joining the freedom fighters early in the current uprising to become a tough instructor. "When the barrage finishes we'll be going over the top," he repeated as he passed Veilleux. As if on cue, the dreaded whistle of a shell, followed by a blast some two hundred yards forward of their position, rippled the ground beneath their feet. Dirt and stones trickled down the sides of the dugout. Almost immediately another followed. This time the sergeant shouted "Settle down, boys. Get some rest. *Vive la France*!"

"Get some rest?" Bernard said, as he nonchalantly rolled a reefer. "With that going on?" He spread some gum on the outer leaf from his pouch and finished the rollup with a flourish of nimble fingers. He offered the thin brown cigarette to his friend. "It'll take the edge off."

Veilleux hesitated before taking it, huffed, then added, "Like you're gonna feel a bullet in the head." He wondered if the lad had felt anything before his life had been extinguished.

"I don't mean a bullet in the head!" Bernard's irritation held a hint of contagious fear. "It'll make it easier to obey the command," he insisted.

"To die."

"They reckon the English are crap shots."

"They reckon this. They reckon that. What the fuck do *they* know?"

Bernard didn't answer but finished rolling his own reefer, flicked a match alight and offered it to Veilleux. Their eyes locked together as they shared the flame and drew in deeply of the drug.

Bernard looked away first as he blew his drag into the cold air. Veilleux watched the cloud dissipate before he let out his own first lungful which caught in his throat. Bernard whacked his back a few times as Veilleux 's coughing fit looked set to bring up the mutton soup they'd drunk from their helmets a half hour earlier.

"Jesus, Veilleux! You're gonna die before the English get a chance to kill you."

"Thanks, Bernard," Veilleux managed to say between rasps. "What the fuck's in this?" He was feeling lightheaded already.

"Just the usual. Only it's grade A."

"What!"

Bernard shrugged. "Can't take the money with us when our time comes."

Veilleux stared at the reefer in his own hands as if it were a deadly snake, but Bernard hid his behind his back as Proulx re-appeared. Their sergeant took the cigarette from Veilleux's frozen fingers, surprising them both by taking a deep lungful. He looked from one to the other as he let the smoke drift out slowly from his nostrils before handing the reefer back to Veilleux.

"I'd rather you didn't," he said softly as he walked away. About five steps later he stopped and turned with raised eyebrows. "Good stuff!"

Another five steps and Veilleux's world erupted.

It was likely tunnelling and mass explosives. At least that's what Veilleux surmised later. When he came round he was lying on his back looking up at a grey sky. It was quiet and peaceful until a high-pitched singing began in his ears. He put his hands – at least they were still intact – to the side of his head to block out the sound. Where was his helmet? It was only when he rolled his head sideways and saw shells exploding in the distance, felt their vibrations but not their roar of death, that he realised the noise was from within, drowning out any other sounds.

When he looked in the other direction a lone girl of about his age stood at the bottom of a gigantic crater beside a dirigible – the dirigible – staring at him with glazed eyes. The craft must have come down nearer than he'd expected or perhaps he'd staggered away from the underground blast before passing out. It seemed unlikely he'd been thrown this far from the detonation and still survived, but that was another possibility. The ringing in his ears slowly subsided and the sounds of war began. He needed to get to cover. As he slid sideways down to where the girl stood he noted that, bar a few minor cuts and bruises, he was otherwise unharmed. For a split second he wondered how Bernard had fared.

He was about to stand when the cold metal of a pistol barrel pressed against his forehead. He suppressed a belch of fear demanding release, but a second pushed out the first. "Please..." His voice sounded as pathetic as he felt.

"I'm not the enemy." Could he believe that? "Are you a mechanic?" Her accent was less the slow drawl of Angleterre than the rapid fire of Lorraine province, meaning nothing in a war that pitched father against son, brother against brother. As he looked up into her face he felt a kind of inevitability in her presence, not sexual, more spiritual. He was smitten.

"I've a degree in aeronautical engineering," he stammered. The polished metal of the engines aroused his curiosity. It was like nothing he'd seen before.

She signalled for him to go over to the dirigible as if she'd been expecting someone with his knowledge to appear. Like the girl, he averted his eye from the body that protruded from beneath the engine and was mostly hidden in the mud.

"Can you fix that? The other engine has ceased altogether."

It looked as if a stray bullet had entered through a weak spot in the engine housing and smashed through a gas pipe, but the engine itself appeared undamaged. By its size he mentally calculated that it would be powerful enough to drive the craft without its twin. His initial observations had been false, the propellers were actually within the housing.

"If I had the tools and the parts," he finally told her. If she were the enemy he'd be a traitor to the cause.

She pointed to a crate surrounded by broken bottles of red wine and a wooden trunk that had strewn spares into a muddy puddle on impact.

"Everything should be there."

Veilleux was feeling less threatened with each sentence and, as he studied the girl, felt his attraction grow. Coal dust spotted a pale complexion. A dirty brown rag kept sweat from her eyes and her short black hair behind her ears. Her tan leather flight jacket was a size too big and as grubby as her khaki battle pants tucked into Germanic-style calf length boots.

"I'm Pascal," he said, as he rummaged through what remained of the contents in the trunk before glancing across the murky water where a small piece of piping stuck out like a periscope.

"Are you from the trench that shot Daniel?"

"I saw it happen. I wasn't firing."

"He was only seventeen. He was my brother." The pistol came

up again in retribution, but dropped almost as quickly, as if she'd remembered something. "Father..." she whispered.

She disappeared through a doorway in the bullet-dented gondola, flaking camouflage paint exposing bright steel. The car appeared otherwise undamaged, so the dirigible had come to rest fairly gently. Veilleux promptly looked around for a weapon in case she wasn't what she claimed. As he did so a badly and hurriedly painted laurel branch on the keel stopped him in his tracks. It was the sign of the resistance. His unit had shot one of their own.

Artillery shells began to rain down nearby as if they had become a target. He began removing the damaged pipe in earnest.

Ten minutes later he stuck his head through the doorway and called out, "The pipe is fixed. We need to fire up the engine."

"Come here." Her voice was close but it was dim inside the craft. The faint chug of another engine came to him as he passed within.

She'd spoken from the front of the gondola, through what appeared to be a store compartment about twenty feet long that led to the bridge. Broken crates and bottles littered the floor. As he stepped into what was essentially a large cockpit, his boots crunched through a pool of red wine, confined by the steel framework of the doorframe. She was bending over a pile of rags on the floor but as he moved closer some of the rags rose and lifted a blunderbuss in his direction.

"It's fine, Father," she told, what Veilleux now realised was a badly wounded man, "We made it, just..."

"And... and Daniel?" the man asked.

She didn't answer but her look of accusation at Veilleux brought up the evil weapon in the man's hand again.

"No, Father," she assured him. "This man is on our side. He's helping us."

Veilleux had moved around so he could see the man's face. A bottle of red wine was gripped in his other hand; to reduce the pain? Veilleux gasped. Even with a deep gash across his forehead, crusting blood around his ear, and almost as much soot on his face as his daughter, he recognised the man he had always wanted to emulate.

"Doctor D'arc!"

The doctor's fading eyes looked Veilleux up and down, gave his hands a second look. "He's a mechanic, Joan. … Tell him," he ordered.

She looked from her father to Veilleux, then back to her father. Her words were for Veilleux. "This dirigible holds a weapon that will rid us of the English for ever. They were making my father develop it. We need to get it to safety before it is destroyed or captured."

"She knows how to work it," Dr D'arc told him. "She'll tell you. … But more than that." He coughed blood, adding to that already on his chin and cheeks. "God is truly with us this time."

Veilleux didn't doubt it as he looked across at Joan. After almost six-hundred years the Maid of Orleans had returned. And this time she would triumph.

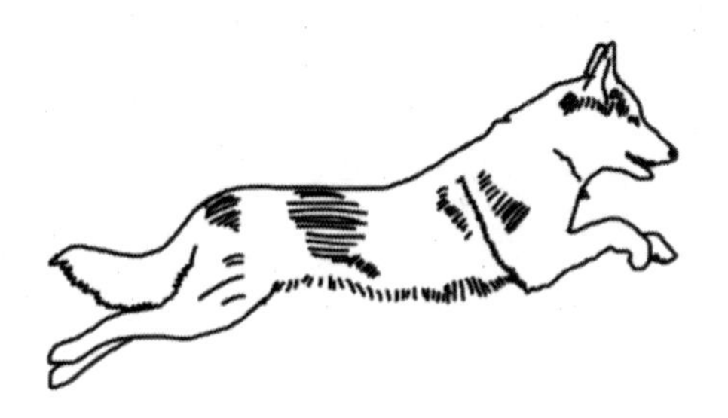

This story was written specifically for the group. The title came first – a direct riff on "Kind Hearts & Coronets" the black and white Alec Guinness film, a classic from Ealing Studios. I make absolutely no claim to this story being a 'classic', but I enjoyed writing it, reading it out to the group and I hope that you, dear reader, find it at least mildly diverting.

Cruel Hearts and Cornettos

Mark Badham-Moore

T*he stars twinkled overhead.*

No. No. No. Twinkled? Twaddled more like it.

Right, stop, think. Start again.

It was a clear night. √

It was a cold night. √

Well, there was a chill in the air certainly, after all it was late September.

The house was dark, inside and out. I like the dark, it keeps me alert, plus I don't really have the imagination to be scared by shadows, even the really dark ones. You know, the ones you see out of the corner of your eye.

I was waiting, in this cold and musty house, had been for quite some time, days I think, maybe weeks, it's hard to be sure.

Tonight, I could tell, others would get here, a kind of synchronicity. The grandfather clock in the hall wasn't ticking, there wasn't even the hum of fridge or freezer coming from the kitchen. My ears pricked, like they do, and I turned towards the front, wide windows. I'd always liked those windows, sitting or preferably leaning over the back of the two-seater, watching the birds, chasing them with my eyes, waiting for the blackbirds and crows to land on the lawn. It was fun, although I rarely got out to play in that part of the garden.

Never on my own. It was always locked, the most precious flowers and plants grew there. The most lovingly tended.

The sound came again, my reverie broken. A tap-tap-tap.

It wasn't coming from the window, nor the front door.

It seemed to be coming from everywhere and inside my head all at the same time. Then it stopped. I almost jumped out of my skin as a hand patted me on the head.

"Hello, boy."

I turned around as fast as my legs could carry me. Which is quite fast, let me tell you.

It was Jack. Good old Jack! I knew him when he was just a little boy, but now he looked about twenty, but a little on the pale side.

"Hey, where are we?" I could see him looking around in the dinge, eyes adjusting, realisation dawning. His face betrayed every ratcheting emotion – horror, sadness, despair, desperation and then, after only a couple of minutes, resignation.

"Why here? *Her* house? And what about you? Is this your vigil too?"

Before I could answer, the tapping began again, perhaps a little louder this time. It lasted longer too.

Both Jack and I were looking toward the door when we heard an 'ahem' behind us. We turned around, and I stepped back behind Jack, fearing the worst, but this time we both shouted out, "Janet!"

From her lazily reclined position on the sofa she jumped up, first to hug Jack and then me, making my two rear legs ache. That always happens.

"Jack ... you look better than ... well, you know ... I have to say, I never expected to be here again."

"I know," said Jack. "Any idea why we would be, after what she did?"

"I haven't a clue." Janet emphasised every word, the punctuation matching every other beat of my pounding heart. I didn't know how much more of this I could take. First Jack and then Janet. She also looked pale, but she was always older, always stressed. My company used to help her. Until ... until what? I've never had the greatest of memories and now I couldn't remember. What? What? What?

"I used to hate coming here," said Jack, gazing out into the moonlit garden, its borders, the lawn in gentle grey disarray. "I could only ever play out in the yard – that concrete slab with the walls. She wouldn't even let the children from next door in to play with me."

"Didn't you break your arm out there?"

"Yes." He paused. "It hurt like hell."

"Less than what happened later, I'm sure."

He looked down at his feet, struck dumb in silent contemplation.

I felt calm, not sure why really, but I could sense that they were both tense, jumpy as spring lambs. Ooh, lamb, that brings back memories, chasing, no wait, wait, that wasn't me, that was the bloody TV. Always on, but not now – hssssssssssss – a screen of static.

Quick as a flash I was behind the sofa. How could that be?

Jack and Janet were both on their feet, holding hands.

"Janet, what's going on?" It was almost a shout, directed at the noisy grey-black-grey-black screen. The glass hummed with static. I felt hairs standing up where I didn't know there were hairs. I tried to cover my eyes; you know how difficult that is?

Silence came again, and in that split-second of absolute quiet I heard a man-sized weight settle on upholstery and springs. Uncovering my eyes, I crept round the side of the sofa, sending a couple of empty, dark-green wine bottles skittering across the carpet. I glanced at the leather-clad feet first, but as soon as I felt that I could I looked up at the faces of Jack and Janet. They were smiling! The relief that swept over and then through me was astounding. I'd never felt anything like it before, except maybe once: Looking up, a fancy ceiling with ice cream up my nose ... What's that all about? As soon as that image, that memory came, it had gone.

"Come on out, boy, it's Dad!" Jack's smile was huge and Janet said, "Uncle John!" at the same time.

There were hugs then. Lots and lots of hugs, some kisses, but not many for me, they knew I can get a bit carried away. Tongues and everything!

The questions came from everyone, a cacophony of interruptions, clarifications and it hurt my neck to keep looking at each of them; too fast for me to keep up. I kept missing the answers as well.

Finally, his hand rubbing my head, Jack's Dad said, "We gotta wait, I think that's all. I don't know what for. It's some sorta gatherin'. *Her* flippin' victims. Sorry, Son, but that's what you were." He hushed Jack with a hand and a look.

"This isn't fair," said Janet. She got up and started to pace. I stretched and then joined her, weaving between her steps. She smiled at me and then stopped, bending down on one knee to scratch me behind both ears. "Do you remember? What happened to you, boy?"

What did she mean? What happened to me? Nothing had happened to me, I was fine. I didn't think I'd eaten for a few days, but I didn't feel hungry or thirsty. A bit unusual I'll admit, but I'd had a good nap, just before Jack arrived. The best and longest. The ... what?

How long? Janet had said it wasn't fair? Fair that I could understand almost every word said, but that I couldn't remember? She was right, it wasn't fair. Stuck in this house. Waiting for *her*. Again.

The Bitch of the House.

I suddenly realised that this wasn't *her* house, not any more. But why? The faintest whiff of ice cream filled my nostrils. It hinted at so much, but it was just out of reach, like how she used to be when she dragged me along on one of her perfunctory walks.

My reverie, on the way to a useful memory, was broken by a phone ringing. An unfamiliar ringing coming from above, which didn't exactly get louder, but seemed to hypnotise all of us.

We weren't fantastically surprised when the ringing stopped

and before us stood a glowing, elegantly dressed lady. Jasmine and lavender scents washed over me and just like the glow, faded away to be replaced and overtaken by the musty smells of the house.

"Mum!" was the first word uttered by Jack's Dad, John.

Suddenly she was smothered, except by me. I hung back, unsure of this new arrival. I didn't know her. Her smile reminded me of *her* smile.

As the tumult of hugs and kisses died down, she gently pushed everyone away and said, softly, "I am so, so sorry. I can't take away the pain that Georgette caused you all, but know this, I love you all." Tears ran down her face, creased, both old and young at the same time. She turned to me, kneeling so she could look me directly in the eyes. "And you, perhaps to you, I am most sorry, you who couldn't even argue, talk back or free yourself. But in the end, you did, didn't you?" She didn't smile. For that I was very glad. She did reach out one frail hand and stroked my nose. At the same time I heard the front door open, but I was too involved in the sudden flash of knowledge, smells and sensations to let any of the others know.

I'd been a happy youngster, taken in by George, as she'd liked to be known, a few days after the death of her mother.

She'd made it known to all and sundry that she'd looked after her mother through those last few hard years all on her own, with no help from even her closest family. She lived on her own, apart from me, and for a very little while, maybe a couple of months, life had been good, a veritable bed of roses. That all changed with the reading of *the will*. She felt cheated, maybe she was, but who can tell in you humans? So quick to hold a grudge, so eager to cling onto it. The trouble was she was clever. Devious. Like a cat. Oh well, an old anti-species habit.

Her feelings toward me dimmed, you could say she reverted to type, but she kept me around. For what reason? I'm not at all sure, perhaps an underlying caring habit she held onto, to feel just that little bit humane.

She kept the house spotless, fed me (barely) and tended her precious bloody roses. Also, she schemed, murderous plans, meticulously planned and executed. I only witnessed the end results ... The funerals and floral arrangements, masking her deceptions. First, her brother, then Jack, his son and finally Janet. George had been the perfect public figure of bereavement, brave, yet battered. Behind closed doors it was a different story ... She sang!

Not to me though, no, she shouted and screamed at me.

I was still a part of her act though and on the final day of Janet's inquest she'd taken me along. She was dressed in black as befitted the occasion. Oh poor, poor Georgette. Oh, how arrogant ...

But, wait ... The front door? No enquiring ring, just the turn of a key? That's bad, it can only mean one person ... The door from the entrance hall slammed open, the hinges heaving. The room seemed to darken. I shuffled back and the dank smell that assaulted my nose made me wrinkle it involuntarily. My hackles were up. Literally.

In retrospect, I think we all retreated, an emotional reverse gear, instinctual.

She glared at everyone in turn, her most spiteful look reserved for me, but it broke as her eyes finally fell upon her mother.

"Mummy?" One small word, one small person.

As your narrator, canine species notwithstanding, I'm not going to give you a word-for-word account of that woman's outpourings. Yes, I do know what verbatim means.

No, before I so rudely interrupted myself, I was just about to detail our final moments together ...

You see, in her conceit she'd decided to celebrate the final, foregone verdict. To this end she'd bought an ice cream, in a small freezer bag, which she duly opened, intending to then descend a long flight of stairs to the building's foyer and exit. The ice cream was soft, she was quietly jubilant and taunted me with the lukewarm confectionery. She'd done similar things several times before, but this time she couldn't help but go too far, and a spot of it landed on my nose. I licked it off straight away. I liked! I wanted more! She refused, hissing all sorts of names at me. Some people stopped to watch the fuss, as I danced around her, my lead getting more and more tangled around George's legs. The next thing I knew I'd grabbed it out of her hand, she lost her temper and pushed me down the stairs.

She screamed, I yelped and screamed too (and dogs do in our way), so a high-pitched bark then, and the next thing I know I'm back in that house.

This isn't the Afterlife, it's the Afterdeath.

By the time she'd stopped crying I was standing with John, Jack and Janet by the front door. Georgette didn't say a thing as we ran outside, one tail wagging.

"C'mon boy, let's go for a run," said John.

Bounding, I didn't look back.

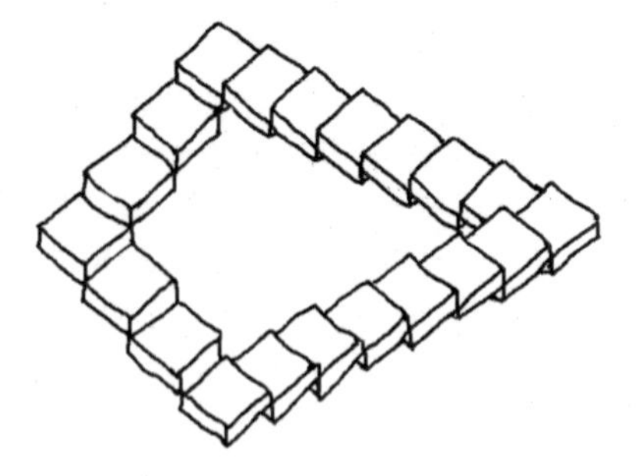

This story came from a writing assignment on an internet writing course. The brief was to simply begin a story, on any subject, that started with the sentence 'I met him on the stairs'. The piece has been through a few rewrites – the reason it no longer begins with those exact words, but the staircase is still there.

I Met Him On The Stairs

Jane Crane

I count the steps as I climb; it is an exercise to stop my mind wandering. One, two, three, four, five. I reach the half landing and turn right. One, two, three, four, five steps up again. I see the stains on the wall where years of sweaty palms have gripped the handrail and left their mark. One, two, three, four, five and another half landing and turn right again. The windowless stairwell smells of disinfectant and the only sound I hear is my own footsteps echoing up and down. If I look up I can see how many more flights I have to go before I reach the floor I need. I climb the stairs, just concentrating on the task of putting one foot in front of the other. From somewhere above I hear a door close and then other footsteps coming down the stairs. The steps mirror mine and I look up into the stairwell. I can see a hand sliding down along the banister and I'm praying that it isn't him. I've left my visit until the last possible moment, hoping that he'd be long gone. I know visiting hours are almost over but I still want to make the effort to see her, even if it's only for a few minutes.

Our footsteps seem to join together in a single sound; both sets of feet land heavily on each step, as if undertaking some monumental task. As the footsteps get nearer I realise I am holding my breath, waiting for the moment I see who will turn onto the stairs in front of me. I haven't seen him in almost two weeks; my studious campaign of avoidance has worked until today. The goddess of bad timing is definitely looking down at that moment, as I see him reach the top of the stairs in front of me. I feel my stomach lurch and I instinctively move across to the left, nearest to the wall, and carry on climbing, my body almost adhering to the dirty paintwork in order to avoid the chance of any physical contact between us.

As we pass he raises his head and looks at me and I see his eyes, lids heavy with exhaustion. A tiny flicker of a smile plays at the corner of his mouth, a slight acknowledgement of my presence but that is all and then it's gone, replaced by a blank expression. There was a time, before it happened, we would have stopped to at least exchange a greeting but those times are gone now. No more friendly banter, no more warmth. The change between us has been sudden and dramatic but it's better this way.

So we pass each other today without a word. I watch as he disappears around the corner at the bottom of the stairs.

Past experience tells me exactly where he will be headed; across the road and into the nearest pub, where he can drink until he stops thinking. It had become a routine for both of us, he would visit first and then I would go in to see her, while he talked to the nurses that were responsible for her care. Then we would go to the pub across the road from the hospital and share a bottle of red wine whilst he told me about whatever numbing platitudes the doctors had spouted that day; the repeated requests from them to not give up, to keep talking to her. As if finding just the right words would bring Lucy back to him.We spent so much time talking about Lucy, sharing memories and talking about how unfair and cruel life can be that someone so beautiful and vibrant could be snatched away from us both so quickly.

The days and weeks went by so fast. Before we knew it three months had passed and we celebrated this macabre anniversary with a shot or two of tequila, in addition to the wine. Can I blame the alcohol for what happened? Partly I suppose but not completely. It was like we had formed some strange bond, a connection forged by how close we both were to Lucy. When our drunken conversation became more intimate, more flirtatious, neither of us shied away. When he moved closer to me in our secluded corner in the pub I didn't push him away, I just laid my hand gently on his arm. I remember watching him, seeing a small muscle flex in his jaw and a deep crease appear in his brow, an outward sign of some inward struggle. Then he sank the rest of his glass of wine and brought his mouth down hard onto mine. There was so much desperation in that kiss, his lips were crushing mine and I could taste the sharp tang of the wine. I pushed my hands into his hair, grabbing fistfuls and pulling his face closer.

My lips felt bruised and swollen and as I pulled my face away from his I could see blood on his lip where I must have bitten him. We sat staring at each other, breathing hard. What had just happened? What were we doing? He took hold of my hand and interlocked our fingers, staring, as if he'd never seen anything like it before. He told me it felt nice to be able to hold a hand that didn't have needles coming out of it, he said he missed being able to do that to her, he was too frightened to in case he pulled out some vital piece of equipment. He kissed the back of my hand and pulled me out of the pub. We made it as far as a darkened alleyway behind a nearby church. This was no romantic coupling on soft sheets; I still have the bruises on my spine to prove that. It was something else, a need to reaffirm life, a desire to wipe away thoughts of machines that breathe for you and drips that feed you through tubes in your nose whilst other tubes carry away your bodily fluids into a plastic bag. When it was over we straightened our clothes and he walked me to my car.

That was the last time I had seen him until today. I had sensed something was changing between us before that night but I had chosen to keep quiet about it, thinking if we acted like it wasn't real then it would stay that way. But it hadn't.

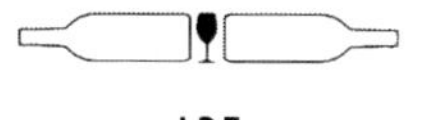

I finally reach the top of the stairs and make my way to her room. I take a few deep breaths and plaster on my best cheery smile before I go in.

"Hey there, Lucy. How's my gorgeous sister today? I've just seen your lovely husband on the stairs. He says you're doing really well."

I wanted to see what might happen when a retired couple who get along well enough realise they are in a rut. Finding a solution which preserves the status quo is often seen as a sign of weakness but my character, Lucy, knows better. This story is a celebration of compromise.

Crossword

Christine Dickinson

Lucy hesitated at the door of McDonald's. She stepped aside to ease the exit of a red faced man shouting into a mobile phone. Squinting through the gap between his suit and raised arm she could see there was no queue. She half turned to look at the patch of sun where she'd parked her car, took a deep breath and sucked in her stomach. A steady trot and she would be through the lobby and at the counter ready to order her Meal Deal.

As she fumbled in her shopping bag for money, the pink sequins on her Turkish pumps winked at her. This was like that time she was caught putting the rubbish out in her nightie by a neighbour. Harry had been away then too but that had been just the one night. She kept her head down and glanced round at the customers. All hands were occupied juggling drinks and snacks with laptops and the morning papers; eyes were too busy to take notice of her or her bedroom slippers.

Lucy's palm was sweaty with coins and the receipt when a crescendo of bells rippled through her jacket pocket. No one looked up. She struggled with the zip and groped at the mobile to stop it buzzing against her thigh. Staring at the green square she could see she had a caller but had no idea who it could be. Her only child, David, and his partner Daniel had set her up with this noisy iPhone on her sixtieth birthday.

"Just because pa is a technophobe there's no reason why you shouldn't be messaging or emailing us and finding friends on

Facebook," he'd said. "Daniel or I can talk you through and there's always the online help. Just have a fiddle around and you'll soon get used to what it can do."

Harry had grumbled about the monthly rental which was more than 'Pay as you Go'. She never went anywhere so 'topping up' had been a rare event which, nevertheless, had always been remarked upon when it was spotted on the Sainsbury's bill.

She balanced her tray and shuffled to a corner table to perch on the edge of a plastic chair. That first bite into the soft roll and its glutinous filling still felt like a treat. She prodded her mobile with her left hand which took her to 'missed calls' and, before she realised it, she was ringing out. As the voice of her renegade spouse filled her ear she snatched her arm away as if she had brushed a hot pan with wet hands.

"Ah, Lucinda, there you are. Have you remembered to feed the fish? I always give them a quarter of a teaspoon before breakfast."

Lucy realised the pain she was registering was in her tongue. She was biting it and whether it was the lingering metallic taste of the beef burger or her own blood she wasn't sure. Waking up late and alone had been a bad start to her day. There was no first cup of tea in bed. Then there was breakfast to get through. She'd had to screw up her eyes to read the packet instructions for microwaving a bowl of porridge. There was a trick to the timing. Did she have four or was it only three minutes during which she could ignore the whirring of the fan, set her spoon and placemat on the kitchen table and fill the kettle? For the last sixty seconds or so she had to crouch and squint through meshed glass and steam as the gloopy, grey mass bubbled to the rim. A lapse in concentration and there would be an eruption of lava with the debris sticking like a slip of chewing gum to hair. That last minute was capricious but Harry had managed it, as he did all the household jobs he'd taken over in the three years since his early retirement, with military precision. Lucy had grown used to his daily recitations of tasks and the ceremony of deleting each one from a mental list to be held up for her approval.

Lucy pushed at the tray in front of her then jerked it back before it overbalanced onto the floor. Her husband was still droning on about his precious fish.

"Harry! Where are you?"

"Where are you? You've left a terrible mess in the kitchen. It's a nasty accident waiting to happen. There's glass everywhere."

Lucy closed her eyes and pressed her lips together. Earlier that morning she'd started to fill the kettle and calculate how much water was enough for one mug. It was then that she realised tackling the day's crossword held no appeal. Even dunking biscuits wouldn't help now there was no one to tell her if she had too many. The kettle clanged as it hit the sink and Lucy swept her freed arm in one swinging motion clean across the worktop. Glass and crockery bounced and cracked on the tiled floor and a snowstorm of oats settled on the shards. Grabbing the nearest coat and her handbag she left without looking back.

As Lucy slammed the front door, pulling the collar of her gardening fleece up round her ears, she had seen Tina at number 44 arranging her bags of recycling on the pavement. She'd managed to ignore her neighbour's exaggerated shrug, the raised arms and then the finger jabbing. Backing her Skoda in a scrunch of gears and gravel, Lucy only remembered at the last minute to check her mirror before pulling out of the drive. She'd caught a glimpse of Tina jiggling bra straps to redistribute the weight of her chest and staring. Accelerating out of their close, Lucy's foot slid across the pedal. She'd told herself to get a grip and had to concentrate on keeping her slippery soles firmly in their place.

Lucy was still holding her mobile at arm's length and building a pyramid of chips with her left hand. Harry was extolling the virtues of using newspaper to wrap breakages before putting them in the bin just as if he hadn't walked out on her the day before. Lucy gave up on the chips.

"Why?" she shouted. "Why?" and blushed at the unexpected volume. On the nearest table a lone man continued to read The Mail and chew his bun.

"I'm busy in the study. I have documents to sort out, insurance, passport. It's a lot to think about. And why aren't you home? What are you doing?"

"I don't know," she said and switched off the power. She knew how to do that. Harry had told her it was very important to save the battery; her phone should only be used in emergencies. Was this an emergency? She didn't think so. She dropped the phone in her shopping bag and shook it to the bottom.

Lucy bit into her burger and choked, slopping coffee over the tray. She'd not eaten in a McDonald's, even this local one, for years. She'd been driving past the nearby power station unsure of her destination and remembering a time before either was built. Years before she and Harry had been part of the crowd watching the demolition of the sugar beet silos. When she complained as steel girders grew in their place and a power station dominated the skyline, Harry's comment had been that she needed to adjust. At the end of their trips to the north he'd always point out the beacons of red flashing above the bypass.

"Nearly there," he'd say and pause. Sometimes she'd join in when he added, "Home sweet home."

Well, that's exactly what she was doing, adjusting, even though he wasn't there to remind her how to think. There would be no more Manchester jaunts keeping her mouth shut during his brother's sermons and shivering over dinners of salad and tinned meat. What's-her-name could go instead. The smell of frying and the sight of damp chips were making her sick. She stood, pulled at the material which had bagged round her waist and smoothed it over the bulge of her hips.

"New shoes," she said to no one in particular. "I'll need new shoes if I'm going anywhere," and she watched her reflection stride towards the door.

It was late in the afternoon when Lucy turned into her drive. There was no sign of Harry's Volvo. She dug freshly manicured nails round the back of her head to take stock of her mood. Nothing stirred, not a flicker of feeling. Her hair felt lank and then her stomach fluttered in anticipation of the cut and colour she'd booked at 'Curl up and Dye' the next day. Twisting to peer into the pet basket on the passenger seat her neck creaked.

"A good workout," she mouthed through the metal grille. "I could do with some exercise. When we're all settled I'll give Tina a ring and see about re-joining the gym."

Two kittens, kidney shapes of black and white, had their paws draped across each other's ears. Lucy poked her fingers through the grid and felt the warmth of their fur like a wrap round her heart.

"A little patience," whispered Lucy, stroking an attacking paw.

The kitten with two white ears gnawed at her finger and gave a lick like emery board rubbed across the skin. She wasn't sure whether it hurt or tickled but it made her smile.

"You'll be free soon. A day or two and you'll have the run of the whole house. What larks, eh?"

Transforming Harry's study into a nursery for her new pets was easier than Lucy had anticipated. Moving the filing cabinet out onto the landing meant that the newly purchased Ultimate Cat Cradle slotted under the desk. She could use his padded chair by the window in the guest room, a place where she often escaped with her laptop if Harry was watching the football in the lounge. Lucy paused to get her breath. No more football commentaries to block out, no more howls or groans during a vital match. Without knowing quite how it happened she was crouching on the floor hugging the brown leather seat. Her chest heaved with the tears she'd held back. And all the tissues buried in her pocket couldn't stop the dripping from nose, mouth and eyes onto the small cushion she'd hand stitched to pillow Harry's bony shanks.

Lucy might have remained inhaling the smell of damp embroidery and suffocating in her clammy breath but for a mewling from the basket. She clutched at her throat, the tight soreness almost a relief, and fumbled her way, hand over hand, along the banister to fall on her knees on Harry's side of the bed.

"So this is all mine now," she said patting the memory pillow he swore he couldn't do without. She shook one of his monogrammed handkerchiefs from the drawer of his bedside cabinet, wiped her specs and took a deep breath for a blow. Once the litter tray and food dishes were in Harry's sanctum and the kittens released to explore their territory she shut the door, tiptoeing down the landing as if she'd just settled a baby to sleep.

A broom blocked her path into the kitchen. It had been propped diagonally across the doorway with the dustpan and brush placed under it on a newspaper. Lucy kicked out at Harry's obstacle course. Out of habit she picked up the folded paper and flicked through the pages to check if they'd already done the crossword. It was the one they had started but not finished the previous day.

She found their last clue, 13 across: 'Bird known as rooster in the US (8)'. She looked at 13 down: 'Dry red wine from Tuscany (7)'.

Chianti, surely? Stepping over the morning's destruction, she took a bottle out of the rack and brushed the dust off with her sleeve.

Lucy had only just unloaded the last of her Waitrose treats from the car when the doorbell rang. It had taken less time than usual now that she didn't have to secrete any carriers into the house as if she were a smuggler. Earlier qualms about living economically had spurred her to do the opposite. In the Springfield Outlet Centre she couldn't resist the leggings in shades of purple and mauve, the tee shirts, each with its own 'thought for the day' and trainers with a big orange tick for her planned gym regime.

"I'm coming, I'm coming," she shouted as a third or fourth ring was followed by a staccato of rapping at the door.

Tina, whose ear had been pressed against the letter box, stumbled into the hall as she opened the front door. Lucy caught her before she fell and found herself in an awkward embrace. Many of her generation as well as the youngsters, she'd noticed, had become great huggers and kissers. Men, of course, could always shake hands. Sometimes the ritual was for two or three pecks on alternating cheeks with a hop and skip as if launching into a do-si-do at a ceilidh. In those moments she dreaded misplacing her nose. She stepped back sinking her body into the warmth of the radiator. Contact with her neighbour's bosom had already dislodged Lucy's specs but that didn't stop Tina launching into a jerky, high-pitched speech.

"Not so much as a 'good day' from Harry. I'd swear he saw me, didn't even look up. Never said a word. And there he was, backwards and forwards. Armfuls of paper. Dropping stuff all over the place. Not like him at all. And you weren't having lunch. Whatever's going on?" Tina stared into Lucy's face. "I've been working from home all day," she said and paused. "You look worn out."

"I've opened some wine," said Lucy, wiping her lenses on her cardigan. "And you can meet my new lodgers. If you've got time? I've been on a bit of a spree."

Tina was seven years younger but she already had six grandchildren living locally and she still found time for wine, tea, cakes or just the gossip which went with them. Since her divorce she'd become a magnet for stray cats despite the presence of Tigger, a mongrel she'd rescued and named after herself.

"Just like Tigger, me. Can't keep still. Drove me ex to drink and now he's gone to blazes."

She had a box of children's toys behind the settee, a swing

in the garden and a choice of men she could sleep with if she felt like it. Lucy sniffed, turned to fumble in her sleeve for Harry's hanky and felt Tina's hand pushing the middle of her back.

"Sit down," Tina said steering her towards the kitchen. "I'll pour and you can tell me why hubby's got ants in his pants."

With another large glass of Chianti in her hand Lucy felt her tongue loosen. She might as well give Tina the satisfaction of being the first to know Mr Harry Martin had left his wife for a younger woman. Well, apart from what's-'er-name, of course, who must have known his plans for a long time although, in his note, Harry had said not.

"I've got chocolate biscuits," she said. "Have you ever tried dunking in wine?"

"Thought you were on a diet."

"There's never been a hope of looking skinny alongside that bean pole. Why bother now?"

"Well then, did you have a terrible row?" said Tina, her lids drooping as she stared down her nose. Lucy noticed the fine arch of her friend's eyebrows. Threading was supposed to be better than waxing. She might give it a go. She pushed her chair back.

"No," she said, "of course not. Harry hates arguments. Well, you know that!"

They clinked glasses over the shared memories – Harry gritting his teeth as Tina boxed their cars into the drive; huffing as she failed to stop Tigger squatting on the path; sighing at the calls during their meals which were set at regular times to aid his delicate digestion. Lucy's skin felt hot and prickly. She held her glass to one cheek and then the other and tried to rationalise a sequence of events.

"Everything seemed normal yesterday at breakfast. Harry was a bit grumpy but that's nothing new. We started on the easy crossword. I got this clue, 'cockerel' and I was talking about chickens. Just daft chit-chat. I said something like why one cock and lots of silly hens. Well, Harry slapped the paper down. Made me jump out of my skin. He said he needed a break from my wittering on and on. He stomped upstairs. I thought he'd gone to his study. But, the next thing I knew, he'd packed that bag he takes when he goes on those choir whatsits and said he'd got a place to stay. Banged the front door and that was it."

"He left just like that? No warning? Where's he gone? Don't tell me there's some old bag after his pension."

"There is a younger model. He met her at choir. They'd had an away day, gigs and so on. Weekly practices. You know the sort of thing, how it can start."

Lucy gulped her wine and waited but Tina was busying herself with the bottle. She reached over to top up both glasses and then sat back, her hand stopping her mouth, as she massaged her nose between thumb and fingers.

"Daft, I know, but I walked up to the butchers to get us a couple of pork chops – thought it would put him in a better mood for later- but when I got back he'd collected more things, coats, clothes, cleared the bathroom, and left a sodding letter. In a brown envelope. I thought it was a bill."

Tina slapped her glass down. "What did it say? And what will you do now? Who else knows? Sorry, sorry, too many questions, but you and Harry...well, who else could put up with his funny ideas. And he's no Adonis, is he?"

No answer seemed to be required. Lucy thought that she'd never wanted Adonis, whoever he was, only Harry and his endearing little ways. Her chair squealed as she scraped it back.

"Come and see my kittens," she said picking up the bottle. "I went to buy food for Harry's precious angelfish and there they were. We made friends."

"Fish are for food not pets," said Tina. "You don't get a lot back from a goldfish, do you?"

"They're angelfish. Harry thinks they're exotic and mysterious."

"Well, he's a bloody mystery to me. A whole aquarium is less comfort than a cold hot water bottle. You want a dog, cuddles on demand."

"That's what he'll be getting," said Lucy. "Come on. And grab another bottle of red."

The next day Lucy woke with a headache. Her bedside phone was ringing and the display read 'withheld'. Well, recipients could play that game as well as anonymous callers. Stumbling out of bed she lectured herself about letting standards slip. The tally for bad behaviour was never-ending. If she listed her own defects she'd not miss Harry's moderating influence in her life. Swinging the bathroom cabinet open showered a stack of foil-wrapped painkillers to the floor. The sickness swept from skull to stomach as she bent to pick them up and collapsed back onto the toilet bowl.

She had lost her appetite for porridge. Why had she never experimented with the varieties of muesli, flakes, chopped fruit and yogurt that Harry had layered into his dish since he'd started eating healthily? More to the point, had she had a choice? He always laid the breakfast table before a last flossing of his teeth, positioning her bowl by the microwave with measuring jug and scales in easy reach. If she'd changed to Weetabix, say, or one of their son's childhood favourites like Sugar Puffs or Coco Pops it would have upset some delicate balance. Those routines they had built up together over nearly four decades as a married couple had felt like intimacy, secret rituals they shared and wrapped around their lives, protecting them. But protecting them from what? Ah yes, invasion, the invasion of strangers into their privacy. All those house rules broken overnight or, presumably, over a series of nights. Someone was having a laugh.

Lucy was considering going back to bed when she remembered the kittens. Tina had named them Pinky and Perky after the duo of squeaky, singing pigs from when she'd been a kid and Lucy had been a dumpy teenager. They'd struggled to extract the cork from their second bottle, another husbandly role now vacant, until Tina had resorted to hammering it in with the aid of a glass paperweight and Harry's Parker pen. Lucy had qualms about abusing Harry's gold and steel stylus, a twenty-first present from his parents, but not about her new pets. She and Tina had lolled on the study rug singing 'We Belong Together', imitating Pinky and Perky voices while the kittens clawed their way up the curtains to the bookshelves and filled the air with dust. Competing with Tina's high notes had been the best laugh she'd had since the house had been full of youngsters when David was growing up. She sighed. No chance of a new generation of kiddies for them. The kittens had a big space to fill.

Was that the sound of the front door opening? Lucy kicked the loo door shut and waited. She half expected Harry's 'halloo there', but it never came. Wrapping her arms round her winceyette pyjamas she hugged herself. All the usual lumps and bumps were rolling into place despite the lack of her 'other half' and the liquid diet of the day before. She had plans. Two paracetamol, a splash or two of cold water and she'd be ready to hit the ground running. Lucy imagined herself sporting the purple leggings with her neon striped trainers and chuckled.

Harry was sitting in his usual place at the kitchen table with a pot of tea and a pencil poised above the newspaper. It was folded in four so that it made a neat square open at the puzzle page. Lucy was singing in a shrill falsetto, "Who else am I gonna lean on when times get rough oh yeah," and entered waggling two empty wine bottles, one in each hand.

Harry's elbows slipped off the table edge, hands dropping to his sides. The pencil pinged on the floor and his dentures slipped so that he had to clamp his mouth shut. When he'd regained control of them his voice had somehow lost depth, its tone sounding querulous rather than his customary authoritative bark.

"Err, porridge?" he said.

Lucy banged the bottles onto the table and heard Harry's cup rattle in its saucer.

"Bacon," she said. "Bacon, two eggs, beans and some fried

bread. That's what I'll have and probably some toast and jam and, yes, coffee. I'll make a cafetiere."

Harry closed his lids. When he opened them again Lucy was still standing facing him. He flicked his eyes over her chest.

"What do you look like?" he said.

Lucy looked down at her T shirt. She'd chosen the white one with the words, *Warning: contains opinions that may offend.* She could have gone for the black, *Just because I don't care doesn't mean I'm not listening,* but the orange lettering picked out her newly painted nails and the flashes on her shoes. She took a deep breath.

"Me," she said. "I look like me. It's today's me anyhow. There might be a different me tomorrow."

Harry grunted. "Porridge tomorrow then?"

Lucy didn't have to think up a witty reply. The phone rang. Harry sprang up and answered in his usual manner.

"Hello. You have reached the Martin household. To whom am I speaking?"

There was a perceptible pause during which he grabbed the chair he'd just vacated and lowered himself back into it, effectively blocking Lucy's exit into the hall. For the third day running she had lost her appetite for breakfast. What was Harry doing here? Had she still got a live-in husband or not? The uncertainty was driving her to drink, not a bad idea if she followed Tina's advice for 'hair of the dog', she thought, and half turned to examine the wine rack.

Harry was in the way. He was holding the phone out and ignored the shaking of her head as she backed off. Lucy knew she couldn't handle a conversation with her co-helpers at the charity shop, Tina or, worse still their son, but Harry was having none of it. He thrust the handset next to her good ear, grasped her right hand with his left and slapped the two together. A jerk of his head skyward indicated that he was going upstairs, presumably to hole up in his study. Lucy felt the energy she'd dredged up for the jaunty entrance made moments before slide down her spine rooting her to the tiles. Both knees buckled. Harry shoved his chair under her bottom and she sagged into it. The seat was still warm. He pointed to the phone, turned with a click of his heels and left the room.

"Hello?"

A young woman's voice answered. "Mrs Martin? I'm so very sorry. It's all been such a shock. Everything's happened so suddenly."

Twenty-three minutes later Lucy took fresh tea up to Harry's study. She found him sitting on the floor, his back to the radiator. Pinky and Perky were sleeping in the nest made by the backs of his knees where he'd folded his legs. One of the cat toys, a furry snake at the end of a pole, was on the floor and still in his hand.

Lucy placed the tray on the carpet and sat next to him stretching her legs full length. Leaning over to pour the tea she paused to admire the flattering purple leggings hugging her stubby but shapely little legs. What a revelation! Who would have thought that adding that touch of Lycra would create a warm, comfortable, practical garment which would be fun to wear. That was more than she could say for the shiny pink, uplift bra she'd bought to transform her look. The saleswoman at Luxury Lingerie had recommended the style to counteract middle aged droop, 'a natural part of the ageing process which doesn't need to define your silhouette'. True, if she leaned forward she could display a shelf of cleavage solid enough to balance a mug, but she was feeling the pinch in the folds of flesh which had leaked out under the wire supports. Lucy poked her free hand up her top and felt between her breasts for the rigid frame. Hooking it with her thumb she pulled the whole contraption down and, by wiggling her upper body, managed to shake the excess flesh back up into the padded cups. As she smoothed the cotton back over her chest she spotted Harry's eyes on her. He was coming out of his trance.

"Why aren't you sneezing?" she asked handing him his mug.

He raised his eyebrows and gulped his tea like a man with a powerful thirst.

She tried again. "Aren't you allergic to cats?"

"It appears not," said Harry. "Perhaps it's because they're kittens. And they've both got short hair."

Lucy watched him stroke Perky with his forefinger. Or was it Pinky? It was hard to tell without comparing their patches of white. We'll have to get collars for them, decided Lucy, red for Pinky and blue for Perky. Or was it the other way round? She snorted. How would I remember that, she thought, when all we had was a black and white TV? She looked across at Harry. Maybe he knew.

"Do you think they'll always get on this well?"

"I expect they'll have their ups and downs," he said, and paused. "Like us."

"A few too many 'ups' in your case," said Lucy, "cock-ups."

"As in cockerel, is that what you mean?"

"Or Cock-a-leekie?" said Lucy, stirring a second spoonful of sugar into her tea. "You've been in the soup, that's for sure."

"Hmm, it's a bit of a cock-a-doodle-do altogether," said Harry.

His shoulders started to shake and Lucy realised that he was laughing. Her eyes filled up and then, when she saw how his comb-over had detached itself from his pate and was waggling over his forehead a bit like the cat toy, she blinked, smiled and leaned over to smooth it back.

"She did tell you? It is twins she's expecting," said Harry after he'd blown his nose with a great trumpeting noise which should have disturbed the kittens but somehow didn't.

"Mothers need a spare pair of hands," said Lucy. "Two, even. She, um, Sonia, will need all the help she can get. A team. People without too many work or family commitments."

She looked down at the flower she'd had enamelled on her thumb nails the day before. Pretty, yes, but what had she been thinking of? She had useful hands. They didn't need to masquerade as art.

"We'd be like surrogate grandparents. That's what I suggested. It's not so much about you being a dad. There could easily be a step-father one day and you're," she paused, "too old."

Lucy stopped examining her nails long enough to glance up. Harry's mouth was twitching the way it always did when he was working his way through a set of clues. His words were at the assembly stage, still waiting to be shunted into place.

"And Sonia said she was desperate. It's all about the ticking clock for women of a certain age. I know all about that. They realise they want children, grandchildren too, and it's nearly too late. You were there at the right time, a safe pair of hands." She clapped a hand over her mouth and quickly pinched her nose to turn her giggle into a cough.

"I thought she wanted me for my wit and charm," Harry said, "but I was just a cheap loan from a sperm bank."

"I didn't know you had it in you," said Lucy. "Tina was poleaxed when I told her you were having an affair. She said we're both dark horses."

Harry stared at her. "You know when you had that craze for karaoke? Did anything, you know….?"

Lucy was sweating. The radiator felt uncomfortably hot now. It was like having hot flushes all over again. Her new bra was surely slicing her in two.

"Sorry, but I've got to get this wretched thing off," she said, clutching at her chest and heaving herself to her feet. "We can carry on talking though. Two babies on the way. That's a lot to think about."

Harry eased his legs, stiff from their unaccustomed sitting position, carefully round the kittens. They barely stirred. He stretched up and ran his fingers along the brown brocade curtains he'd chosen when they'd first bought the house thirty years before. A rough nail caught in one of the pulled threads.

"Blinds," he muttered to his wife's retreating back. "New blinds. Why not?"

Lucy was elbowing her way out of her T-shirt as she sprinted down the passage.

He raised his voice. "Are those trousers you've got on? Or are they tights?"

Lucy turned to face him. Her top was round her neck, the glow of her cheeks almost as pink as her chest.

"Leggings, they're called leggings, Harry. You should keep up with the times." She vanished into the bedroom.

Harry blinked and swallowed. "I'm right behind you," he said. "And then we'll go out and get the kittens a scratch post, shall we?"

"I'm having my hair done at one o'clock."

"At lunchtime?"

Lucy poked her head round the bedroom door and threw a tangle of pink satin and lace onto the landing.

"Why not?" she said and disappeared again.

Harry pushed the door of the study so that it closed with a gentle click.

"Why not indeed," he said, and followed her into the bedroom.

A poster for a book-signing revived memories of a brief romantic encounter with the author forty years ago, before he became famous. I toyed with the idea of going along before dismissing it, but the situation got my imagination working. This story is the result.

Jammy Bastard

Julie Williams

No reason to feel furtive. Dr Carr popping into Bindings bookshop in her lunch hour was hardly the stuff of scandal. Susan squared her shoulders and tried to engage her long legs in their usual confident rhythm. A gang of year-elevens buying sweets unbunched so she could pass on the pavement. She recognised one or two of them but it was her rule not to make eye contact. She noted the poster, just the bright colours and his face, as she pushed open Bindings' door and stepped inside. She knew the details already, had surprised herself by thinking of little else since she heard. The smell of good coffee and murmur of conversation drifted through from the café but thank God the sales area was empty. His book was shouting at her from prime place on the display table. Should she pick it up straight away or pretend to browse around first?

"Hi, Susan! Rare to see you out of the surgery in the week. How are you?" Bill Hughes appeared from the back office.

"Fine, thanks, and you?" She didn't break stride as she slipped the heavy book off its stand on her way to the counter. It landed with a wumph, front cover up, even more startling the closer you got.

"Well, I wouldn't have had you down as a fan." Bill was amused, practically chortling. She shook her head, about to tell her lie, but he hadn't finished. "Did you see our poster? He's signing copies early Friday evening. There'll be a talk."

"No, Bill, it's not for me. It's for a friend's sixtieth. She's the fan." She fumbled her credit card into the machine and felt acute relief when her purchase dropped out of sight into one of Bindings' quality paper bags. "Hope Sylvia's okay," she said. The receipt zipped out of the machine and Bill handed it over with a quick nod to his wife's good health. Susan had made it to the door and was about to turn and say goodbye when he called out.

"Tell your friend about it. Come with her, if she's local. It's quite an event, he's only doing two bookshops outside London. We're his home town – did you know?"

Spike heard it first and became hysterical. Susan jumped up, scattering her Chemistry notes on the lawn, and pelted after him through the French windows. He bounced up and down by the hall table, yelping insanely, until she lifted the receiver and made the ringing stop. Bloody dog.

"Hello, may I speak to Sue, please?" It was Barbs. Barbs who had better things to do than revise for O-Levels. She was polite to Susan's parents at all times.

"They're not here, it's me. What's up?"

"Your lucky day, that's what. The Jamjars' concert at Peterborough tonight. Tony and me'll pick you up at seven."

The group's name sounded familiar, but not from Top of the Pops or Ready Steady Go. She wouldn't show her ignorance by asking. "I can't, I've got Chemistry and French Oral on Monday. And I'm behind."

"You can't miss this, not even for French Oral." Barbs sputtered the last word and took a minute to recover herself. Susan, mystified, waited patiently for her to continue. "They're our mates, from the estate, and they're fantastic. This time they're supporting two London bands but it won't be long. They'll be big as The Beatles someday soon. Come on, Sue."

"I've got to look after Spike. Mum and Dad are away till tomorrow." She still called them Mummy and Daddy at home but couldn't admit it.

"Great. You can revise for the rest of the day, then come out. No-one stays home Saturday night. It's not natural. See you at seven."

At half-past five she stood up and dusted grass clippings off her shorts. Her legs hadn't tanned, just turned a blotchy pink. She piled up notes and books and trudged indoors with them, Spike at her heels. His dog food made a horrible sucking noise as she levered it out of the tin but he turned to his dish with joy once he'd slurped a fresh bowl of water. She made herself a Vesta Paella, taking forensic care to follow the instructions on the packet, ate every scrap and left the washing-up.

The bathwater stung, but by some alchemy it turned her legs a uniform brick red. She hoped it would pass for a proper tan. Her legs were her best feature, long and slim. And her hair. "Like ripe corn," Daddy said sometimes, giving it a tousle with his big hand. Posing sideways in front of Mummy's full-length mirror, she thought the new op-art minidress looked fab. Why didn't she have a boyfriend? Barbs wasn't any prettier, and she'd been going out with Tony since she was fourteen.

From the back seat of Tony's dad's Ford Cortina, Susan watched those two and longed to be as close to someone. Their bare arms touched all the time, winding and unwinding, rubbing and sliding. Tony was steering with one finger of his left hand, the other elbow hooked out of the window, while Barbs tickled and tormented him. Now and then she'd go too far and he'd give her a playful shove with his shoulder.

Susan tilted her face up to the slanting sunlight and let the breeze kiss her throat. *Wild Thing* by The Troggs boomed from the car radio and when Barbs turned round, screaming out the words, Susan screamed along too. Tony played air guitar, one hand vibrating on the neck by Barbs' ear, the other plucking chords up high. A rock 'n roll miracle kept them on the road until they scorched into the Broadway Cinema car park, raising dust. Once they'd stopped, Tony dived under Barbs' thigh to pull up the handbrake.

"What, doll?" he said to Barbs' unspoken comment. "We got here, didn't we?"

In the crowded foyer, dim after the bright outdoors, Tony marched up to the box office and laid a casual forearm on the counter. Barbs and Susan shuffled along too.

"We're with the band," he said.

"Where are they then? Don't look like it to me, son."

Boys and girls were streaming past them, handing over tickets at the door to their left and disappearing into the thick darkness of the auditorium. A queue to buy tickets was forming at their backs as Tony got stuck into an argument with the voice behind the glass. Susan stepped away. A wave of embarrassment swept her over to the side wall. She leaned against it and concentrated hard on the details of a stand-up cardboard advert for a film called Alfie. Barbs followed and took her arm.

"Tony's big brother Steve's their roadie," she said, their faces close together. "We'll be in before you can say George Harrison." She pulled down on Susan's arm to push herself up on tiptoes and scan the big hall. The third time she did it, her fingers dug in painfully, then she let go and pointed. "Yeah! There's Steve now."

Pencil behind his ear and scratching his head, he bustled across the foyer towards Tony. Barbs tried to drag her over to join them, but Susan hung back on her own, afraid she'd start blushing again, and glanced across the foyer in the direction Steve had come. A boy whose face she half-recognised was standing in an open doorway, staring at her. She pulled down the skirt of her dress and peered to see if her red legs were glowing in the artificial light. She put her hand up to check her hair, then thought What am I doing? He's rude to stare like that. Defiantly she raised her eyes and stared back.

He held her gaze for a long, long time and something clicked into place. She stopped breathing to make the moment last longer and struggled when her breath ran out. He emerged into the foyer and made a lazy progress through the crowd. Several kids nudged each other and moved to let him pass. Tall and skinny like her. Dark blond like her. Nose too big for ideal proportions, eyebrows heavier than you'd expect. Just gorgeous. But he wasn't coming to her. Stupid to imagine that a boy like that ... She watched helplessly as he crossed to the box office, tapped Steve on the shoulder, shook Tony's hand and put an arm round him, talking all the while. The crowd moved across her sight line and when it was restored, he'd gone. She'd been so sure, and now she'd lost him.

Only she hadn't.

"Susie!" Barbs squeezed through and grabbed her. "Come on, we're in, and you'll never guess ..." She kept talking in breathless bursts over her shoulder as they ran, dodging after Tony and Steve. Steve shoehorned them past the man on the door and yelled that he'd see them after the show. The auditorium was packed and noisy. They eased down the sloping side aisle to the front row, where Tony lifted Reserved cards off three seats and swung into his on the end. The cinema's screen had been rolled up and a wandering spotlight picked out a drum set, amplifiers and three bright guitars above them on the empty stage.

"Barbs, I couldn't hear. What did you say?" said Susan, her lips jammed against her friend's ear.

"What? About Jamie Jones, fancying you?" said Barbs. Susan's stomach flipped over. It must be him. The crowd had fallen quiet for the moment and Barbs' voice was the carrying kind. Susan would have been mortified, but she was too excited.

"Jamie – who is he?" she said.

"Only The Jamjars' singer, that's all. He wanted to know everything about you."

That's where she'd seen his face before. On tattered fliers posted around Fenbeach. On lamp posts in the marketplace and the walls of alleyways down by the river.

"What did you tell him?" she said.

But Barbs wasn't going to make it easy for her.

"Funny, you could be twins, except he's got this really big nose and yours is quite a normal ..."

A roar rolled over their heads as The Jamjars ran on stage in a rush of energy that took Susan's breath away. Jamie picked up the bass guitar, flicked its lead to check it was plugged in, then came forward to adjust the angle of his microphone on its stand. Impatient, she willed him to see her now, and for once she would have welcomed a spotlight on her face. From below, the clean lines of his throat and jawline showed tan against the white of his shirt as he looked all around, checking the other Jamjars were ready to go, scanning the circle up above and the back row of the stalls. Finally he let his eyes drop and pick her out in the front row, as though he'd known she'd be there and had saved the best till last. His gaze rested with her while the drummer set the beat and his bass and the other guitars took it up for the opening riff. He brought his lips close to the microphone and started to sing. His voice, resonant with a ragged edge, found an echo deep inside Susan. Heaven must be made up of moments like this, she thought, seamlessly joined to last forever.

Backstage after the show, Susan didn't breathe a word while the boys arranged who was going with whom, except, "Yes," when Jamie asked if he could see her home. It was the first sentence she heard him say, in his voice with the sexy catch that was just as lovely speaking as singing. His eyebrows made an upside-down V as he asked. She believed he was genuinely unsure what her answer would be and her yes burst out so loud that the others looked up in surprise, but she didn't care. This was the best night of her life.

She squeezed through the driver's door into the back seat of the Cortina, aglow with happiness, and waited. After a short discussion she didn't hear, it was Barbs who squashed in beside her, and the headlights picked out Jamie strolling round to the passenger side. She tried to swallow her disappointment. The headrest on his seat blocked her view. She couldn't even study how the hair grew in the back of his neck. Tony switched on the radio and turned the car out into the street.

"He's too tall to fit in the back, that's what he said. But I think he's shy," said Barbs in a whisper. Paralysed by fear that Jamie had overheard, Susan turned towards the window to shut her up. Barbs sat forward and joined in the chat about the concert with the two boys. Susan sat back and agonised.

If he was too shy to sit next to her in the car, he'd be too shy to ask her out. Yet he wasn't too shy to stand up and sing in front of hundreds of teenagers, was he? He wouldn't have been too shy to sit next to Barbs. No, the trouble was her, Susan. She'd done something wrong, sounded over-eager. She'd intimidated him. She put boys off. No wonder she'd never had a boyfriend.

The car bumped over the bridge at Salting St Paul and took the first turn off the roundabout along the river road. She forced herself to search the sky for the sickle of the new moon, but it wouldn't stay where she found it, it blurred and jumped as she blinked back the tears. She must be giving out the wrong signals. She was too stiff, too self-conscious. But what could she do? Not far to Fenbeach now.

The street lights on Town Bridge surprised her by how quickly they came into view, their reflection a trail of spangles on the water. Now she was going to be dropped off alone at the North Bank where the posh people lived, and those three would ride on home to the estate, laughing all the way. At her.

Only she wasn't and they didn't.

Tony drove away with Barbs beside him, leaving Susan and Jamie together on the pavement. Jamie was peering down the short garden path.

"Blimey, posh house," he said.

"Nobody's home. I'm on my own tonight, except for Spike," she said.

"Spike?"

"He's our Jack Russell. He doesn't like bells. Gets hysterics when anyone calls. I took the phone off the hook tonight so he wouldn't explode or zoom into space."

"He could be up there in orbit right now," said Jamie, his voice gruff. He slid sure fingers under each of her ears, pushing through the thick hair in her neck, and cupped her chin between his thumbs. He raised her face to the stars, and then he kissed her. There was a rushing in her ears and a falling away in her stomach and she didn't want it ever to stop. She shifted closer and her arms went round him of their own accord. This was living.

Jamie surfaced first, gently taking his mouth away and dropping his hands. When she opened her eyes he was looking across the road at the river.

"Quiet neighbourhood," he said. "Bit out of my league. I better leave you now, Susie. It's been very nice."

Very nice! Was that it? She couldn't let him walk away. Especially not after that kiss.

"Don't go. Come in and have a drink. We've got wine," she said, "Daddy has some very good wine. You'd like it." She found the key in her shoulder bag and opened the gate, stepping boldly through. "Come and meet Spike."

She strode along the path and felt her power as she heard him follow. Spike was whining and pawing at the front door from the inside, until she turned the key. He hurled himself at her through the crack but when Jamie followed her in, he skittered back and took a stand by the stairs, emitting staccato barks on a rising scale.

"Dog's not very impressed with me," said Jamie. He seemed smaller, more human, as he hesitated by the door of her father's surgery. Partly to pacify Spike but mostly because she wanted to, Susan took his hand and led him across the hall into the sitting room.

"Blimey," he said again, as she flicked a switch and all the little lights on shelves and tables came on together, suffusing the large room with a cunningly intimate glow (Mummy's description). She pictured Barbs' lounge on the estate, lit only by a single bulb with a pink plastic shade and the constant flicker of the TV, and mentally fitted it four times into this space. She squeezed Jamie's hand. Never before had she felt so tuned in to the feelings of another human being. He squeezed her hand back.

"It might be nice to sit outside," she said, nodding at the dark garden beyond their reflections in the French windows.

"Yeah, that'd be good, Susie," he said, "I'd like that." She unlatched the glass door and Spike nosed it open then scooted off to his favourite peeing spot among Mummy's dahlias. Susan kicked off her sling-backs and padded over to the drinks cupboard. Her parents drank wine at dinner a couple of times a week and recently her father had poured her a small glass on special occasions.

"Red or white?"

"Oh, red I think." He met her eyes with renewed confidence, as though he'd given himself a shake. "I'm more of a Newcastle Brown man myself, but I'll try anything once."

She found a dark-green bottle, the liquid black inside, and handed him the corkscrew.

"Like I said, I'll have a go," he said, sticking the curled metal into the cork and applying just the right pressure as he turned it, while she found two glasses. He poured, then with a sideways glance that brought her blush back, he held his glass out to toast her. The wine glowed ruby-crimson in the lamplight.

"I'd like to buy you a dress this colour, Susie," he said.

Susan had been waiting and hoping for him to say something personal, and here it was. She'd treasure it always. She felt for the cardigan she'd left on the sofa arm, picked up the bottle and her glass and slipped out into the fresh air, thankfully cooler now. The grass had retained the sun's warmth beneath her bare feet. Jamie was close behind. He spread his jacket on the ground and sat, reaching his arms round to cradle his knees, his shirt cuffs loosely rolled up to the elbow, glass held in one hand while the other clasped his wrist.

"I couldn't buy nothing much, yet. Haven't even got a car. But I will, won't be long." He patted the jacket beside him, looking ahead dreamily at the shapes of trees. Longing for another kiss, Susan sat too, and took a rash mouthful of the wine. She didn't have the taste for it yet, had only sipped it at meals, and she almost choked. Jamie's hand came round and patted her between the shoulder blades. His arm stayed with her after she'd recovered. His hand was warm on her hipbone.

"If Monday goes okay, the Jamjars'll get signed up to a record label. Don't know if you was there while we was talking about it, only heard yesterday. Our demo's got them interested and on Monday we're going down the Smoke to lay down a couple of tracks at their studio. If they like them, that's it! I'm jacking in my job – well, I just won't go in Monday and that'll do it."

"Fantastic," she said, "well done, and good luck. Fingers crossed." His face turned towards her now and dipped down to her ear.

"Oh, we'll make it." he murmured, his lips brushing the lobe, then moving to search out her mouth. "Just watch us."

For two weeks afterwards, Susan kept the thought of him, the things he said, the smell, the touch, the feel of him, in a secret place in her head. She was able to address the exam papers without difficulty as long as she could go to Jamie's place whenever she chose. Then the exams ended amid general rejoicing.

He still hadn't phoned and she began to fret. Explanations crowded in – the Jamjars had got the contract and were busy recording, they hadn't and he was busy looking for a new job, he was worried Daddy would tear him limb from limb, he'd lost her number. But then, he could look it up, or get it from Barbs. Couldn't he?

That was the other thing. Barbs' odd behaviour. She was such a nosy cow normally, her nosiness had cemented their friendship, cheerfully busting through Susan's reserve. But she didn't once ask Susan what happened with Jamie. It was true they didn't see each other much while the exams were on, just snatched chats in the corridor when they happened to coincide, but it wasn't like her. A slight awkwardness grew between them. It held Susan back from asking Barbs how the Jamjars had got on in London, though she badly wanted to know.

Barbs left the High School before the end of term for a full-time job where she'd been a Saturday girl, at Peterborough's answer to Vidal Sassoon. A couple of weeks later when school broke up, Susan's parents whisked her away on their annual camping trip with the Harrises to the south of France. Susan acquired a golden tan pretending to be Brigitte Bardot in a bikini on the beach with Julia Harris. Every night she dreamed of Jamie and woke next morning with an ache in her heart. Impossible that he didn't feel as close to her as she did to him, that he wouldn't want to carry on seeing the girl who made him feel that way. There was nobody she could tell about him and she felt if she didn't confide in someone soon, she'd burst. She didn't even know his address. Barbs must know it through Tony. On the ferry home, Susan resolved to go and see her.

Spike turned his back and sulked in the car when they picked him up from the kennels. It was August already and pouring with rain. Susan grabbed her PVC mac from the hall closet the minute they got home and shoved her feet into Mummy's gardening wellies. Spike sniffed the big pile of letters on the mat without enthusiasm.

"I'm taking Spike for a walk," she called. His ears sprang up. She clipped on his lead and gave him his head as he tugged her all the way to the park. Once there, he stopped tugging and looked up at her expectantly, but she wasn't going to release him this time.

"Nope, we're going to see Auntie Barbs," she told him, and set off along the path that led to the estate, past the deserted tennis courts. It was around seven on a Friday night, so with any luck they'd have had tea and Barbs wouldn't have gone out yet.

"Hiya, Sue."

Her head had been down so she hadn't seen him, and he'd stepped on to the grass to walk past before she recognised him.

"Tony, hi! I was just on my way to see Barbs. How are you?

How's she?" she said. He was back on the path and wheeled round slowly, perhaps reluctantly, to face her.

"She's not there," he said.

"How do you mean? Aren't you going out tonight?"

"No, er, we're not going out any more."

"Together? You mean, you're not going out together." Her voice trailed off, stupidly.

"No, she's got a new boyfriend."

"Oh." Her stomach lurched and her heart sped into overdrive. She knew before he said who it was.

"Yeah, she's been with Jamie Jones a couple of weeks. He's going to be a big star, did you hear? The Jamjars got signed by Decca, got a single coming out. Old Barbs, with a pop star, eh?"

"Oh, Tony, I'm sorry."

She wasn't sure who she was sorrier for, Tony or herself. Either way, she didn't go to Barbs' house. Compared with Barbs, the Chemistry, Biology and Maths A-set would make a dreary group of school friends next term, but at least none of them was likely to break her heart.

Susan and Peter kept reference books for work in their separate studies in her old family home. The shelves in the sitting room were reserved for novels and biographies they read for pleasure. She felt their comforting presence behind her armchair as she took Jamie's memoir out of the Bindings bag and laid it in her lap. It stood out, all right. The front cover sported zigzagging bands of orange, yellow and chocolate brown, with the title *Jammy Bastard* looped in round yellow letters outlined in black. The portrait of Jamie smiling his lazy smile on the back cover had been photographed in the early Seventies, maybe six years after they spent the night together. Susan felt a powerful response to it. How would it be to look into his eyes, perhaps shake his hand, after all these years? She could do it now, no hard feelings. She could go tomorrow night, why not?

Peter, who would certainly laugh her out of any notion of attending Jamie's signing, was ferrying the boys to their respective halls at Durham and Edinburgh for the start of the spring term, and wouldn't be back until the weekend. Early in their marriage she'd told him about her night with Jamie, one morning after they made love. She wanted to show him that she too had experienced love and loss before they met. She was in earnest, he was the only person she'd confided in, but he smiled indulgently and said how sweet she was. He joked that he would thrash Jamie within an inch of his life if he ever came back from the USA. Then they made love again. Afterwards, at a party, it amused him to mention, "Sue's ex, the great Jamie Jamm."

Twinkle-eyed, he watched her deflecting people's questions: "No, I just met him once after a concert, we never went out together, nothing happened, really." She had not been amused and he'd apologised.

Susan put a log on the fire and banked it up with coal from her mother's brass scuttle, took a tangy mouthful of Shiraz and opened *Jammy Bastard.* A strictly chronological account, it presented no challenges to a determined reader scanning for specific references. The print was large and well-spaced.

She stood when she reached the end and stretched her legs that had grown stiff with sitting. She pulled aside the curtain to gaze through the french windows at the darkness outside. Nothing. She'd found nothing in Jamie's book. What she'd wanted to know, what she finally felt ready to understand, was why he chose Barbs out of the two of them.Yet *Jammy Bastard* didn't mention Jamie's relationship with Barbs. Its glossary bristled with famous names but Barbara Jolly didn't appear there or anywhere else in the text. She did show up on the picture pages, in two photos four years apart, a face in the crowd that surrounded The Jamjars on tour. No sign of her after 1970, Jamie's big year, the year he dropped the band and went solo as Jamie Jamm. The year he married the first of his three Hollywood blondes. Poor Barbs.

Susan brushed her hand over a patch of condensation beading the glass. They hadn't gone all the way out there on the lawn. They'd kissed and talked and gazed at the stars. She'd fetched blankets and they'd huddled together as the first birds hazarded a dawn song, then watched the sun come up over the trees. Just the one night, in the summer of '66, when Jamie awakened a new person and left her to face the world alone. Susie, the new girl she'd become, couldn't change back into her old self, but she couldn't go forward either because she couldn't go with Jamie. Her response had been to step sideways, to funnel her passion into her schoolwork, and to blame Barbs.

The phone beside her chair buzzed and she grabbed it on the first ring, a residual habit from the time of Spike.

"Hi, darling, sorry to phone so late."

"It's okay, Peter, I'm wide awake. I've had the strangest day and I've been thinking. There's something I want to tell you, about Jamie Jones – Jamie Jamm, you know."

"Ah, so you're going to the book-signing. I saw it was on, in the Citizen, but I didn't tell you. I got in trouble last time I mentioned him, remember?"

"No, not that. It's just that expression: 'Nothing happened.' I used it afterwards about Jamie and me, but I shouldn't have. It wasn't true. Something really did happen between us even though we only met for one night. Even though we didn't ..."

"What are you telling me? Planning to check if he's single and run off with him?"

"No, I've just been remembering, that's all. It's all come back to me. I think I was lucky to meet him when I did. And lucky that I didn't hear from him again, though at the time I was hurt. After all these years I'm sure that I had the best of Jamie Jamm. So no, I'm not going tomorrow night. How are the boys?"

While Peter told her about today's journey to Durham, meeting Sam's girlfriend in the student café and plans for the trip to Scotland with Tom tomorrow, Susan hunched the phone up to her ear with one shoulder, and lifted *Jammy Bastard* in both hands. Still listening, she carried the heavy book through to the hall and lowered it into a cardboard box already half-full of donations for the Oxfam shop. On impulse she hunkered down beside the box and turned the book back cover up. She reached out two fingers together and stroked Jamie's portrait. She folded the flaps over so it disappeared then took the phone in her hand again, feeling a sudden rush of affection for her absent husband.

"Bye, darling," she said. "Love to both of them, and hurry home when you're done."

I am fascinated by living in the fens, shaped and regulated by man, yet carrying an ancient force which can have a powerful impact on us, if only we let it. This story was triggered by a visit to Wicken Fen, but bears no relation to any living person or being there.

White Fen

Siân Thomas

"All work and no play make Jack a dull boy!" Andy's taunt bellowed from the path. Megan clung to him, giggling.

"I just want to finish this, then I'll come and join you." Jack pushed the spade back into the peaty soil. The earth resisted. He angled the blade and applied more pressure, lifting the clod free.

"Aww, come on. You've done enough today!"

"I might have. But the rest of you certainly haven't," muttered Jack. He remembered how Andy had decided that he and Megan would work on one of the bird hides that day, leaving Jack with the two new volunteers to dig out the trench. They'd made a good start in the morning once Jack had shown the girls how to cut out slabs of turf and lay them out, ready to load onto the trolley. Predictably after lunch the girls had soon got bored and wandered off. They'd probably been doing a spot of sunbathing. He assumed they must have already returned to the hostel and would be getting ready to go to the pub.

Just a few more yards to dig out and the ditch would be restored, ready to carry the water away from the pump. Jack liked the idea of using old technology in reverse to maintain the water levels in the fen rather than draining the land, as it had in its heyday. He was looking forward to seeing the pump in action. Not that there was any wind to speak of to run the pump, as Andy had pointed out that morning. If the forecast, and Andy, were right, that would have to wait until tomorrow.

Jack looked up. He could see Andy and Megan at the far end

of the boardwalk. Andy's arm was wrapped around Megan's back as she leant into his side before they turned the corner and were out of sight.

The air thickened, pressing on his back. He stretched his spine, pulling his shoulders back to ease the nagging muscles. Perhaps he had done enough but it seemed a shame not to finish the job. Besides Megan seemed totally preoccupied with Andy now; no chance for him anymore.

A breath of cooler air made the sweat prick his face. The willows murmured. Another waft, stronger this time, reached the wooden common sails of the pump, nudging them a fraction. Jack resumed his digging, encouraged by the refreshing breeze. Perhaps he might be able to run the pump after all.

Funny, he thought Megan would have had more sense than to fall for Andy. Another easy conquest, as Andy would be itching to tell him tomorrow. Well, what did he care? She'd only given him one of her cheeky grins the other evening when he'd bought her another glass of Merlot, her favourite he'd discovered. Now that he thought, it wasn't much to go on really.

Jack slammed the spade back into the earth, losing his footing. His ankle turned and instinctively he leant on the spade to regain his balance. Fingers of air teased the back of his neck. Still the earth refused to budge. He was so close to clearing the ditch.

"Come on. I could use some help you know!"

The rushes strained against the increasing breeze, then clattered together. He tugged at the spade. It sprang back, knocking him in the chest. He gasped, air spun into his lungs. He couldn't stop now.

He had no idea how long it took. He had the sensation that time was suspended, waiting until his task was completed. He took hold of the long tail pole to turn the cap into the wind. To save time, he'd unfurled just two of the lower sails with their sail cloths. The sails turned, running gleefully like a pack of lurchers chasing each other's tails. He laughed as the water gushed through the wooden trough, frothing like warm beer through its new muddy chamber to return to the fen.

The cadence of the sails picked up. His hands burned from his last efforts and he held out his arms to catch the healing breeze as it kissed his fingers.

A coot dashed out of the rushes, feet splayed to counter balance its elongated neck. Close behind tottered its troop of young. Jack laughed as the family shot across the cropped grass of the bank and into another clump of reeds. Perhaps there was still time to get cleaned up and join Megan in the pub?

Rushes clattered nervously. Jack stared as a gust of wind grabbed the topmost dry clods of earth from the neat pile of cut peat, flinging shreds into his face. His eyes stung, and he tasted the cloying peat. His vision blurred as a second hail was tossed into his face.

"What the ...?" Jack pulled his shirt sleeve across his face. Umber slabs of cloud raced upward to blot out the sunlight. A fractious gust grabbed more clumps of peat and spun them into a cape around Jack's shoulders. He'd seen a fen blow in the fields before, but surely it was too damp here, in the heart of the fen? He shut his eyes, but his legs wobbled as he tried to keep his balance on the narrow bank. The last thing he wanted was to fall into the ditch. He opened his eyes, still gritty and watering. If he could just focus on something he wouldn't feel so dizzy.

Through the haze Jack could just make out the silhouette of the wind pump, cap twisting as the demented sails cut through the air. All his work would be for nothing if any of the sails broke. They would take weeks to repair.

Jack blundered along the bank towards the pump. The brown murk swirled around him, snatching at his breath. He felt for the mini Maglite on the key ring in his pocket. The yellow band of light flickered, casting a thin aureole across the path ahead of him. He ran towards the pump. If he could just reach the tail pole to turn the drumming sails out of the wind. He stretched out an arm up towards the lower sail. The mocking wind smacked the tail pole and the brake chain into his face, hitting his jawbone before dancing away. The gyrating pole soon came back into reach. This time he jumped, seized the tail pole, yelling as the upward momentum tugged at his arm socket and he landed on his sore ankle. Still he clung on. The Maglite and keys were snatched from his grasp.

The wind moaned and dropped. The tail pole lay submissively in his hand. Quickly he secured the brake chain and furled the sail cloth, feeling the lower part of the sails for any immediate signs of damage. He was grateful he'd only uncovered two of the sail cloths. Despite the sudden squall everything was intact.

Jack dropped to the ground. The last trickle of water belched through the pump and sputtered into the trough. He'd proved it worked. He'd had enough, and he'd certainly earned a drink now, if he could just drag himself back to the car. His keys ...

He scrabbled furiously through the grass on his hands and knees, feeling the heat rising from the ripe soil. Already the sun was burning away the remnants of ochre mist, restoring the familiar blue sky. Frantically he searched the ground around him, but it was hopeless, the keys and the Maglite could be anywhere.

If he couldn't find his keys he'd have to meet up with the others. It was only a short walk to the pub from the visitor centre. Surely someone would give him a lift home to collect the spare key and he could come back to collect his car. Andy might not be too willing to leave his growing harem, but he wouldn't want Megan offering Jack a lift first. Jack smiled, realising that he wasn't too bothered about who gave him a lift.

A pair of dainty feet appeared in front of Jack's hands. The hem of a russet skirt fluttered. As Jack struggled to get up a slender arm reached down and took a firm grasp of his hand, propelling him upwards, surprising him with its strength.

The crown of copper hair tumbling around her pale face was

strewn with bits of peat. Instinctively Jack reached out as if to remove one of them, but she stepped backwards. She laughed, keeping one arm behind her back.

"I'm sorry, I can't remember your name ..." Jack struggled to remember the girls who had helped him that morning. Surely she must be one of the volunteers, but he couldn't remember either of them being as stunning as the young woman in front of him now.

"They call me Elaine." The woman held out her hand. In her palm lay a bunch of keys.

"You've found them! How did you..?"

Amber eyes fixed on Jack's face as he traced the curves of her hips melded in orange gauze which shimmered in the afternoon sun. She seemed to be almost fluid, the delicate weave of her dress continually shifting in front of him. He wanted her to stay with him; to know more about her.

"Do you want to come back to the pub with me? I'll just have to lock up first then we can join the others."

She stared at him coldly. She dropped the keys into Jack's hand and turned away. A pulse of sunlight flashed across the fen. Jack rubbed his eyes.

"Elaine?" She was gone. He glanced up at the boardwalk but there was no sign of her. She couldn't have reached the bend so quickly, surely? He dashed to the wind pump and peered into the gloomy recess. Of course, there was no sign of her.

Why had she disappeared like that? He kicked the heap of peat. Such a beautiful woman. Trust him to mess it up.

What if she had gone the longer way around the boardwalk? Perhaps he could persuade her to come with him if he caught up with her in the car park.

Jack sat in the car for several minutes, just in case she'd taken the other circular route along the boardwalk back to the visitor centre. He shivered; it was getting cooler now in the early evening. Perhaps she'd headed straight to the pub in the time he'd spent locking up. He'd better stop wasting time and join them before Andy took control. He rammed the car into gear and sped out of the car park.

As he stepped into the pub Jack could see Andy holding court among the group, the rest of them with their backs to the door.

"Hey Jack. Jeez, look at you!"

The group turned to face him. There was Megan and the two volunteers, their plain faces flushed by the afternoon sun and alcohol.

"Where's Elaine?"

"What happened to you?" asked Megan. "You look rough!"

The two volunteers kept staring at Jack. He lifted up his arm to find the shirt in tatters around his chest.

"Whoever Elaine is, she's obviously hot stuff," laughed Andy.

"Why don't you go and tidy yourself up before you sit with us. Andy can get you a drink." Megan turned towards the other girls.

Andy stood up. "Go on mate." The volunteers giggled as Jack limped towards the toilet.

The cold water stung as he rubbed his face clean, wincing at the sight of his puffy eyes and a vicious weal across his cheek where the tail pole and chain had caught him. He brushed back his hair with his fingers, and tried to straighten out his shirt into some semblance of order.

He joined the others, perching on the spare stool next to Megan. How could he have ever been interested in her? Jack ignored her, and looked around the pub.

Andy was staring at him. "Take it easy. You've obviously done too much today. Have your pint first."

Jack nodded. His throat was parched. All he wanted was a quick pint, to get away from the others and to find Elaine.

There she was. In the dim corner of the room he could make out a slender figure with tousled hair. He got up.

Megan put out a hand. "You okay?"

He brushed her hand away, staring at the girl shrouded in the corner seat.

As he walked right up to her, she looked up. He froze. Disappointment flooded his face.

"What's your problem?" The boyfriend rose from the dark recess, pushing his hand out to meet Jack's chest.

"Hey guys. No worries. It's just a case of mistaken identity." Andy pulled Jack away. "Come on, Jack," he murmured.

Jack swung round. "I don't need a nurse maid. Just tell me where Elaine is, or are you keeping her to yourself? Megan's not enough for you?"

"Cool it, mate! Look, you're embarrassing everyone. You locked up didn't you? Why don't you finish your pint, go home and sleep it off."

"Better still, I'll leave now! Save you all getting embarrassed! Here. Yes I locked up." Jack flung the centre's keys at Andy and strode off, leaving his car outside the pub.

He clambered over the gate next to the visitor centre. The planks of the boardwalk groaned under his feet as he moved quickly towards the wind pump. The fen was waiting for him.

Damselflies darted around her as she stood facing the pool of water, watching the moon usurp the place of the retreating sun. Her hair hung down her naked back. She raised one hand and the damselflies gathered in veneration at her feet. As the insects continued to dance in attendance she seemed to hover with them towards the edge of the bank. She did not turn towards Jack, but he knew that she had already sensed his presence.

Jack stretched out a hand to touch her lustrous hair. This time she let him, but she gave no indication of welcoming his attention. His fingers burned and grew numb, but still he wanted to caress her.

She looked over her shoulder, and smiled at Jack as she stepped into the water.

The reeds parted gently, ragged heads bowed as Jack waded in after her. The water soothed the pain in his hands, he felt his muscles ease. A few damselflies darted towards him as if to encourage him as he trod through the weeds.

For one moment he hesitated as he sensed the pull of a current drawing him into deeper water. The fen tensed around him, silent, watchful. She turned again to look back at him. He knew he must stay with her.

He stumbled as tendrils of weeds pulled at his heels. He fell, swallowing putrid water as he fought to regain his foothold. He tried to reach out towards her, but she was too far ahead of him.

Sweet chants rising from the depths of the pool lured him further. The sound was so beautiful, he longed to hear more. He slipped beneath the surface. He felt the music's pulse embrace him and carry him gently down.

Written for Plonk, but a struggle. I started it way before I started 'Contraband' and almost gave up on it. Thanks to the rest of the Red Wine Writers I persevered and eventually completed what turned out to be my longest story in this anthology. Having had some experience with the occult several – make that thirty something – years ago, I can claim to know a little about what happens later in this story; although sometimes I wonder if I've forgotten more than I learned. 'Bodies' is, of course, fiction. I don't want you to get worried ...

Bodies

Terry Martin

Red wine flowed that night. It was a party after all. Blood flowed too, in large amounts, dissipating in the waters of the swimming pool in rivulets of crimson that would have appeared black if not for the underwater lights.

DI Sanders stood at its edge looking down into the innocuous liquid, the twenty-three bodies that had floated there already numbered, bagged and taken away for autopsies. An unsmoked cigarette glowed in the light breeze between fingers that hovered about six inches from his mouth. Pulsing pressure in his skull made it difficult to think.

He rarely had headaches, and amidst the pain were flashing recollections of a father he hadn't thought about for years. Why now? His father had brought him up single handed following the death of his mother from cancer when Sanders was five. He remembered that much. Not long after his seventeenth birthday he had come home from college to find his father had, with no prior warning nor message of explanation, packed a suitcase and left their three-bedroom council house in Croydon. The police hadn't been interested, and Sanders knew none of his father's friends or work colleagues, or even if he had any. His solution had been to join the army and forget.

The cigarette still smouldered in his hand. Around him uniformed constables traipsed the ornamental gardens and white-clad crime scene personnel stood in huddles, perplexed by what they had found. Sanders guessed the five men in casual suits from SO6, while surely expecting to be sacked, were discussing how they might have deployed better, but Sanders doubted there was anything anyone could have done. A couple of others, dressed in jeans and hoodies, Sanders assumed were MI5. The death of the Home Secretary was going to be an international embarrassment.

It was impossible to blank out the devastation from earlier in the evening, yet he had no recollection of how the party-goers had died or ended up in the pool. What he had felt was the onrush of some powerful force; like standing in the path of a high-speed locomotive just before impact, a disconcerting jump as it passed through him. It had seemed instantaneous yet when he looked into the swimming pool the bodies were floating unnaturally on the surface.

"You okay, Guv?" It was DS Lake, just plain Vespa to Sanders, the first detective on the scene after he'd called it in.

Sanders could have replied, "It feels like my brain has melted and is boiling in my head." Instead, he sighed and said, "I knew Lord and Lady Westbrook."

"Yes, you told me." Accusations laced her words, like: 'How come you were at a party of the Home Secretary?' And, 'What else didn't you tell me about his wife?'; like he was responsible for their deaths. But no-one, absolutely no-one, knew of his affair with Beatrice. Sanders wasn't in the mood to ponder though. Before Lake could remind him not to, he flicked his glowing tip into the pool.

"Sir!"

"Well, my DNA's going to be all over this place. A bit more's not going to make any difference, is it?"

Not waiting for or requiring an answer, he turned away from Lake, aware of frustrated eyes on his back, and walked around the Georgian mansion that was Moondyke Manor to the paved drive where, earlier in the evening, he'd parked the red Range Rover Evoque he'd hired. The idea had been to blend in with the luxury cars but it just looked brash and cheap amongst the mostly-black Bentleys and Mercs. Despite the loss of Beatrice, and his discomfort, a smile twitched his lips.

Two Savile Row-suited spooks leaning against the Evoque straightened up as he came into view. He didn't break stride as they moved towards him, surprise in their eyes at the Victorian military dress uniform he wore, which pleased Sanders. It meant their briefing hadn't been complete; hopefully, because they didn't have all the details.

His clothes were genuine, a captain's. Beatrice had managed to persuade some toff to lend the uniform from his collection. Authenticity had been the requirement and Sanders' contacts were not the kind who could acquire historical dress, at least not legitimately. It was all to help him blend in with the steampunk-themed party. His security credentials were without question. Seven years earlier, on leaving the army and joining the Met, he had been assigned to lead Lord Westbrook's diplomatic protection unit. It was during this three-year stint that his relationship with Beatrice had begun.

"Commander Fielding wants to see me, I presume?"

Glances were exchanged between the two spooks.

The man on the right nodded and said, "He's Chief now."

Sanders, unsurprised by the revelation that his old army commanding officer had risen to head of MI5, threw his keys to the other man.

"You drive." The glances again. "I've drunk too much."

"You hadn't been officially invited to the party, Lieutenant," Fielding stated. The reference to his old army rank irritated Sanders, adding another level of pain to his headache. Sir Patrick Fielding, the 'sir' being a title gained since leaving the forces, technically had no authority over him. But Fielding's position, as the head of MI5, meant he could have authority over anyone in the country if he chose.

Having risen through the ranks, much like Sanders, Fielding's ambitious drive and single-minded ruthlessness had made his current position inevitable. He relaxed in a green velvet wing-back chair, left leg dangling over the arm; a familiar position to Sanders. Fielding flouted propriety, and his new title had failed to give cause for correction.

Sanders wasn't fooled by the disrespectful pose. It was how Fielding used to brief his officers. The forefinger and thumb of his right hand waved his trade-mark John Wayne cigar into a room already clogged with a few hundred years of Cuban aroma, compounding the throbbing in Sanders' head, and ignoring the ban on smoking in public places – Sanders doubted this was a private residence. It could have been a room in any gentlemen's club – which it probably was – in the heart of London, but this was Frampton Marsh, a little village, not a mortar's launch away from the Lincolnshire town of Boston, and just twelve miles from Moondyke Manor.

"I wasn't on the original list of invitees. Lady Westbrook had asked if I would attend. For old time's sake." Sanders itched to fish out a cigarette, but the overpowering smog reminded him he was trying to cut down and that his passive inhalations ought to be more than enough to satisfy his craving. He'd given up on the electronic ciggies months before, realising, even as he did so, that one of the reasons he smoked – and there were many – was that it wasn't socially acceptable anymore; a weird kind of rebelling.

His own chair had been pulled out from under a D-end dining table by a butler – Sanders couldn't think of another title to describe the man – who had left a large decanter and tumbler of what was most likely Fielding's favourite tiple, Jameson's, on a pedestal next to him. The senior of the two spooks who had brought him here now stood, looking uncomfortable but no less alert, at the entrance to the room. Outside the room the second agent had planted himself by the door as they came in. The building seemed devoid of any other people.

Fielding's imposing physique said much about his current lifestyle, though in his time he had been lean, muscular and something of a hero. At least that's what his official army file had said ... but it hadn't put Sanders' mind at rest about the man. Fielding had been reckless and was as likely to put his men at risk as himself. That this hadn't been questioned by those higher up the chain of command made Sanders edgy. He'd risked his career for a copy of that file and unsurprisingly had found nothing of use. Having served under Fielding in Afghanistan Sanders could vouch for the file's accuracy ... to some degree.

"Your floozy sidekick, Lake, is being made up to DI in charge of the case."

Sanders wanted to argue the floozy reference but knew Fielding was merely trying to rile him. The promotion wasn't unexpected. She would make a great inspector. He winced at a spasm in his skull which Fielding mistook as surprise.

"Well, we can't have the public know you were at the party. A scandal would be almost as damaging as the murders." Sanders wasn't sure what Fielding was implying. "Officially – within the force – you've been suspended."

He'd expected that too, though he had been hoping for a temporary move to another station for six months, maybe a year, and then back to familiar territory. Fielding's knowledge of what Sander's superiors ought to be telling him came as no surprise either.

"Shouldn't have you around at all, really," Fielding confirmed. "After all, you'll be a suspect."

Sanders hadn't even considered that. Shock and the headache had blunted his ability to think straight. Was he that traumatised?

"The media would just love it. And we don't want the affair to come out, do we?"

When he told DS Lake he knew Lord and Lady Westbrook he hadn't said they'd developed a good friendship. He'd also not even dreamed of telling her, or anyone else for that matter, that he and Beatrice were in love ... okay, having a sexual relationship. If it had been more than that it was only now, after her death, that the depth of his feelings hit home. Working class roots had convinced him he was getting some kind of revenge on the aristocracy by sleeping with Beatrice. Now he realised, when it came to feelings, class meant bugger all. They were sure they'd been discreet. Lord Neville had been oblivious. It shouldn't have surprised Sanders that MI5 knew of their relationship, but it did, they'd been that careful.

"Don't be so stupid, Ken," Fielding said, as if he'd been reading Sanders' mind, and Sanders had a paranoid streak about that possibility. "You think the wife of the Home Secretary has a private life? Get real."

Of course, he was right. Love truly was blind. A C4 manila envelope landed on the floor at Sanders' feet, Fielding's hand freezing in mid-air for effect, caught in the act of tossing it over. The spook at the door tried to remain impassive, but his eyes flicked across as Sanders pulled open the tab.

Sure enough, telephoto shots, obvious from the narrow depth of field, showed him and Beatrice together and enjoying each other's company in ways that married people shouldn't do with someone else's partner. Some were wide-angle, taken in a hotel room. He felt sick.

"Those are stills from the HD video," Fielding explained, revelling in the revelation.

"Bastard."

"Oh come on, Ken. Surely you really didn't think that you and Lady Beatrice were going to jeopardise the security of the country."

Sanders' expletive had been personal. Now it dawned on him that MI5 might actually be responsible for his friends' deaths. His half-checked lunge at Fielding resulted in the spook aiming his Glock 17 at the DI's head.

"That's not our style, Ken." Fielding remained relaxed in his chair, looking up into Sanders' face as he leaned over him. "Lord

Westbrook was an excellent Home Secretary. He also had a lot of time for you. Said you were great company for his wife ... Though we had a lot of covering up to do for your little sordid escapades."

Sanders' legs crumpled and he fell back onto the chair, with the spook's gun following into its shoulder holster beneath the Savile Row suit. Could he have been responsible for silencing innocent people?

"Yes. Lord Neville knew all about your affair. Thought you were the best man for the job. His own sexual gratification came from ... elsewhere ... but that is confidential. Apart from your ... indiscretions ... he thought you were the perfect cop. It's appropriate then that you work behind the scenes to find out the killer or killers. Someone with the experience we need. Someone who is motivated by more than just duty. Someone like you, Ken."

A bundle of emotions spread out like octopus tentacles through his organs, thrashing at the pain in his head. He recalled the bodies in the pool; Beatrice's bustle protruding from the water like a mini desert island, her body spreading out like a worshipping siren, silhouetted by the underwater lights, a halo of leaking redness searching for release from life. And that multiplied by twenty-three.

The room spun, cigar smoke caught in his throat drawing down the pain in his cranium. An ancient Ming vase seemed the only safe place to vomit. The automatic was back in the spook's hand as Sanders lurched across the room to empty his stomach into the Chinese ornament. He'd witnessed things in Afghanistan that most people couldn't imagine: women and children mutilated in the name of religion, bodies blown apart and shredded by shrapnel, friend and foe exposed as just worthless lumps of meat. The cheapness of life – a lack of respect for that singular spark of vitality that was being human. But seeing those bodies in the pool had shocked even him. That copper-stench of blood – its smell had never been that strong before – remained in his memory. Not even the sour spew could shift that.

Removing his hands from the side of the vase he wiped the sleeve of his bright red ornamental jacket across his face, looked down at the sick smeared on the uniform, his puerile side surprising him with the pleasure of glimpsing the disgust on Fielding's face.

"Did you have to do that?"

"Did you see it?" Even as he spat the question at Fielding he guessed it would receive an affirmative. But it didn't.

"I've seen footage from the CCTV. Shame there was a power cut and the UPS batteries failed just before and until just after the murders took place." The irony in his voice couldn't hide his disappointment. "Quite a gruesome residue though."

Strange, Sanders thought. He hadn't even realised the power had gone down.

"You wouldn't have noticed. The lighting in the garden and by the pool was all gaslight. In keeping with the authentic feel of the Victorian party theme no doubt. Such extravagant expense for so few."

"Steampunk."

"What? Dressing up's dressing up, whatever it's labelled. All very childish."

Sanders decided not to argue the point. It was irrelevant to the case.

"You'll have Mason and Kazaks working with you."

"I'll work on my own thanks."

"You've met them already. They're very efficient."

There was little point in arguing. Fielding's commands were never disobeyed. Never more than once, anyway.

"They'll take orders from you."

But their agenda will be to ensure I don't step out of line, Sanders thought.

"I'll expect regular reports from you on a twenty-four hour basis."

As if his men wouldn't be giving their boss a minute by minute account of his movements and actions.

"Thanks," he said with enough sarcasm to make even Fielding react.

"You'll thank me at the end of this."

"Just fuck off, Henry." It wasn't normally a phrase that Sanders dared use to address Fielding, who was immutably unpredictable, but his headache did a somersault of joy as he rose from the chair, the pain subsiding enough to allow his facial muscles to form a grin which no doubt Fielding took as a grimace. The spook opened the door for him. As he left the room Sanders was pleased that even the cigar smoke wasn't doing well up against the acrid contents of the vase. Mixed feelings about the arrangement and the arrogant yet noticeably forced smile on Fielding's face didn't alleviate his malaise. Sanders knew the commander hated being called by his first name more than being sworn at, but even that hadn't shifted the big man from his chair.

Leaving Fielding on his own, the spook closed the door before he and the second agent followed Sanders into the spacious hallway.

"Arrogant fucker."

"What did you say?" Sanders asked, turning on the man.

"The boss, sir. He has a bit of a stutter." Their eyes met and Sanders recognised a kindred spirit. Maybe there was a chance they would get on after all.

"What's your name?"

"Mason, sir."

Sanders raised a questioning eyebrow.

"Just Mason."

"Call me Ken."

"I'll try, sir ... Ken."

"You'll get the hang of it. Let's go. And you're Kazaks?"

"Yes, sir."

The spooks weren't able to see amusement spread across Sanders' face. Considering the evening's events Sanders guessed he was grabbing at something to lighten his depression and release some of the pressure in his skull.

The two bottles of Rioja that might have killed another person barely dulled the pain in his head and early morning TV didn't induce the stupor that Sanders required to sleep in the hotel room that Fielding's men booked for him. His house would have been as empty, and the bed even more so. Sarah, his wife, had left him just a month earlier. It wasn't because she'd found out about his affair, though now he realised that was possible, nor his drinking, but because she had been indulging in an affair of her own and decided the grass was greener.

He was unable to blank out the earlier carnage from his mind. But how had they all died? It was as if his memory had shut off along with the CCTV. Yet the result was imprinted there. It hadn't been, and it wasn't, a dream, yet there was an unearthly feeling that seemed to be manifesting itself within his mind.

Trouble was, this wasn't the first time he'd experienced the feeling. Previously his whole platoon had been wiped out.

Sanders was surprised when Lake led the interrogation in Interview Room 3 with DS Tapscott the next morning. There were officers specially trained in interviewing techniques.

He had been left to stew for twenty minutes, seated at a stainless steel table that was, like the chairs, bolted to the floor. Words and patterns were etched into its surface. A history of interrogations that sanding discs and etchants had failed to remove. A strong smell of bleach and citrus did nothing to clear his head which felt like someone had cleaved it with an axe and was now trying to extricate the weapon.

Vespa's scrutinising gaze didn't help. He guessed he looked a mess. A shower hadn't shaken off the effects of the wine or given him the will to shave. A new grey tracksuit and sneakers supplied by the spooks, while comfortable, just seemed to add to the colour of his mood and emphasised his sore red eye.

Vespa's classic features had created a stir amongst the mostly male station when she had been drafted in six months earlier. She'd not only shown her worth as a copper but had put several officers in their place. DC Oats had been suspended awaiting investigation for sexual harassment. She'd suddenly dropped the charge of attempted rape for reasons she never disclosed.

Oats was a twat though, always had been, so he didn't have many friends and Sanders didn't know anyone who liked him. But if the media had picked up on the attempted rape story the rest of the station would have gone against her. As it was, she'd gained a lot of respect from those who were aware of what had happened. They knew what Oats was like.

The file remained open on the hit and run that had killed him not long after. Sanders had noticed a smug look on Lake's face before they heard of the fatality, though she'd had a rock-solid alibi. Still ...

Tapscott had joined the station around the same time as Lake. A loner, and someone who looked like he should have retired years ago. A born cop, and he'd probably go to his grave a cop. His eyes had a deadness about them. A kind of acceptance that his time had come. Sanders had seen it in the eyes of soldiers he'd fought alongside in Afghanistan. But coppers who'd known Tapscott said he'd always had that look. It made him dangerous and it put Sanders on edge and made him feel even more uncomfortable.

"Why you?" he asked, as they sat down on the other side of the table.

"I'm asking the questions, Inspector." Lake's voice was soft and feminine, but quietly insistent, yet she'd been respectful enough to use his rank. Biting back a retort, Sanders only then realised this wasn't going to be a friendly chat.

She turned on the tape and introduced those in the room.

Sanders couldn't help glancing at the one-way mirror, wondering who was on the other side. He felt unnecessarily guilty even before the questions started.

"Where were you last night?"

He wanted to say, "You know," but this was all for the record, he reminded himself.

"What time?" He felt like he had to defend himself, play the same game. But that wasn't going to help the investigation or him.

"Between ten and ten-thirty." She wasn't rattled. "That's the time of the power cut." She was even trying to help him, avoiding mention of the horrors. Yet that silky assured voice, which he'd once found sexy, held completely different undertones. She already knew the answers. But the questions had to be asked.

"At Moondyke Manor."

"What were you doing there?"

Sanders looked her in the eyes. Her tone suggested this was personal. Sure, they had a great working relationship, and friendly innuendoes and banter were part and parcel of their daily routine, but had he missed signs?

"Gate-crashing a steampunk party. Well, I was sort-of invited. At ten past I was phoning you, DS Lake."

"Just before then?"

"We'd discovered the bodies in the pool."

"We?"

"Me. Beatrice and me. Lady Westbrook." He'd cut off her hysterical screams with a slap to her cheek, held her tight as he looked around for ... somebody ... something.

Lake looked surprised. "Lady Beatrice was still alive?"

Sanders frowned. She was alive then. But ... "Then ... yes."

"What happened?"

"She died too."

"Don't be smart, Sanders. We know that."

He wasn't being smart. In his head he was back at the pool; felt the force, like an express train bearing down on him and Beatrice again. Yet this time, he'd let go of her, put up his hands as if to fend off the onrush – to protect them both – a split second before impact; fell dizzily to the ground as if he'd been spun a hundred times, or downed a bottle of Teacher's. When he looked up Beatrice wasn't in sight. No. Because she, like the others had been slashed – skin shredded – and dumped in the pool. Yet he still lived. God, why?

"Well?"

Sanders looked up, unprepared for the pity in Lake's eye; wiped his own when he realised tears had trickled as far as his mouth; licked the salt from his lips. Where had they come from?

"I don't know what happened. Just the consequences."

Lake glanced at the mirror, her impetus lost, seeking help. Sanders looked in that direction too, expecting to see no more than their reflections, but something shimmered there, distorting their features. Was it the strip lighting affecting his eyes? Fluorescent tubes did that to him sometimes. But then he stiffened as he felt that locomotive bearing down on him again.

"What the ... ?" Lake blurted.

And then it was gone.

"What was that?" she asked, turning to Tapscott.

He shrugged. "What?"

"Did you see that?" she demanded of Sanders.

He nodded. He'd felt the train, knew now that it was something to do with the pain in his head. Yet he sensed the source was far away. Some exterior force was trying to ... Then Kazaks, the Latvian-born MI5 agent who had mostly stayed silent while Mason did the talking, burst in, Fielding close behind trying to grab his oik. So, there had been a crowd behind the mirror. In seconds the small interview room seemed claustrophobic.

"What's going on?" Kazak's demanded. He didn't seem to notice Fielding's hand clamp on his shoulder, such was his fear. They'd seen it too, from the other side of the mirror.

"Something ..." Lake started to say, but Kazaks cut in.

"What are you, Sanders?"

"Eh?" Sanders was confused by the question. Mason was hovering by the door, looking disappointed at himself for allowing his partner to break rank. Two uniforms peered into the room from behind him.

Kazaks was still throwing questions his way.

"Are you some kind of witch or something?" There was just a hint of a Baltic accent.

"Calm down, Kazaks!" Fielding's grip on Kazak's shoulder was shrugged off.

"I said, what are you, Sanders?"

"What do you mean?" Sanders was more than a little bewildered. He felt the world was coming apart. Neurons fired erratically, bouncing this way and that within his skull, searching unsuccessfully for hidden recesses. Everyone was acting weird. Everything was weird. What was going on?

"Kazaks!" Fielding's voice held that familiar foreboding that Sanders recognised from Afghanistan. If the spook continued his verbal assault on Sanders then Fielding was likely to do something. Not immediately, perhaps, but his memory lasted a lifetime.

"Sir?" Lake's sharp request had everyone's attention. She spoke to Fielding like she knew him. In that moment Sanders realised she did, and that didn't bode at all well. Now Oat's death really did hold sinister connotations. "I don't think Sanders had anything to do with the attack."

What was she talking about? Kazaks looked out of his depth, as confused as Sanders felt.

"Attack?" Sanders queried. "What attack?"

Fielding this time. "The shimmering in front of the mirror. Most likely a Russian attack. Or at least a precursor."

Some kind of new technology? It still didn't make sense.

"Will someone tell me what's going on?" Kazaks asked. Frustrated and perplexed, he looked like a lost child. Sanders was not surprised that Fielding hadn't briefed his men as to the whys of their placement. Mason's frown confirmed that his old commander's policy of only ever telling his underlings enough still held true. Lake was a different kettle of fish. She knew whatever it was that the two spooks didn't.

"Sanders a witch?" Fielding surveyed the room. "Well, that's not strictly true. But you're right about the magic. That's what you were implying, wasn't it, Kazaks?" A nod went to Mason, who disappeared, as Sanders saw it, to ensure the room behind the mirror was empty. There was relief in his face as he ushered the two constables away. He obviously felt he'd heard enough. "I'll remind you that you're all bound by the Official Secrets Act. This is national security after all. Are we sitting comfortably?"

Sanders grimaced at Fielding's clichéd question, at his subconscious dominance, but it highlighted that they were all standing. No one took a seat though. Fielding moved to the door and casually leant against it before speaking. It clicked ominously and loudly shut.

"There's been talk for years that the Russians have been experimenting with magic, or whatever force it is that holds the world together. You can all close your mouths now. There is such a thing as magic. Nothing like Harry Potter I'm sad to say. Although that might actually be fun. This is all about calling demons and conjuring spirits – for want of better definitions – to do evil deeds."

"Then there is a god." Tapscott sounded relieved. His death-wish look almost disappeared.

"Fuck no," Fielding said with a laugh. "What makes you think that?"

"If there's evil there's good." Sanders had never taken Tapscott for being religious in any way. "If there are demons and spirits, then there are angels. And God exists."

"I said, for want of a better definition. They're not actual demons and spirits," Fielding told him. "I'm surprised that an intelligent man like you would put one and one together and make three."

"You just said tha ..."

"Shut it, Tapscott," Sanders advised.

The DS shot a look at him, double-took the warning in his old boss's eyes and drew back from the argument with, "Bloody spooks."

"Very wise," Fielding said. "Both of you." He moved around and leant back on the edge of the table lifting up his left leg to sit on the cold metal surface. There was a groan from the metal joints. Sanders was reminded of the green wingback chair in the club at Frampton. He supposed a psychiatrist might describe his pose as wallowing in his throne, emphasising his superiority.

"Right. Have you heard of the Metaphysical Research Group? No? It was founded during the Second World War. Unofficially funded by the Treasury. The Germans had their own magic investigation department, the *Zauber Staffel,* headed by Hitler himself, so our intelligence suggested at the time. We've never been able to discover what the Russians named their department. We call it Mars. The red planet. The planet of war.

"We had to have a counter department ... in case magic was real. The group wasn't disbanded after the war. In fact it grew in size. Not with our agents I hasten to add but ordinary," he gave a snort, "people with a scientific interest in the occult. On the surface the MRG was a crank society and many cranks did join it, but it still had some influential people working at the science. And magic is a science ... of sorts. Most countries seem to have their own occult agencies these days."

Fielding surveyed the disbelieving faces. "I was more than sceptical too. I'd been asked to take charge of a military unit, unofficially under the MRG's umbrella, aptly named 666 Platoon – someone in Whitehall had a sense of humour – to see if we could use magic to get the edge on the Taliban."

Sanders was dumfounded. "Come on, Lieutenant, surely you suspected the platoon was different with a handle like that?"

He had, but he'd been a soldier then and soldiers didn't ask questions. Fielding didn't wait for an answer.

"Could the faith of fanatical Muslims be stronger than Earth's ancient magical energy?" Fielding directed his question at the others in the room. "It's that immeasurable force that seems the most logical source of power from what the boffins say. The enemy may actually have been tapping into that very same force, but in the name of their god, believing that it was their deity giving them power. Platoon 666 was an experiment ..."

"We were guinea pigs?" It was all becoming clear now ... and he'd also suffered headaches then.

"... that yielded no conclusive results." And then to Sanders' question, "You were soldiers. Doing what soldiers do best. Obeying orders. Except that you, Sanders, appeared to be a powerful vessel. The whole unit was being given drugs. In the rations. Small doses. Not enough to impair combat effectiveness or induce hallucinations. Just enough to make you braver and maybe open up that magical side the scientists said was waiting to be tapped. None of the other soldiers showed any signs of ..."

"None of the other soldiers survived Afghanistan," Sanders cut in.

"Unfortunately not. But you were the exception, Sanders. In lots of ways."

Sanders felt the eyes of everyone in the room, sensed the train pulling out of the station. That's how he imagined whatever it was going on in his head; a gigantic steam-powered express train building up pressure, readying to thunder along imaginary tracks.

"Fight it, Ken!"

Fielding's hands gripped the top of his arms, shaking his consciousness back into the room.

"What?"

"They're using your tiredness to funnel the energy. You have to stay focused and with us!"

Sanders felt an inkling of control within himself, but he couldn't allow Fielding to know. For now he allowed Fielding to believe what he expected – what he'd been expecting, so it seemed, for some time. He feigned a faint into Fielding's arms, felt the physical power that his old commander still retained despite his excesses.

Just before losing contact with the force that was using him – it had to be strong because it didn't emanate from the UK – Sanders had felt a hint of self-understanding, a kind of enlightenment that made him want to retain the link – which was why he broke it. The time wasn't right. The important thing was that he'd broken the link. He'd been a puppet for years. And not just with one puppet master. But he felt the balance was changing.

"You're their conduit to strike at us. That's what they did in Afghanistan."

Yes, he knew that now. He brought his hand up to his forehead to cover his eyes and stepped back from Fielding.

"I'm okay."

"Are you sure?" Incredulity laced the question.

Sanders dropped his hand and nodded. He was also sure that if Fielding had been able to read his mind before, he couldn't now.

"Then we need to get you to the club. And fast."

"The club?"

"The MRG boffins are meeting there. They'll want to question you."

Protests were on the tip of his tongue, but they'd have been pointless. Fielding wasn't a man to take "no", or any other response than the one he wanted, for an answer.

"One of them's a mage," Fielding continued, grabbing Sanders by the arm. "He'll be able to give you protection."

Will he now? Sanders wasn't so sure he needed protection any more, but he allowed his old commanding officer to lead him from the room, through the station and out to the car park preceded by his two spooks. And what the fuck was a mage?

Sitting in the back of the limo alongside Fielding, the two spooks in the front, Sanders allowed the Russians to get the steam up on their locomotive. It was useful imagery. It allowed him better control. He could visualise being in the cabin alongside the fireman and the driver, though in actuality they were a group of thirteen: six women and seven men. Their location was still not clear to him but it seemed likely they were on Russian soil. They were confident and sure of themselves. They'd used him many times, he realised, though the two mass deaths were the only occasions that he recalled. They just thought he was a medium, nothing more. Until now it appeared he had been, but Beatrice's death had triggered something, some latent ability that he hadn't known he possessed.

Just ahead, Lake and Tapscott were in a marked police car, full-on blue lights and siren. A bike outrider preceded them sending traffic veering into the cycleways that edged the main road until they turned off onto country lanes that were, thankfully, devoid of traffic. The dykes on either side, full with recent rain, would have been an unfortunate option for oncoming cars. Given a different situation Sanders would have enjoyed the ride.

Magic hadn't interested him. Not since his father disappeared. Until then their relationship had, he was sure now, been a good one. But the trauma of being left to fend for himself had messed with his memory. His recollections of the occult had been limited to his father's Dennis Wheatley collection, and they were pure fiction. Now he sensed things were changing and he was keen to learn the rules. There were always rules. And a reason for them. If you knew rules inside out you could push them to the edge ... and sometimes break them.

In the army he didn't ask questions and used his initiative to bend the orders to suit the situation. Police work had been little different. If not for his cavalier behaviour he would have received commendation after commendation, but the irony was he'd not have been so successful had he policed by the book.

Instantly that triggered a memory of when he was a child. In their three-bedroom semi, a council house in Dagenham, the master bedroom was set aside as a library. Bookshelves covered every wall, even across the window, and in pride of place were the Dennis Wheatley novels and around them Steven King, Peter Straub, James Herbert, Graham Masterton and writers of the occult that were less well known. On the top shelf, out of reach of inquisitive hands, were magic text books. He had forgotten all about them until now.

As memories flooded back the pain in his head dissipated. How strange. Even more strange that he now recalled studying the magic books with his father, practising ceremony after ceremony within the library room that also doubled as a temple, until he was the one leading the spell-making, his father trusting him to call forces into the triangle of art outside of the protective magic circle, into his father; demons and spirits, as Fielding had called them, the depths of the human subconscious, the unconscious force that mostly lay untapped. There seemed no reason why such a close relationship with his father shouldn't have survived, and it only now dawned on him that it probably still did, if he knew where his father was. Had his father created some kind of memory block?

"Are you sure you're okay?" Fielding wasn't normally so concerned and Sanders wasn't stupid enough to think the concern went as far as his welfare. His only interest would be in using the DI as some kind of weapon, or maybe just purely as a means to trap or ambush the Russians. That's why, he realised, the MRG had a presence nearby. The possibility struck him that they'd been keeping a close eye on him since he left the army. For seven years? He controlled his anger, his need to avenge Beatrice's death.

He gently released a little steam, not enough for the Russians to notice, but enough to delay their impending attack, because that was their intention. They had slaughtered the Home Secretary and his friends with the certainty it would draw all the UK's occult big guns together. If MI5 knew of his affair with Beatrice then it was likely the Russians did too. Their plan, which flowed into Sanders as if he were a part of the Russian group, was to hit the heart of the MRG as soon as he reached the club, but he wasn't going to give them that opportunity. He needed to know how good the MRG boffins were. His guess was they would mostly be practicing magicians. And one in particular, the mage, as Fielding had called him, would be better than the rest.

"I'm fine," he answered eventually. There was every chance that Fielding knew of an impending attack. Being in control was imperative. Giving either side an inkling of his abilities – and he was certain now that his father had trained him well for a moment like this – would take away any advantage he might have. A sense of lightness, of expansion, overcame him as the pain finally dissipated. His visualisation of the locomotive grew stronger and in that moment he realised he was capable of fending off whatever the Russians threw at them without the aid of the MRG.

"You don't look fine." Fielding laid a hand on his arm. When Sanders turned to him he was almost convinced that the concern in his old commanding officer's eyes was genuine. Focus, he told himself.

Gravel rattled the bottom of the car as they swung into the poplar-lined driveway of the club. It looked as empty now as it had the night before. There were similarities to Moondyke Manor. No doubt, it was designed by the same architect. The limo came to a halt with a desperate crunch, a signal for the doors to be flung open and Sanders to be helped, though it felt like he was being hauled, out onto the driveway. At the Doric portico entrance a tall man with slicked-down grey hair, and jeans and sweat shirt that would have looked better fitting on a skeleton, appeared and beckoned them to hurry. He looked thirty years older than Sanders but came towards them with a grace and strength that belied both his age and fragile build. There was something familiar about the way he moved, and familiarity in the lines of his face.

"Go!" the man shouted to everyone as he took Sanders' arm and led him into the hall, then quietly, "I'm John, by the way."

"We're coming too."

John's resigned and tired face turned to Fielding who stood at the front of an uncomfortable group. Sanders could see who amongst them knew nothing about magic. Lake had that confident air, a persona she wore when under stress, something Sanders had always admired. Tapscott stood behind the spooks, the apprehension in his eyes emphasising his death-wish look. Kazak's business-like air didn't hide his fear.

"Go!" Sanders insisted. He didn't want unnecessary deaths on his hands. John glanced his way, a hint of suspicion in the lines of his face. "He must know what he's talking about," Sanders added, which seemed to satisfy the man.

"Our choice," Fielding told him. "Move."

John shrugged, gently grabbed Sanders' arm and turned to lead him down the hallway deeper into the building.

"Cannon fodder might come in handy," the tall man mumbled.

Sanders glanced at him but he was intent on his goal. Pressure was building in his head again. He allowed it to rise, the boiler of the engine ready to burst. The Russians would be thinking the MRG were defending against their attack. The MRG would assume the Russians were building for a massive onslaught.

At the end of a long hallway double doors led into a small candle-lit antechamber, then up several steps into what Sanders realised was a temple with several equal-distanced sides. Columns reached up into a ceiling hidden by dancing shadows that emphasised its height. Sickly incense hung in the air from burners dangling on chains. Magical designs in the mosaic floor picked out a central circle about ten metres in diameter. Sanders had only ever seen the small one that was revealed by rolling back the rug in his father's 'library'. This one contained eleven white-robed MRG members. They stood equidistantly near the edge of the circle facing its centre, eyes cast down in concentration. John turned, put a finger to his lips – his little finger paralleling his forefinger like an effeminate glass raising. He signalled Fielding and the others to take seats set into the gloomy alcoves of the room, their black umbras looking forlorn and lost on the bare stonework as they did so.

Sanders was ushered to the edge of the circle. Those inside would be afforded a degree of safety while those outside would be in grave danger of, at worst, losing their minds. John really was going to use them as cannon fodder. But Sanders said nothing as John called on names of power to temporarily open a doorway into the circle, psychically – there was no physical barrier – and closed it again after they stepped through. Sanders glanced back but the others were now invisible in the deep shadows of the recesses. He brushed aside a pang of guilt as John picked up a robe for himself and handed another to Sanders.

"Put it on." All part of the ceremony. Sanders remembered from his father that altering perceptions even a little could add strength to a working and they needed power in gargantuan proportions to do more than just fend off the Russians. They were intent on destroying everyone in the building and Sanders realised that, while those in the circle had been chosen as the most able, there were others nearby creating further barriers, protecting the foundations and surrounding grounds. It was clear to Sanders that John was what Fielding had called the mage. A scientist of magic. The high priest if your beliefs were pagan.

As they moved towards a stone altar a spotlight thumped into life startling Sanders with both its sound and blinding brilliance. It took him a moment for his eyes to adjust as the beam cut its way through the smoky atmosphere to light up the triangle of art outside the circle, adjacent to the altar.

When Sanders had been learning ceremonial magic his father

had allowed himself to be the vessel for the demons that he had taught his son to control within the confines of the triangle of art, outside of the safety of the magic circle. Sanders had even put one of his school friends into an induced stupor and used him in the triangle of art but had never told his father. Knowing that it was possible to coax someone into the triangle, it still came as a surprise to see Lake kneeling within, a look of trancelike rapture on her face.

"Time is different in the circle," he remembered his father telling him, but it didn't stop him from looking around. The shadows revealed nothing. Were the others still there? Why had they done nothing to stop this? He staggered as the Russians made use of his slip of concentration but he focused on the chanting of the others in the circle. When had that started? While one part of his mind tried to untangle the confusion that threatened to overwhelm him, another part, the part his father had helped him train, began to dominate once more. Confidence returned.

"That was going to be you," John said from beside him, looking towards Lake. "But a woman is more appropriate for our evocation. You're more use here than there. And I sense my brother taught you far better than my father taught me."

"You're mistaken." Sanders said, taken aback by the suggestion. "My father was an only child."

"I was the black sheep, if you like." John explained quickly. "Banished for practising magic for my own ends. I never expected your father to pass on his knowledge. Simon was a very adept yet moral magician. Magic is amoral by its very nature. But enough of the past. We must link to destroy the Russian threat."

Without waiting for a response he turned, picked up a wooden staff resting against the stone altar and smashed it against its side, twisting the broken fibres until the two pieces broke free. Enochian letters were carved into the wood, tingling Sanders' flesh as John handed him one of the halves.

"Together," was all he said. Sanders found himself linking with his uncle, bringing together the rest of the MRG in the circle, allowing the other man to call several demons into Lake, one at a time, each one controlled and cajoled into fulfilling the combined will of the MRG. While John led the main attack, Sanders used his newly remembered skills to garner strength from the rest of the group, enabling him to redirect the Russian attack back to the senders.

The psychic voltage exhilarated, as if an orgasm built. Controlled danger. Like a lion tamer in a circus. Adrenalin surged. Lake screamed each time a new demon was conjured, but Sanders felt no pity, just the all-consuming power as together their group sent their emissaries of death to burst the Russians' boiler, splashing madness throughout a Moscow bunker beneath what was once the KGB's headquarters. No shredding bodies as revenge, though they would still die horribly. The demons would not be freed from their task until it was complete, but they were demons and constant domination was needed to keep them in line. The Russians fought and clawed each other to death, but it took an armed security team to eventually free the demons from their task. In the end the combined potency of John and Sanders upon the MRG made the results of their counter attack a foregone conclusion. Beatrice was not avenged. Nothing could do that, or bring her back to life. But there was a kind of satisfying closure.

Then it was over. Within the circle others crumpled to the floor exhausted. John let Sanders close their working as he went round to each of the men and women to check on them, a grim smile on his face. Sanders was aware he carried his own smile; felt complete for the first time in his life; ready for whatever the world threw at him.

Lake was being attended to by Mason as Sanders left the circle, now just impotent patterns on the floor. Kazaks stood to one side obviously shaken by what he had witnessed. As Sanders reached them he realised Fielding was standing behind, a calculating smile on his lips. Before Fielding could say anything Sanders lunged forward with the broken staff dissipating the final charge from about two feet. Sparks crackled around the MI5 commander whose normal composure crumpled with a fear that pleased Sanders no end. The last vestiges of power subsided, but not Fielding's hair, still tingling erect with static.

"You may think you've unleashed yourself a weapon," Sanders said to Fielding, pushing him away with the unbroken end of the staff, "but I'm my own man now. Find another mug." Fielding backed away ignobly, saying nothing.

Sanders then turned to Lake, ignoring the stench of shit. Her clothes were soaked in perspiration and fresh piss. Her blond hair was now white and matted to her head. There was no animosity in her face, only something that Sanders thought of as enlightenment. As if death had finally found her, but she'd beaten it. There was no doubting that she would live with the experience for the rest of her life. But she'd live.

Mason looked up. "She volunteered. She wanted to do this. She wanted to do this for the country."

Sanders knelt down, put the broken staff on the mosaic and took her by the shoulders to get her attention, to focus her vacant eyes.

"You saw something in me, didn't you?" Her face lit up with a moment's recognition. Then she passed out. "The demons won't have harmed her," he said to Mason. "But let the medics see to her." Doctors and nurses were already hurrying into the chamber to check on the magicians.

Electric lights had been turned on, revealing a domed hall. A balcony, about twelve feet above the floor, and running the full circumference of its eight sides, had been covered in glass like a Victorian conservatory – a control room. Sanders could see white-coated technicians fiddling with equipment, making him wonder if the boffins had found some mechanical or computerised way of boosting magic. He had his doubts about that. Below was a scene of devastation. It looked like the aftermath of a battlefield. Some of the MRG appeared to have suffered more than others and one was being administered resuscitation. Sanders guessed the medics had been waiting within the comparative safety of the enclosed balcony.

John cut him off as he made for the door.

"Going so soon? Aren't you the least bit interested in what we're doing here?"

"I need a holiday. Then maybe we'll have a chat over a coffee." Not red wine, Sanders thought, no more red wine.

"I understand your father now. We were young when we fell out. I think he would have understood me better now if he was still alive."

Sanders knew he *was* alive, but there had to be a reason why he wished his brother to believe otherwise. He'd felt a call from his father as he spoke to Lake, but he kept that to himself. There were questions he needed to ask his father, and he now knew where to find him.

"I'd like to say you remind me of him," John said. "But you don't. I'd like that coffee." Sanders could see sincerity in his face and accepted the offered hand.

"See you soon," Sanders said, turning towards the exit. Before he reached the doors he was surprised by a tap on the shoulder. His physical senses were still dulled, yet he felt invigorated and strong. Mason stood there holding up a set of car keys.

"You might need these, Ken. The Evoque is round the back."

Sanders realised it was men like Mason who kept the country safe. Dedicated, resilient and capable of doing whatever was needed without question. Yet they were human too; had doubts, regrets, emotions.

"You drive. Drop me off at my house and take the car back."

"The boss won't leave you alone. You know that?" Mason said as they made their way out of the old building.

"He's gotta find me first," Sanders replied.

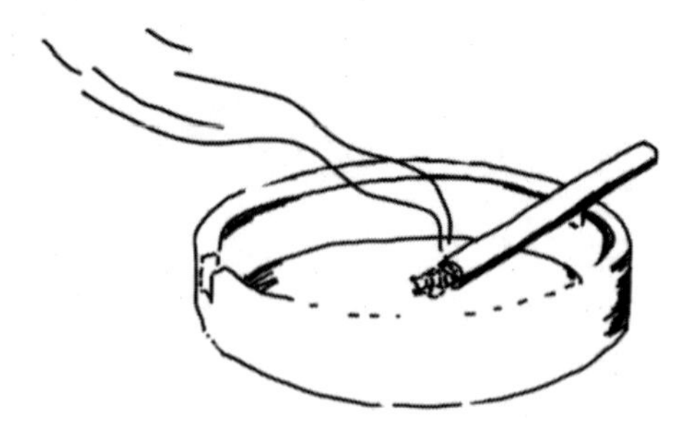

This story started life as a short play written for just two actors. The theatre company it was written for decided it wasn't for them but I felt it would be a shame to let the story of these two characters sit in a drawer and never be heard.

We'll Meet Again

Jane Crane

I'm lying here, with my head on your chest and listening to your heartbeat. It's my favourite place to be. I look up and see you're smoking a cigarette and I decide to help you finish it. I take it from you, take a deep drag and return it to your mouth; my scarlet lipstick has stained the tip but you don't mind, do you? I hold the smoke in my mouth for a second and then blow it out towards the ceiling; I remember when you tried to teach me to blow smoke rings but I wasn't any good at it. I watch it float away and imagine it clinging to the already grimy paintwork. I know I should get up, tidy my hair and get ready but I don't want to leave the warm space we have made on the bed, it's safe here, nothing can go wrong. Perhaps I'll just close my eyes and pretend to be asleep: perhaps then everything will stay the same.

"You should be getting ready, Rose." Ted's voice makes me open my eyes.

"I know I should but I ..."

"No buts, Rose, you have to get ready now."

I stretch out my arms and legs like a cat in the sun and sit up. Looking at my reflection in the dressing table mirror I realise that my hair is a mess. I stand and head over to the table and I tell Ted it is all his fault.

"Look at my hair. You are so naughty, Ted. I had it done

especially for today and look at the mess you've made of it." Ted chuckles lightly and gets up from the bed; I watch him walk towards me. He's still wearing his uniform trousers, scratchy khaki wool, and his white army issue vest, and I marvel at how handsome he is. Even the regulation haircut suits him. He looks every inch the soldier as he nears me and drops a kiss on the top of my head.

"You look beautiful, Rose, you always look beautiful." He stands behind me looking at the two of us together.

"Hmmm, such a sweet talker, aren't you? Bet all those girls in foreign parts just loved your patter."

"I've never let another girl near me foreign parts – never mind me patter!" he says, feigning horror, and he heads back to sit on the edge of the bed. I turn to face him.

"You know what I mean, you saucy git! 'A girl in every country.' Isn't that what they say about you Army lads?" Ted looks appalled by my suggestion.

"You know I've not so much as looked at another woman since you. I've loved you since I was eighteen, Rose Poole, you know that."

"Oh really! And here I was thinking you'd adored me from afar since I bought you that bag of humbugs on the pier when you were fourteen."

I can still remember how angry his brother Jim had been, having to take his little brother with him on our first date. His mum only did it to make sure we didn't get up to anything. Poor Jim – he spent the whole time trying to sneak a quick grope without his baby brother seeing anything.

"Mum knew you were a bad influence, even back then. I knew what you two were up to every time you gave me a penny and sent me off to the arcade."

The memory makes me giggle; it was so much easier then, before the fighting, before everything changed. I loved Jim then, at the start, but it wasn't a passionate love, just something we sort of fell into, like a habit. But I used to catch Ted watching us, especially after Jim and me got married and we moved in with Jim's family. All of us living together under one roof, it was quite sweet really. Jim used to joke that we'd wake up one morning and find Ted sleeping at the end of our bed.

"I didn't mean to fall in love with you, you know. My big brother's wife – what a bloody joke. I had plenty of other girls who were desperate for me to call on them and take them out." Ted says this like he's angry with me – like I made him fall in love with me.

"Oh well, excuse me for ruining your life, Ted," I shout at him. "I'm sorry that loving me has been so awful for you. I didn't ask for this either!"

Ted gets up from the bed and comes towards me, like he wants to hold me but I'm having none of it. How dare he blame me for this? Ted looks apologetic and tries again to hold me close to him. This time I let him, but only just.

"I didn't mean that. It came out all wrong," he stutters. "I'm sorry, Rose. Please look at me. There isn't much time left for us now and we're wasting it. Please don't be upset with me."

I can't hold it in any longer; I begin to cry, resting my forehead on his chest. Ted is searching for a handkerchief in his pockets but finds nothing. He grabs a corner of his vest and tries to lift it up to dab my eyes but it's no use. As he struggles to lift it high enough I see the scars on his side. They look so raw and painful; I want to kiss them and make them better but when he sees me looking at them he quickly pulls his vest back down to cover them.

"I wish you hadn't waited so long to tell me how you felt, Ted. We could have run away together – I would have done that for you, you know?" I reach up onto my tiptoes and kiss him gently. "You should have told me sooner. Instead we've had just these last few months and you've been overseas for half of it."

"I can't help when I get called up, Rose, when they send for me I have to go." He leans close to me and whispers, "but I'm here now aren't I? Let's make the most of the time we have."

He gestures towards the bed but I shake my head. I have to finish putting my face on. I sit back down at the dressing table and begin applying my make-up. Ted shakes his head and goes to lie back down on the bed. He takes a packet of cigarettes out of his pocket and shakes one free. He lights it and I watch him blow smoke rings in the air. I wonder if he is thinking the same thing I am.

"And how much time is that exactly, Ted?" I ask. I get up from my stool and head across to the big brown wardrobe in the corner of the room. It smells of varnish and mothballs as I begin to pull out the clothes I will need for today.

"Everyone will be here in a minute and Jim will be downstairs, wanting to know where I am."

I can see Jim now, sat in the corner of his mum's best front parlour, clutching a bottle of something, waiting for me to be by his side. Then I know I will have to leave Ted behind in this room.

"You know there's nothing I can do about that," Ted says. "That's just what has to happen. You married him, Rose, you chose him."

I turn around to face him and for a second I have to fight the urge to slap his face.

"And what was I supposed to do? Be a spinster? Wait for you?"

I remember my mother sitting me down at our kitchen table and telling me I needed to get married. She told me not to waste my time waiting for true love; normal girls like me didn't get swept off their feet like the starlets I watched at the Saturday morning pictures. She said I should get myself a husband, settle down quietly and have a few kids.

"Every girl needs a husband, Ted. Everyone told me that and so I married the next best thing to you – I married your big brother!" I'm so angry with him, men don't understand, no one pressures them into getting married before they get labelled as a spinster.

"And what a beautiful union that's turned out to be," shouts

Ted. "How often is he knocking you about these days? Once or twice a week?" Ted stubs his cigarette out in the ashtray by the bed and lies back, arms folded across his chest in defiance. I feel as if we are standing on opposite sides of a great divide and if I don't do something now then it will separate us forever. I walk across to where he lies and he grudgingly moves his legs so I can sit. He almost looks fourteen again – that petulant stare, arms stubbornly folded. I want him to understand how things are.

"Don't judge him, Ted. Or me for that matter. What he's been through over there, the things he's seen, they've changed him. You of all people should understand that. He's not the same man he was." I instinctively reach up to my cheek, the last place he hit me. He had come home drunk, like he did most nights, and we had gotten into an argument about something silly, I can't even remember what. But I remember the slap. I remember feeling like my eye was about to explode in its socket. And I remember how he cried like a baby in my lap afterwards, begging for forgiveness and promising it wouldn't happen again.

I begin pulling on my stockings, putting on my skirt and jacket. I see the black hat with the veil on its stand on the dressing table but decide that I don't want to put that on, not yet.

"Maybe I should be grateful to him. After all it's only when you realised he was knocking me about that you finally told me how you felt about me. Do you remember?" Ted nods and smiles.

"Like it was yesterday. You were sat crying in the dark in mum's coal cellar, the night I got back from Malta. I didn't see you at first, just heard this pitiful whimpering, like a puppy. I thought mum had gotten another dog until I heard you blow your nose. No dog could make that much bloody noise!"

"You cheeky bugger!" I say. But before I can do or say anything else he is next to me, pulling me down onto his lap and holding me tight. He reaches out to stroke my cheek.

"Your lovely face. He made such a mess of it. I would have killed him if he'd been at home." He kisses me lightly on the cheek and we sit for a second, our faces close together, listening to the tick of my bedside clock. Time passes and we don't move for what seems like ages.

Finally I say, "We kissed for so long that night in the coal cellar my lips went numb!"

"And I had to try and explain to Mum why I had coal dust handprints on the arse of my uniform when she came to do my washing."

I giggle at the thought of Edna trying to work out what was going on with her baby boy. Our laughter is interrupted by a knock at the door. Before I can open it Edna walks in.

"Aren't you ready yet, Rose? Who ya been talking to up here? Thought I heard you shouting? Why are you sat on the end of the bed not ready yet?"

All of these questions are fired at me before I have a chance to answer any of them. Edna walks across the room and over to the window; she turns then and looks me up and down. "Is that what you're wearing? Oh well I suppose it will have to do." She's fussing with the net curtains, straightening the pleats. "The cars are here. You need to come down and be with Jim now. And have something to eat before we leave." She walks back towards the door. "I've done plenty of food, and there's lots of Uncle Billy's homemade rhubarb red wine, but no one seems hungry. It's all just sat there on the table," she mutters, as she closes the door behind her.

"I'm not surprised." Ted is sat on the stool by the dressing table now. "Her bread and butter pudding was the reason I joined up!"

"You could have got me into so much trouble, Ted. She'll think I'm barmy." I can see Edna now, telling everyone about her nutty daughter-in-law upstairs talking to herself.

Ted walks across to the window and stands on the same spot his mum had done just a few minutes before.

"So that's me down there is it? In that box." He looks lost and sad. "The plumes on the horses are a nice touch. Very grand I must say. Not bad for the boy who was always given last go in the bathwater." He walks back to sit on the bed, he looks resigned, his shoulders slumped, defeated. I want to be near him so I go and kneel down in front of him and take his hands in mine. He looks at my face, like he's trying to memorise it.

"What did I say to you that night in the coal cellar, Rose?"

I lift his hands to my mouth and kiss them before I give him his answer. "You told me we would always be together. That you would never let me go, not when it had taken so long for us to find each other."

Ted holds my hands so tightly they begin to hurt. My wedding band digs into my finger like a reminder of my other life.

"So let's just stay here then," he says, with such desperate passion in his voice. "We can do that can't we? You can just stay here in this room with me and we can be together forever, like it was meant to be."

I want to say yes; I want to lie down beside him on this bed and never get up again but I know that I can't.

"It can't be that way, Ted, not now. You know that as well as I do. It's time to go."

I get up from the floor, holding his hand until the very last moment. The knock on the bedroom door makes me jump.

"Rose, come on love, it's time. You need to come down and be with Jim now, he needs you."

"I know, it's time." I take the black hat from its stand and I sit at the mirror carefully pinning it in place. In its reflection I can see Ted standing behind me, watching me get ready. I see him light another cigarette and then, with a tiny smile, he is gone and all that's left are smoke rings rising in the air.

Emily set us an assignment to write a flash fiction story based on a lie. I started thinking about how someone who is lied to can become complicit in the fabrication because they want so much to believe. Children and Father Christmas came to mind.

The Lie

Julie Williams

"Mummy – Dad, I can't get to sleep and I'm really thirsty and I need to talk to you ... Oh, you're not my daddy, who is he, what's he doing here, Mum? What is that man running down the stairs for ... Mum?"

Footsteps patter on the landing and small hands push the door open. Now Tommo's standing by our bed, curls tousled, one leg of his Fireman Sam pyjamas rolled up, and he's tugging at my elbow and running to the door, then back to tug harder, he's frantic, and what on earth can I say to calm him down, to reassure him? It's a nightmare.

Brian's away for his December conference and Jim next door, distraught but as it turned out not inconsolable at the fragrant Jenny's departure, popped round with a bottle of red after nine when he knew Tommo'd be in bed. I look such a mess, too, but he seems to like me all the more for that. Says Jenny was always too damn perfect, she thought kids would spoil her figure and her career prospects. That was what the split was about.

Even as he and I were tiptoeing to the bedroom past Tommo's door it occurred to me the little 'un had woken at midnight a week ago and padded along to ask for a drink of water. But Jim and I carried on and went to bed, whispering and giggling like kids over the sprig of mistletoe he'd brought, and to be honest I haven't had as much fun since I first met Brian. Maybe ever.

Jim was just about dressed and was pulling his jumper on when we heard the clear little voice. He had the presence of mind to keep the knitted folds over his face and dashed out of the door before Tommo reached it. I'm sure Tommo didn't recognise him.

"Come and have a hug with Mummy and I'll tell you all about it, sweetheart. That's right, jump up on the bed."

"But Mum, are you all right? Did that man hurt you, Mum, is he a burglar, should we call the police?"

"No darling, I'm fine, he's not a burglar, he's nothing bad at all, but I'm afraid I've been sworn to secrecy. I can't tell you who he is." Tommo's scrambled in next to me and is clinging to me tight. I'm thinking fast.

"What's this, Mum?" Tommo has twisted round to pick at the twig stuck to his buttock, embedded in the cotton jersey. The bedside lamp shines pink through the tops of his ears and my heart lurches with love for him. "Ugh, I've squidged it." Then, thoughtfully: "Why wouldn't he let me see his face if he wasn't bad?"

A split white berry smears my finger with juice as he hands it over, and inspiration strikes.

"So you wouldn't see his big white beard," I say. "This is mistletoe. He picked it on his way here from the North Pole. I can't tell you his name, but he wouldn't mind me saying he'll be bringing you lots of presents next week on Christmas Eve. Don't tell Daddy, sweetheart. This is our secret."

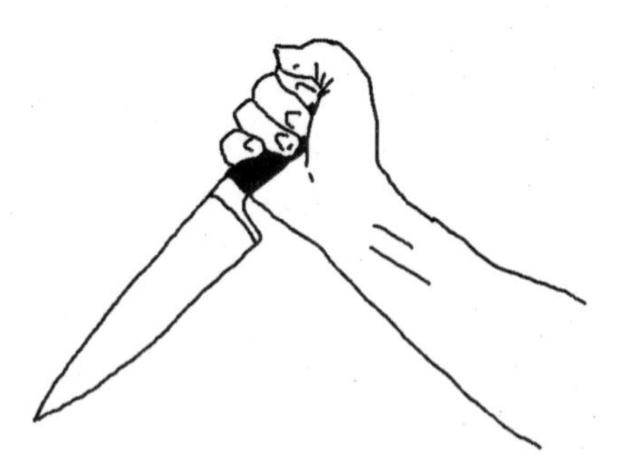

'Darkness Falling' is part of something bigger, an as yet untitled novel (actually it has several titles but none are sticking). Not quite the opening, it's sufficiently early in the story for me to feel happy to let it out here and I hope it stands alone. The novel is about unlikely lovers, one is Cat; the other doesn't feature in this extract for the sound reason that Cat hasn't met him at this point. Why Lewis? I guess because it's far from London, which just may be where her future lover is to be found. And the story is an exploration of a fragile union, perhaps like the union between Scotland and England.

Darkness Falling

Adrian Lazell

I pushed my face into the pillow and merged into the cotton, searching for somewhere different, calmer, and warmer. On the beach at Elafonissa, wet from a morning swim, I headed inland, my toes sinking into the pink sand with each step. Ahead of me the dripping back of a man. I reached and ran my finger along his spine. He turned; his face belonged to Mr Banks who, way back, had taught me English. He asked me what I was doing and I wanted the sand to collapse under me. I hit the refresh button but each time Mr Banks reappeared as a badly made Photoshop; his grey face pasted onto the bronzed body of a man thirty years younger, the furrow between his brows deeper.

I heard the crash of a bin tumbling outside and I'd left Crete for Lewis; the rain hitting the window coming from the East, off the Minch. It doesn't always blow on Lewis. It comes in waves; wind, calm, wind, calm and those lulls, those still moments, are the ones that make this the best island in Europe. Not just my opinion but that of the tourists who pour in every July and August. This though was a darker season. I considered going to check on Charlie but after a minute decided against, the warmth of the duvet overriding my maternal instinct. And he would sleep through Armageddon.

The curtain brushed my back and I felt raindrops. Did I leave the window open? What time was it? The alarm was out. A power cut? It seemed that we had only moonlight for illumination. I fumbled for my watch – quarter past three, I let my head drop back to the pillow. I should close the window.

I sensed it then – something not right. I lay and listened to a gutter overflowing, the telephone wires whistling, and breathing, not mine. "Charlie?" Someone, or something exhaled, a shallow, urgent burst was followed by a grunt. "Charlie – is that you?" An intake of breath shredded the night. It should be Charlie because the house held just the two of us, and we had no guests tonight.

The sound came from the far end of the room and, as I tuned in, the volume rose. I lifted my head to peer over the foot board but could see nothing, then pushed against the mattress to look along the wall. Something was there, a shape, a person – the head rocking. Not Charlie, wrong size and he'd be in bed alongside me, not waiting. Not a stray animal, this was human and adult. I watched a silhouette emerge of a man sat against my wardrobe. I could see his beanie, eyes staring back and something metallic in his hand. "Hello?" Nothing ... No response. I waited. He waited.

"Who are you?" Still nothing, again I stayed still. Then I pushed through the fear, slipped a leg from the covers and a foot to the ground.

As quick as an Alsatian he was on me, his knees pinning my arms, one of his hands held my neck, the other holding something over my face, catching the moonlight – a knife, a kitchen knife.

"Hello Cat."

"What do you want?" He stank of alcohol, sweat, urine – an addict's deodorant and he was shivering.

"I've come for my son."

"Get off me, Matt." His eyes, blue but bloodshot, suggested some thought process, but he didn't speak. The thought had been derailed. Either stoned, pissed, or possibly both, I reckoned.

"Get off me now, Matt." His only movement was to nod like a stupid toy dog. I began a silent countdown, and then pushed with my left side. He resisted. I pushed again and he lost balance. As he hit the floor I threw the duvet over him and launched myself across the end of the bed and through the door. Closing it I held the latch for a moment, until the futility of that became clear. I pictured him approaching with Jack Nicholson's smile crying "here's Johnny" before snapping myself back – this is real Cat, this is happening, wake up girl. I could hear him on his feet. Charlie's room stood opposite mine. I wedged limbs across the entrance. My door was ripped back and he emerged, incontinently, one step back for every one forward. He swayed towards me, just centimetres from my face.

"Matt, let's go downstairs. I'll make you a tea."

"I don't want tea. I want to see Charlie."

"It's Christmas ... Let him sleep." I inclined my head towards the stairs. "Come down and we'll have tea." I sensed the cogs turn in his head. I offered my right hand to his left. His right was still clutching the knife, though it was pointed at the carpet. I smiled, "Matt?" After a minute of uncertainty he took my hand and stair by stair we made a descent through the gloom. I tried the light – it worked.

I guided him to a chair, filled the kettle and pulled the open kitchen window towards me. Through the pane I could see debris from the upturned bin turning to pulp in the rain, though now it was just mizzling. On Lewis we have fifty words for rain and another fifty for arseholes like the one sitting opposite me. His eruption now dormant I felt pity, not fear. He looked sad. Still, I reminded myself, he had a knife.

"Fuck look at the size of that." His eyes were on the turkey. I closed the cutlery drawer and retrieved an empty bottle of Shiraz from the floor – presumably drained by Matt before he ventured upstairs.

"You can't eat all of that ... just you and Charlie."

"No. Mum's coming," I said, "and Shona and Alex." This had been true, before the weather set in and their flight got cancelled, leaving them on the mainland. But I calculated it might be better if he thought family were due, "Sugar?"

"Oh for fuck's sake, Cat ... you're my wife."

"Ex – wife."

"My ex-wife then, we were together for ..."

"Four years."

"Exactly."

"Tastes change ... You might have given up sugar."

"What and started taking fucking sweeteners."

"Maybe," I smiled to try to pacify him. I knew that when the fuck count went up so did his blood pressure. The table scraped across the floor, shoved away as he stood.

"I want to see Charlie – I came to see my boy." He jabbed the knife in the air with each syllable.

"Well you can't see him like that."

"What do you mean?"

"You're pissed. You stink and you're waving a knife around." I kept eye contact. "I could call the police."

"Don't threaten me, Cat."

"And if they come you'll go back inside. You're breaching the injunction just being here."

"Don't push me." He stood, pointed the blade and took a stride to get past the table and another to put him in touching distance.

"Using the knife makes it worse."

"I'm getting angry, Cat."

"Matt, ... give me the fucking knife, you don't know what you're doing, GIVE me the knife." I slid the table back to its bearings and offered my hand for the weapon. My eyes were fixed on his. He didn't blink, just stared back. Matt was my height, plus another twenty per cent and, beneath his drunken daze, made up of sinewy strength. I didn't fear what he might do to me, just to Charlie. He had history there.

A minute of staring in silence, but for the patter of the rain, was punctured by Bruce Springsteen. Santa Claus is coming to Town began to play, unrequested, on my radio upstairs. The wiring in the cottage had these moments of free will. A few seconds later the radio died. We'd both looked up at the ceiling then back at each other. More silence, then Matt put the knife on the table, lowering his head an inch, like a dog acknowledging that he was no longer the leader of the pack. I took the knife, dropped it in the sink and rewarded him with a mug of tea. "Sit down, Matt."

He sat and took a sip. "Sugar?"

"I put in two," but I placed my mug on the table, took his and went back to the cupboard, found the bag and added another two. His diabetes seemed low on the list of priorities.

"I'd heard a rumour that you were back on the island."

"But you didn't want to believe it."

"Frankly ... no. So how's AA going?" He missed the sarcasm. We talked family – mine mainly – our respective love lives – non-existent – and the difficulties of getting work out of season. In truth Matt couldn't hold down a job anywhere, at any time, for long. But he calmed with conversation. I had a judgment to make, to send him out into the elements or to put the decision off until the sun, or what passed for the sun here at midwinter, rose.

Fifteen minutes later Matt took to our mummy-shaped sleeping bag and the sofa cushions on the lounge floor for what remained of the night. I did the zip up, not quite a straitjacket but if he got up I'd hear him. I left every door open between the lounge and bedroom, which was not quite a perfect plan because the route between the two passed through the kitchen, offering a choice of weapons and alcohol. But I figured he'd just sleep – if he was anything like as tired as I felt.

I looked at the dead alarm. Despite the daylight everything seemed blurred and my head was heavy. I found my watch – it said two o'clock. What had happened? For at least a minute I lay against the sheets, trying to put the pieces of the night back together. A car drove past and I could hear neighbours laughing somewhere, but nothing inside. A malignant thought grew and I propelled myself towards the door and Charlie's room – empty.

"Charlie." I half fell down the stairs – kitchen, lounge both empty, other than the remains of Matt's sleeping arrangements. "Charlie, Matt?"

The toilet, utility room, studio were all without life. Back in the kitchen my handbag sagged on a chair, my purse opened. Keys – my car keys – I ran to the door and pulled it open. The car was gone, Matt gone, Charlie gone. Why hadn't I rung Mum? Why hadn't I called the police?

I ran into the road and screamed, "Charlie!"

The road was empty both ways.

"Matt, you fucking bastard, where have you taken my boy?" How could I have been so stupid? How could I have slept? "Matt, I fucking hate you, I hate you." I dropped to my knees, "I fucking hate you."

Only when I heard a voice did I break from sobbing, "Catriona, are you okay?" A calm voice, though a stupid question – if I was okay would I be on my knees crying onto the tarmac? I knew the face, Mr Banks, now thinner than in his high school days. His retriever pushed his nose into my face and Mr Banks muscled up enough energy from his ancient body to pull him back. He offered a hand and I took it. "I need to call the police," I inhaled a chunk of damp air, "Charlie's been taken." I moved towards the house and Mr Banks followed, made tea, held my hand and sat with me until the police arrived.

The hours that followed were the longest; empty except for dread and my meandering on the subject of Matt. And first Mr Banks and then W.P.C. Grant just listened.

They learnt about Glasgow, how my Dad got hit by a joy-rider one night on Sauchiehall Street. A week later his life support got switched off and I started to hate everything about the city. It buzzed an ugly chainsaw noise that gave me migraines. I'd started college there though, and that's where I met Matt. He spent a whole term constructing a Viking out of driftwood. I heard him say that he'd collected the wood on Lewis the previous summer and I jumped his conversation. I'd embrace anything that took me back here.

We talked, had coffee, met for lunch, went for a drink, smoked joints, toured galleries and within a week I'd left my Mum and sister to move into his digs. And for a while, for a week or two that autumn, I loved him. His art tutor loved him too, not surprisingly really because he had a gift. He made beautiful pieces but everything was glacial with him, never a full river. He worked when he felt like it and that became rare.

When I got pregnant he entered a state of denial. He thought if he refused to acknowledge my bump it would go away.

"It's down to you, not my decision," was followed by him leaving the flat and staying away for days. Nature made our decision – I miscarried.

W.P.C. Grant and Mr Banks looked confused. Charlie came later. Matt had come over to the island a couple of times after I escaped Glasgow and once, when I was weak and drunk and he made me laugh, we also, unknowingly, made Charlie. Of course I didn't tell him. But six months later he came back, discovered my secret and seemed, well grown up about it. He'd give up everything he'd been on, every substance. He'd get a job on the island. He'd be a dad. And this gullible, naive, girl believed him. I even married the deadbeat – why? I hate him. I fucking hate Matthew McNeil and as soon as I get Charlie back I'll get rid of the bastard one way or another. W.P.C. Grant told me they'd find Charlie. He couldn't go far. And Mr Banks noticed I hadn't drunk my tea and wandered off to make some more.

I kicked the toilet door shut and sat, dropping my elbows to my knees and holding my head for a second, before hearing the front door spring and a familiar voice. In my rush to free myself from the operation and dress, I fell to a kneeling position.

"Charlie."

I hit my head on the door handle and was hanging on to clothing as I launched myself down the stairs.

Charlie had to wrestle free from the longest embrace of his life. I told him there were presents in his bedroom and he grinned before taking the stairs at Olympic speed. Then I caught W.P.C Grant's conversation with a police sergeant on the porch which took my gaze outside to Matt, handcuffed in the back of a squad car. The policewoman barred my exit with her arm on the doorframe. "Not a good idea, Cat." So I stood at the door and stared. I didn't shout, just stared at the tosser. Maybe they'd been adding bromide to my tea but I thought I scored top marks for dignity.

Five minutes later they drove off. Mr Banks went home to get a bottle of his best claret to bring back for dinner. I told him not to rush; the turkey would take a bit of cooking. It did. Charlie stayed with me throughout, following me from room to room. At 10.00 that night we sat down to eat and to listen to some very detailed stories of Mr Banks' forty years in and out of education. Elafonissa didn't get mentioned. And a few minutes into Boxing Day, I said goodbye to Mr Banks, double locked the door, checked every window twice and picked up the already sleeping Charlie. He shared my bed that night.

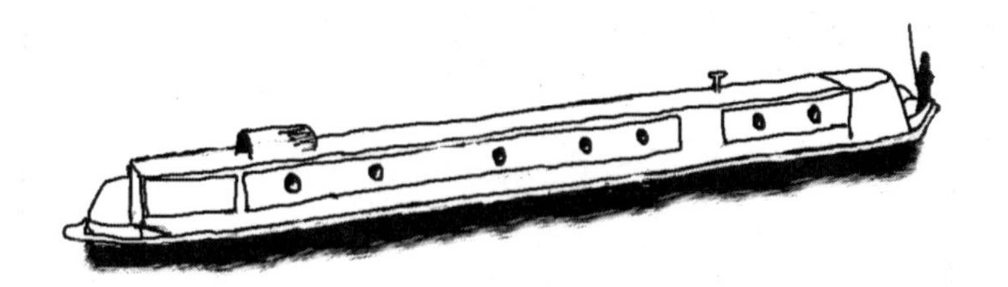

While 'Contraband' was written specifically for Plonk I also had another market in mind, the anthology *Looking Landwards*, a collaboration between science fiction and fantasy publisher Newcon Press and the Institution of Agricultural Engineers – looking at possible futures in farming. I was delighted when it was accepted in *Looking Landwards* and even more delighted when the publishers agreed that I could also publish 'Contraband' in Plonk.

Contraband

Terry Martin

"Drone incoming," Clements shouted from the bow of the seventy-two-foot barge.

Poised with her short pole, she could have been a Valkyrie waiting for a battle to end. Raven, her pet crow, stamped on her shoulder then pecked her unkempt wavy red locks as if wanting to hide there.

"Fuck off, Raven!" she said, waving a hand, but the bird hopped around to her other shoulder and buried its head in her hair.

Even Dog searched the skies when the buzz of a drone's propellers and high-pitched whine of its engines reached the ears of the rest of the crew. It took Baxter a moment to find the craft through the thin mist that rose from the inland waters of The Wash. He was constantly amazed at how quickly Clements spotted anything out of the norm. It was why she was such a good pilot in the biofields. Dog snorted through his tusks and lumbered along the roof of the hold, morning dew still twinkling on his bristly grey fur.

Normally a drone didn't bother Baxter. But normally Baxter didn't break the law. Well ... nothing more than the occasional motoring offence, and he'd been without a car for three years. Oh yes, there had been that spliff a girlfriend had shared with him, what, twelve years ago? But right now he was committing a crime that guaranteed a ten-year stretch, and possibly, depending on the judge, considerably longer. Until they sold-on their contraband Baxter couldn't relax. Not that there was much chance of that happening.

This trip was make or break. The way their luck had gone the last six months Baxter wasn't at all confident that smuggling ninety six bottles of premium French red in the empty engine compartment was a wise decision. Prohibition laws meant a bottle of good wine could fetch at least a hundred times more than when alcohol was legal. And red wine was a commodity that the biotechs at the algae farms were crying out for, or so Baxter had been 'reliably' informed.

But reliability was in short supply as highlighted by the fiasco with their seized diesel engine three months earlier. A new engine had been expensively out of reach of their haulage business so Baxter had negotiated a reconditioned one. It never materialised and the suppliers, who had insisted on payment up front, were no longer traceable. He had borrowed with the barge as collateral and now the loan sharks wanted their money and, of course, their exorbitant interest.

The irony of where they now punted the barge wasn't lost on him. Around them, like a vast magic carpet, spread the bright green algae farms of East Anglia and the East Midlands supplying the UK's biofuels industry with ninety per cent of its raw material, and therefore diesel oil. Ironic also that the flooded fens were now the home of an algae industry that, begun fifty years earlier, might have helped reduce the effects of global warming, and minimised the rise of the World's oceans.

Baxter turned, gripped the twenty-five-foot quant firmly with his calloused hands and thrust it into the bed of the Welland Channel – a misnomer in itself. Having seen an old road atlas, he knew it had once been the A16. Larger boats still used the River Welland itself but a punted barge would flounder in such deep water. Once he had a solid purchase he leaned hard on the pole and started walking towards the back of the barge, his thighs burning with lactic acid and his calves twitching with the onset of cramp. Passing him casually on the port side, Rozinski, with his perpetual weathered grin, pole balanced horizontally in his hands, made his way towards the prow in readiness for his next turn.

Baxter still wasn't sure about the Latvian. Clements had agreed on hiring another crewman after the engine seized. She was a tough woman, and despite a life spent on barges looked nearer thirty-five than forty-five. But she wasn't up to punting a loaded barge, and Baxter sometimes wondered if he was. It was back breaking work. Rozinski had heard of their plight and needed a job. He had approached them as they sat in the Floating Coffin – a seedy pub in the port area of Boston Fort – where they were nursing two large black Americanos. A good Italian coffee was the next best thing to a pint of bitter in Baxter's eyes. Not quite the same buzz though. Rozinski was six-foot-four and built like a Norse hero; shoulder length blond hair, slightly ginger stubble, and a jaw-line that would have done Judge Dredd proud. His cut-down sleeveless t-shirt struggled to cover sculpted muscles. He'd accepted their first, and embarrassingly low, wage offer and had proved an asset in more than just his powerful frame. It was a month before they found out he had been the North of England cage fighting champion until he refused to take a fall. His retirement had been less about the ethics than making him wonder if he was as good as he thought; how many of his opponents had thrown a fight? Having Rozinski at your side was often enough to stop an impending brawl.

It didn't take Baxter long to finish his stint at propulsion, the drone still keeping slow pace above them, bio tubes rippling across the 'fields' in the barge's wake. They'd got a good speed going, making pushing easier. Once the tide turned they'd have to moor up or drop anchor. Fighting against it, if it didn't kill you, was likely to undo all the hard work of the previous day.

Striding back to the bow, Baxter could see in the distance the towers of the reactors monopolising the horizon like a dead lichen-covered forest, dwarfing the occasional wind turbine that also fed power to the biogrid.

Baxter could hear Clements, from her position on the bow,

mumbling "Shit" over and over like she was counting seconds. She had one hand raised in an attempt to block the low sun, glancing around to give Baxter a hopeless look as he approached. Drones didn't usually follow the barges, they just flew back and forth sending their live feeds to the Water Guard main station at Lynn Fort. He clenched a defiant fist across his chest, mouthed, "Come on," and was relieved to see the hint of a smile before she flicked a glance at the back of the boat. Rozinski was just about reaching the end of his walk to the stern.

Baxter's mind wandered as he worked the pole, thoughts flitting here and there as he felt the barge moving beneath his feet. Maybe the Water Guard was changing the way it monitored waterway traffic. Cracking down on smuggling more like. Keep a clean sheet all your life and no questions asked. Yet as soon as you veer off the straight and narrow, bang, they go for the jugular.

They were making good time but would still have to moor up and catch the returning tide later. As Baxter headed back to the prow he noticed the reactors were getting closer, their pipework finally revealed, destroying the illusion they were bright green hydras. Clements called them Triffids.

"Don't worry, Bozz," Rozinski called across the barge, a finger in the direction of the sky, "that's just routine." But they both knew it was a lie.

Baxter pushed his quant into the water, searching for a firm pivot, found it and began pushing even before Rozinski had removed his pole from the murky water at the stern, giving the Latvian a satisfied twist to his grin when they passed.

Baxter panicked a moment as his quant refused to budge from the sludge of the channel bed, but a practised jerk and heave sent him tottering on the edge of the stern with his right boot anchored on the low gunwale. Rozinski's grin became a loud laugh of light-hearted derision; the more meaningful as he'd been in the same position about half an hour earlier, only managing to recover by letting the pole travel vertically through his hands in a hundred-and-fifty-degree arc and then pulling the quant in reverse. Not the best way to avoid being dragged overboard. It slowed the barge but it was better than having to throw out the anchor and wait until your crewman swam back. They had both been in that position more than once before they'd mastered their quants.

Multinationals had drained the country of the most skilled engineers so repairs were limited to a few garage lathes, and their old seized engine now sat on the bench of one of these garages. He shook his head again at his naivety and how easily he'd been duped by the bastards who'd sold him the non-existent engine. Guilt still hung heavy in his thoughts and cut a deep red minus in their bank account. This trip was going to pay for its rebuild and a nice profit. Well, that was the plan. The constant buzz of the drone didn't bode well though.

Marsh gases bubbled up a stench of rot from the vegetation that had once covered the flat lands hereabouts, but Baxter's sense of smell had long ago learned to cope with the noxious odours. A bark from Rozinski set him back on his task. Tiredness and boredom were compounding his guilt trip and he was allowing the drone to get to him, but once you had the barge moving at a decent pace it was in your best interests to keep it that way. The barge was a pig to get moving.

As they reached the rising green towers of the newer reactors, and quite beautiful they looked, in Baxter's eyes, Clements called a warning from the front of the barge, "Eh up! Water Guard!"

Baxter didn't stop pushing but, even as Clements shouted, he also heard the familiar whine of the Briggs and Stratton engine that powered the patrol's fluorescent green hovercraft. Taking supplies to the Spalding Bio Farm for the technicians and maintenance crews wasn't a crime, in fact their journey had been booked and logged back at Sutton Fort before they'd headed West along the Holbeach Channel, the route of the old A17, to the Welland Channel. It was far safer to stick to the marked routes than risk snagging on the roof of an old farmhouse or damaging the floating production tubing of the cheaper reactors.

At least the two officers from the Water Guard were thoughtful. Rather than hit the side with their magnetic winch, and interrupt the crew's pushing, they drew up at the stern, cut their engine, and began drawing in their craft. Carbines were slung across their backs, fluorescent green flak jackets over dark green uniforms. Expensive micro headsets were barely visible but it was obvious they could be in instant contact with their base. There was no option but for them to come aboard to check credentials and, with all hands keeping the barge moving, they were unlikely to be offered a guided tour. Now that the hovercraft was silenced the ominous buzz from above reminded Baxter they were also on a monitor in a control room somewhere.

Dog snorted mucus menacingly in the face of the first officer, a young lad in his late teens, as he clambered on deck. He started to unclip his pistol.

"He'll not hurt you," Baxter called out. "A genetic softy. Just looks like a real wild boar, is all."

The young lad didn't look convinced but the automatic stayed in its holster. His backup, a man in his late forties and most likely the senior in rank, had slid his carbine around and up in an easy action that said 'experienced professional'.

"Dog! Bed!" Baxter shouted. He wasn't convinced either, having seen what Dog's tusks could do to a man's thigh. It was true about Dog. His aggression genes had been tampered with. He doubted the officer would still have a face if Dog was a normal boar. This was Dog's barge though, as much as the rest of the crew, and he hadn't budged.

"Dog! Bed!"

Baxter hadn't heard Clements temporarily leave her post. She was halfway along the roof of the hold when he glanced round, Raven flapping in her locks like a trapped bat. Unruffled, Rozinski was nonchalantly finding a purchase with his quant at the front of the barge.

"Bed!" she repeated, as Dog turned his dripping snout in her direction. Reluctantly, and to Baxter's relief, Dog slowly lumbered to his pen welded to the front of the cabin, giving Clements a look that unsettled even Baxter as he passed her.

"Come to the front," she called to the officer as she turned and hurried back to her position. "We can talk while I guide." The older man, carbine slung on his back once more, nodded to his junior and then accepted a hand to climb aboard.

"We've a consignment of electronic stuff for Curry's and the latest Marvel releases for Forbidden Planet." Baxter called over his shoulder as he led them forward. "Don't know why the biotechs love paper so much. Costs the earth these days."

Despite the effort of pushing the barge, Rozinski was still able to smile at the officers as he passed them on the other side.

"He's always so fucking happy," Baxter said, mostly to himself.

"We've a tip off there's a haul of illicit wine coming through. Seen any strange vessels around?" asked the senior officer at the back. Baxter managed to keep moving despite his arteries feeling as if they'd been zapped by liquid nitrogen. Thankfully they weren't able to see his chin drop. Running alcohol wasn't just a smuggling offence. Prohibition laws were on a par with terrorism. But vineyards were suffering in the ever-changing weather patterns making wine a very lucrative commodity if you wanted to take the chance to make a quick buck.

Hoping his pause was taken for recollection Baxter finally said, "Saw a Dutch tug as we crossed the River Welland. Not seen her before. *Rode Tulp* I think she was called." He was pleased to see a look between them as he glanced around.

"I'll leave you with Clements. She has the cargo inventory."

As he pushed his pole into the muddy bed he overheard the older officer mention *Rode Tulp* into his microphone. Almost instantly the buzzing from above went up a notch in volume with a direction change that left them with just the lapping of water along the barge's length. Baxter was surprised at the relief he felt as the drone disappeared from view despite having two Water Guards on board.

Rozinski's smile was no longer one that Baxter felt easy with. There was a coldness now in his eyes as they passed and a purposefulness in his stride that made Baxter look back quickly at the officers. The Latvian had more to lose than any of them if their contraband was found packed tight with bubble wrap in the empty engine compartment. Feeding a family of six with another child on the way on benefits that wouldn't keep a cat alive led Rozinski to visit the back-street loan sharks more times than Baxter had fingers, or so the Latvian had told them.

"Don't do anything silly," he mouthed, but Rozinski didn't even look his way. If they played it cool they had a chance that their illicit haul of wine wouldn't be detected. The coldness in his blood returned, making his muscles protest even more.

"Fanzy a push, offizers," he heard Rozinski call, poking his quant in their direction. What was he up to?

He had to act before things got out of hand.

"Drop anchor!" he shouted, lifting his quant free of the bed and turning back to the front of the boat. Rozinski looked less surprised than Clements. "Offer the officers a cuppa. It's about time we had a break. My back's killing me."

Clements recovered quickly, knowing Baxter rarely made rash decisions, recon engine aside, and that he had a reason for his order. At the end of the day he was the senior partner owning fifty-one per cent of the barge. She released the anchor and they all grabbed for something secure as the barge juddered to a halt, Dog snorting a grunt of protest as its trotters skidded on the roof.

"I'll put the kettle on," he called as he made his way aft again, and, "Apologies for our initial hospitality, officers. We'll not make Spalding before the tide turns anyway, so we might just as well moor up and head out again early tomorrow. Appreciate you boarding from the stern though. That was thoughtful." Giving them a bit of praise wasn't likely to change anything but doing the opposite most certainly would.

He reached the cabin and put the battered brown enamel kettle over the hob and lit the jets beneath. The younger water guard entered the cabin first with the barge's inventory under his arm and sat on one of the three high stools surrounding their circular wooden table, clean but stained with years of culinary misadventures. Rozinski leant, arms crossed, against the engine housing. Nothing like broadcasting the obvious, thought Baxter. The senior officer launched himself onto the kitchen top next to Clements, his legs dangling over the cupboards, giving him a commanding view over them all. He eyed the Latvian thoughtfully.

Baxter started to wonder if he'd made the correct decision. The guards might have glanced at their papers quickly and left. Now they were going to be on the barge for a good half an hour. Yet he still had the feeling that the Latvian might try something desperate.

"How's traffic been?" he asked, in an attempt to break a tension that was slowly building and at the same time spotting the officer's name and rank on the left breast of his flak jacket: Johnson and Superintendent. What was such a senior officer doing on a patrol hovercraft?

"Busy," Johnson replied. "And lots of traders taking stupid risks. Caught three in the last week." He paused, cast his gaze slowly over the crew. "I blame it on the biotechs. They're the ones desperate for alcohol and meat. Our jurisdiction doesn't cover the algae towns though. We could stop all this if it did. The constables," layering his last word with disrespect, "could do more, but the techies earn too much money for their own good."

"You're telling me," Baxter agreed. "But it's good business for us."

"Good enough?"

"A struggle at times." Baxter nodded, feeling his conversational skills crumbling, his mouth wanting to babble on.

Clements passed the officers their teas, the younger one's eyes lingering on her tight royal blue sports top. Off-boat she'd have covered up. She wasn't one to flaunt her body, unlike Rozinski, whose muscular build said who wants to challenge me? Cafés were still under policed and Rozinski was willing to earn extra cash in backroom cage fights. Clements, on the other hand, didn't want to end up in the back of anything to make more money. She preferred Baxter to fulfil her occasional needs and, while he would have liked this to be more frequent, their friendship was more important to him, leaving him to rely on his hands to alleviate pent up passions.

"We couldn't help noticing you've a problem with your engine," Johnson said.

Baxter was pleased that his crew didn't react. Maybe he'd been wrong about Rozinski. It seemed likely that the failed engine was the main reason for the Water Guards' interest in the barge.

"Packed up three months ago. Got ripped off buying a recon." No reason to lie.

"We all make mizdakes," Rozinski said, and took a sip of his black tea, still leaning against the housing, dominating the cabin with his bulk.

At the table the younger officer was flicking through the paperwork, glancing across occasionally at Clements. She was old enough to be his mother but she was still a looker.

"Everyone seems to be out to get what they can these days," Johnson complained. "There's just not enough of us to make an impact. I've been on these waters for the last thirty years and smuggling's increased, yet my budget gets cut each year. The algae farms are great for the economy and keep the green campaigners happy – well mostly – but the majority of the biotechs get paid far more than a senior guard. Clasper here," he nodded to the lad, "probably earns in a month what they earn over a couple of days. Didn't bother me once. It's eating at me now though."

He was quiet for a while, allowing Baxter to reflect on his

words. It wasn't often that guards discussed their opinions with the likes of the barge traders. Particularly not senior guard officers.

"Tea's good," he said to Clements. "Proper leaves?"

She looked at Baxter, who gave a slight nod. Owning up to a little thieving might make the guards less inclined to think them capable of bigger crimes was Baxter's logic. His decisions had been wrong in the past though, and he was constantly aware of that."We delivered a consignment of tea to the Humber Fort last September. Seems we missed a box when we unloaded."

"Haven't had a decent cuppa for years," was all Johnson said. "Artificial tea's just not the same." He closed his eyes for a moment as if in bliss. Then he snapped them opened with a look of relief as Clasper turned at the same instant. "Looks like your tip paid off. Just come through." He touched the headset. "The *Rode Tulp* was carrying alcohol. They reckon a thousand bottles of red wine. That's some haul."

It was indeed. Their engine compartment held less than a hundred bottles. But at £200 a bottle, or thereabouts, it wasn't to be sniffed at. A thousand bottles was big business. If the Dutch ship had sold to the Spalding Farm their own consignment would have been worth far less in a flooded black market.

"That'll all be recorded on the drone. Can't board a vessel these days without it being monitored. The good thing about being the senior officer on patrol is I can order where the drones go. Now then, I think it's about time we left you to your business."

Johnson slipped off the top and put his mug there. Clasper stamped their papers and squiggled a signature at the bottom before standing. Baxter noticed the relief flood into Rozinski's face. Clements even sighed.

"Oh," Johnson said, turning back, "Clasper here's a bit of a mechanic. He'll take a look at your engine for you before we go."

The colour drained from Clements' face turning her tanned features grey. A wrench appeared in Rozinski's scarred right hand, but Johnson's automatic was already out of the holster and pointing at him.

"Put that down." It was said quietly and with a hint of regret, or so Baxter thought. But they were done for now. They'd taken a terrible risk and it hadn't paid off. It was his idea. He'd persuaded the others that the chance was worth taking. Once again his decision had been flawed.

"They're not in on this," he blurted. "It was my idea ... To get us out of debt."

"Move over there together." Johnson gestured with his Glock, ignoring Baxter's plea. Clasper did likewise with his carbine as he edged around the cabin. Rozinski, like a cornered dog, followed suit until the crew members were all on the opposite side of the table to the engine compartment.

Clasper slung his carbine around to his back and opened the doors; looked at Johnson immediately. "'Bout eighteen cases."

"On another day that'd be a decent cop," the older guard said. "Today?"

Baxter raised his eyebrows as Johnson put the automatic back in its holster.

"We don't take bribes but under the circumstances a half dozen bottles seems a reasonable gift. It'll be another half hour before the drone heads back this way."

They watched, dumbfounded, confused and relieved as the young guard extricated a case from the bubble wrap that protected their hoard.

"I know you're honest traders," Johnson said. "Just the climate's not conducive to honesty right now. There's them." He raised a horizontal hand high above his head. "And there's us." His hand moved to his thighs. "And never the twain shall meet. Except when there's a bit of profit to be had. And it's usually them," his hand shot up again, "that benefit."

He followed Clasper up and along the deck to the rear and helped him slip the case of mixed reds under some tarpaulin folded at the rear of their hovercraft. The crew had followed in stunned silence, Dog's trotters clipping a merry tune on the deck by their side, Raven cawing defiance as if she alone had sent the guards scurrying off.

Johnson shouted above the sound of the Briggs and Stratton as it burst into noisy life, "No need to tell you you won't be bothered by the Water Guard on this trip again. But be assured, we will be keeping an eye on you in the future." With that they shut off the electromagnet, hauled in the winch, swung about and were soon travelling away at speed, Johnson standing with a hand on the cage to steady himself, looking back at Baxter and the crew.

Raven flew after them briefly then returned, landing lightly again on Clements' shoulder, wings flapping for balance.

"Fuck," Clements whispered. "That was just too close."

Rozinski uncharacteristically hugged Baxter and Baxter surprised himself by hugging back. They pulled away, looked at each other, then at Clements, and burst into laughter.

"Maybe our luck's changed at last."

I like a list. It gives shape to a day which might turn flabby. A good list starts well and ends with a surprise. I had no idea that the colour theme in 'Under the Bed' would take me to a dark place.

Under The Bed

Christine Dickinson

Think of wine, Pinot Noir, a rose or twelve
for a valentine, a warning to stop,
a heart aflame, hot stuff, cayenne, chilli,
the flush of cheek, shame, cherries, a sun blush
tomato, fever, rouge, chapped hands, a debt,
yew berries, a nose for a clown, rubies,
the tip of danger, a touch of anger,
his favourite dress, her lust for a sports
car, dawn if the rain is due, a sunset
to please a shepherd, the flash of a robin,
Christmas with Santa Claus, blood, a girl
in a hood meeting a wolf, a good look
under the bed after the cold war
and you might find one, Mao's book.